CONFLICT DIAMOND

CONFLICT DIAMOND

A DIAMOND RING DARK ROMANCE

THE KIDNAPPED SERIES
BOOK 3

ALIX KEY

DIAMOND
FREEPORT PRESS

Published by Diamond Freeport Press
P.O. Box 42133, Arlington, VA 22204

ISBN 978-1-95018-475-0

Discover other titles by Alix Key at www.alixkey.com

091625ak

ALSO BY ALIX KEY

Find a complete, up-to-date list of Alix's books at www.alixkey.com.

The Kidnapped Series

Diamond Solitaire

Rough Diamond

Conflict Diamond

Priceless Diamond

The Irish Mob Trilogy

Irish Brute

Irish Vice

Irish Reign

The Boston Mob Trilogy

Her Irish Savage

Her Irish Protector

Her Irish King

The Taming the Mob Princess Trilogy

Taken Enemy

Twisted Enemy

Tamed Enemy

The Sinful Mafia Series

Sinful Mafia Santa

Sinful Mafia Deception

Sinful Mafia Seduction

Sinful Mafia Salvation

WORD OF WARNING

Conflict Diamond **is a dark romance.**

It contains hard-to-read scenes, graphic language, and explicit sexual content.

A complete list of potential triggers can be found at:

https://alixkey.com/books/kidnapped-series/

Please don't read this book if you are sensitive to any of those triggers. But if you believe in the redemptive power of love to overcome near-unimaginable trauma, then this is the book for you.

Welcome to the Diamond Ring.

THE KIDNAPPED SERIES, A RECAP

Have you read *Diamond Solitaire* and *Rough Diamond*, the first two books in the Kidnapped Series?

You can get started with *Diamond Solitaire*, by typing

https://alixkey.com/PB0US

into your phone or computer browser. And you can continue with *Rough Diamond*, by typing

https://alixkey.com/PB1US

into your phone or computer browser.

If you don't want to read them—or if it's been a while—here's a quick summary of the Kidnapped Series so far (minus, of course, the spicy scenes!)

Alix Key and Travis "Trap" Prince enjoy a one-night stand where, against all odds, they bond on an emotional level, each healing a deep wound in the other. But when Alix returns home from the tryst, she is kidnapped.

She wakes to find that her desperate, addicted brother sold her to drug kingpin Klaus Herzog. Herzog, a sexual sadist, holds Alix as a slave for three years, repeatedly abusing her in horrific ways.

Trap spends those three years searching for Alix and building his billionaire's tax haven, Diamond Freeport. Herzog, meanwhile, becomes one of unknowing Trap's most important clients.

When Herzog brings Alix to a dinner party at the freeport (her first time out in public since she was enslaved), she seizes a steak knife and stabs him to death. Trap and his richest clients cover up all evidence of the death, but they learn that Trap's home has been under surveillance. (He believes the bugs were planted by a former client who was connected to the CIA.)

Finally reunited, Trap and Alix try to overcome their trauma. Trap, though, lives with a crippling phobia of physical contact, and Alix is emotionally and physically scarred from her slavery. She begins to drink heavily, in part to deal with her confusing attraction to Trap's kinks.

Alix flees Trap's home when he rejects her drunken attempt at seduction. Separated, Alix and Trap are miserable. Ultimately, he finds her and grovels for her forgiveness.

Alix returns to the freeport and successfully conducts an art auction for a wealthy client. Alix and Trap celebrate with an intense night, when Alix embraces Trap's kinks and he overcomes his phobia.

Relaxed and happy the following morning, Alix and Trap receive a terrifying email. Someone has video of Alix murdering Herzog—which they will release if Trap doesn't pay one billion dollars and provide a freeport warehouse for illegal drug operations.

The clock is ticking: Alix and Trap have fourteen days to comply or their lives will be ruined.

1

ALIX

I stare at the email that is going to destroy my life:

"This video goes to one hundred media outlets, the Dover police, and the FBI at 11:59 pm on August 15. The only way to make it disappear is to deposit one billion dollars in the Credit Suisse account designated in the subject field above. In addition, we require a climate-controlled private gallery within the Diamond Freeport suitable for storage of up to one shipping container of pharmaceuticals."

A countdown at the bottom of the message spins wildly as seconds melt into minutes, measuring out fourteen days before my world goes up in flames.

And beneath it all, the video runs on an endless loop. It's eerie—black and white and completely silent. But what it lacks in color and sound, it makes up for with detail.

I can make out ever strand of my platinum blonde wig. Every pleat in my Marilyn Monroe halter dress. I can even see the beauty mark that was painted on my cheek.

From my place, kneeling obediently at Klaus Herzog's feet, my knife flashes. The man I called Master slumps in his chair until my stabbing frenzy drags him to the floor.

Blood.

Rivers of it.

Oceans.

Herzog's death is hideous and disgusting and terrifying and I'd do it all a thousand times over, because killing him was the only way I could ever be free.

The video reaches its end—a head-on shot of my blood-spattered face, crystal clear and utterly undeniable. I look drugged, or maybe like I'm sleepwalking. Somehow, that makes it worse—if I screamed or sobbed or puked, I'd be acknowledging the horrible thing I did.

Instead, I'm a zombie.

There's no hint of the Alix Key who came to the Diamond Freeport of her own free will three years earlier. The Alix Key who was a good girl, who spent her entire life saying no—to sex, to drugs, to anything she wasn't supposed to do. The Alix Key who stood by her twin brother Leo, despite his endless battles against addiction, despite losing family and friends and fiancé.

There's not even a hint of the Alix Key who found power and pleasure in the bed of Travis "Trap" Prince, the owner of the freeport tax haven, the man who forged the Diamond Ring, a coalition of his richest, most powerful clients—including Klaus Herzog.

Staring into the face of the robot on the video, I don't see a good girl. I don't see a newly awakened woman. I see a stranger, dead to the world.

The recording ends again.

And starts once more.

I remember how the knife felt, heavy in my hand. I remember the metallic smell of blood, mixed with shit after I sliced through his intestines. I remember the gleam of light on bone and muscle and organs I can't name.

I was a slave for three long years because my brother sold me to pay off his debt to a drug kingpin. I was raped every day, in disgusting ways only a sadist could have dreamed up. I was fattened up like a pig for slaughter and when I refused to eat, I was drugged, force-fed, and given a boob job without my consent.

Clearly, I was insane when I sliced Herzog's throat open with a steak knife. When I plunged that same knife into his belly. When I mutilated his crotch.

But somewhere between the first knife strike and the hundredth, shouldn't I have come to my senses? Shouldn't I have realized I was protected and safe in the freeport? Shouldn't I have remembered that civilized human beings rely on police to protect them, on courts to convict criminals?

Herzog turned me into a monster.

I don't deserve to be in polite society.

And I have no right to drag anyone else down with me.

The video starts again. Before I can rake my knife across Herzog's throat, Trap's voice rings out behind me. "Turn it off."

In the past six weeks, I've become conditioned to obeying Trap's direct commands—in the bedroom, at least. His words anchor me when I fear I'm too damaged to return to the real world. They awaken this body that I thought would never enjoy physical sensation again. His commands make me come.

So I'm not surprised when my hand moves automatically, hitting the red button to close the email. But I'm startled beyond words when I see the expression on Trap's face.

He's furious.

And my reaction to his rage—despite the past six weeks, despite Trap treating me like a princess, despite Trap never lifting a finger against me that I didn't crave and consent to explicitly—my reaction is to drop to my knees, planting my hands on the back of my head and displaying my breasts to his satisfaction.

To the satisfaction of the animal who trained me, Herzog.

I thought it was bad, seeing Trap's anger at the video. It's infinitely worse, seeing that fury directed at me.

Not at me, whispers a quiet corner of my brain, the one that majored in psychology, the one that completed all the coursework for my PhD and only needed to finish my dissertation when I was kidnapped. *He's not angry at me. He's angry at my actions, at what Herzog taught me to do.*

Logic isn't a great help. I fall back on words. "I'm sorry," I say, but that's almost as bad, because Trap told me never to say that, never to apologize for being held a slave.

His throat works. His face scowls. His hands fold into fists, and my body braces for a blow my brain says will never come. But when he speaks, his voice is deceptively mild. "Who sent it?"

"The *From* field says Klaus Herzog."

"Well that's clearly impossible."

Again, there's that mildness I'd be a fool to trust. "It's someone associated with him." I'm stating the obvious. "They're demanding a gallery. They plan on storing drugs here."

"They *plan* on getting my fist up their—"

I cut him off before he builds up a true head of steam. "And they won't just *store* drugs. They'll distribute them. Take advantage of the freeport's documentation system."

I've only been at Diamond for a month and a half, but I've already seen its sophisticated receiving and shipping divisions in action. Every item that crosses in or out of the tax haven is documented. Any failure to maintain complete records would result in the loss of the freeport's tax-exempt status.

And any record reflecting sale or transfer of illegal drugs will destroy Trap's business even faster.

"Motherfucking, cocksucking..." Trap drops a heavy finger on the telephone console on his desk, launching a dial tone through the speaker. Another brutal push, and a flurry of digits dials automatically.

"MacGregor," comes a harsh reply, halfway through the first ring.

"I need to know who sent an email," Trap says without preamble.

"To your work account?" It's eleven in the morning on an August Saturday, but Diamond Freeport's Chief of Security is all business.

"To Alix's."

"Forward it to me."

Instead of clicking a few keys, Trap looks at me and raises his eyebrows. He's asking permission to forward the file. Because right now, the only people in the world who know I killed Herzog are the surviving members of the Diamond Ring—and our would-be blackmailer.

Trap trusts Mac; otherwise, he wouldn't hire the guy to run security for the entire tax haven. But there's a difference between trusting a man to protect your physical space and trusting a man to protect your life. Because if this story gets out, my life will change forever.

Trap's will too.

After I killed Herzog, Trap called in countless debts to have his home restored to pristine status, virtually overnight. He has aided and abetted a criminal. He's an accomplice after the fact.

I want to trust Mac. But I don't want to make Trap's burden any greater than it already is. I love Trap. I can't hurt him.

So I reach out to close the email. Mac doesn't need it. We don't have to bring him into the circle. We'll figure out something else.

My hand, though, slips on the mouse. I end up scrolling to the very bottom of the message.

My heart stops.

Trap is scowling, waiting for me to give him a thumbs-up. Mac is silent on the other end of the phone. I gape at the computer screen like I'm staring at a ghost.

Not a ghost.

A savage rapist.

No. Two. Two vicious animals.

The image at the bottom of the email looks harmless enough. It could be copied from a stock photo website, maybe a home goods catalog. It's a harmless kitchen accessory, available in millions of houses in America.

I'm staring at a copper oil cruet. Not much taller than my hand. Freshly polished to a red-gold gleam. Metal spout facing the right side of the screen. My breakfast of coffee and toast and peaches rises in my throat, and it takes a massive effort of will not to vomit on Trap's sleek keyboard.

He's watching me. Even if he doesn't understand, he knows something terrible has happened.

"I'll call you back, Mac," he says. The silence of the terminated call surges against my eardrums.

I'm back in Herzog's mansion. I'm dressed in his perverted version of a catsuit—corseted black latex with cutouts for my breasts and between my legs. An O-ring gag forces my lips apart. My feet are laced into boots with monstrous stiletto heels.

That cruet is from Herzog's kitchen, where I eat every meal with his other slaves. That cruet is filled with olive oil. That cruet is pressed against the tight pucker of my ass, tilted, emptied, all to prime me for a triple penetration I have no way of stopping.

I'm helpless. Hopeless. Dosed against my will with one of the designer street drugs that made Klaus Herzog a billionaire. Klaus has my mouth; he's ramming his way through my vicious gag. His brothers, Jonas and Ansel, ride me hard, front and back, pumping through the stinking lube of tainted oil.

The four of us are the only ones who know the full depravity in that room that Halloween night.

Klaus is dead.

I've vowed never to tell a soul.

But one look at Trap makes it clear he's not giving me a choice.

2

TRAP

Alix has gone as white as bleached bone. I glance from her
face to the computer screen, half expecting another video
to have launched, because I can't imagine any other reason for
her reaction.

The Beast that lives inside my brain chooses that moment to
stir from its lair. I know its triggers—blood, disease, germs of
any kind. I spent twenty years with the fucker making me pay
for any physical contact. I had rules and regulations to keep
myself clean, to make the world safe. And when I fucked up—
early and often—I paid the price, bleeding off the Beast's strangling tension by tapping out a five-count with a finger or a fist.

The Beast reminds me of the filth that destroyed my dining
room—Herzog's blood sprayed on ceiling and walls, on floor
and table. The Beast had a fucking field day that night.

But Alix saved me.

Three years ago, her innocence tamed the goddamn animal

inside my skull. And last night, when I finally touched her again...

Alix isn't a threat.

I think it again, calmly, slowly: *Alix is not a threat.*

The Beast skulks back to its cave.

But Alix stays frozen. The screen still shows the ass-end of that fucking email. There's an ad there, from one of those fancy kitchen shops. Like this is the moment I want to stock up on goddamn copper pitchers.

"Hey, Princess," I say, keeping my voice low and even, like I'm trying to calm a frightened dog. I love her. I hate that I have to do this to her. "What's going on here?"

At first, I think she doesn't hear me. But she blinks before I have to reach out and catch her chin, before I need to forcefully turn her away from whatever the hell she thinks she's seeing. She shudders—a long, rippling shiver that looks like it hurts.

"Herzog's brothers," she finally says, whispering so softly I have to lean close to hear.

"That cocksucker had brothers?"

She nods. "Two." And then a frown creases the space between her eyebrows. "Maybe more. I met two."

She's getting closer to speaking in sentences. That's good. But she's still staring at the computer screen like it's a nest of fucking tarantulas.

Now's as good a time as any to shut that goddamn email. I'm pretty sure Alix doesn't notice when I ease her hand off the mouse, but she sighs when the message closes. We're both left staring at the Diamond Freeport logo, centered on the screen.

I say, "I can't keep you safe, if you don't tell me what's going on."

Her eyes finally meet mine. The whiskey warmth I'm used to is gone, replaced by something cold and lonely, like the dirt on top of a new grave. "I've got to go," she says.

"The fuck you do."

"They're after me," she says. "I'm the one who killed their brother. They won't care about you after I leave."

She's talking in a weird voice, like she's reading words printed on the wall behind me. She's got a ghost-look in her eyes, same as she did after Herzog bled out on my dining room floor.

She's not in her right mind. I know that. But something jackknifes inside me at the casual way she says it—*after I leave*.

"Not gonna happen," I say.

"You don't know these men."

"I know men like them."

She shakes her head. "You *think* you do—"

I cut her off, fueled by rage that she ever needed to deal with those jizzstains on her own. "You're not leaving."

"But I—"

"Not a chance."

"You'd be safe—"

"No." I cut off her immediate argument. "I spent three years looking for you, waiting for you, praying to a god I don't believe in that you'd come back." Her face softens just a little, but I have to go on. "I just spent two weeks without you. Two weeks not sleeping. Not eating. There is no way in hell I'm letting you walk out that door now."

She still protests. "But I'm the one who did it. I killed Herzog."

"And *I'm* the one who covered up what happened. Your leaving now doesn't get me off the hook. We're in this together."

"Because of what I did."

She wants to be guilty. "Society" and "rules" say taking another life is wrong. But some fucking cumwipes don't belong in society. Some rules don't apply. "You just read their goddamn demands," I say. "A billion dollars and a freeport gallery. You think they'll give up a chance like that without fighting?"

And that's the argument that wins, at least for now. Acceptance—or maybe it's resignation—relaxes every muscle in her body. I recognize a similar response in my own. She's not leaving. I'm safe.

Safe enough, anyway, to ask, "What are their names? The brothers?"

"Jonas," she says, using the German pronunciation. "And Ansel."

"Where do they live?"

She shakes her head. "I don't know. I only saw them at his house."

Him. Klaus, the rat-fuck bastard. "They're in the same business?"

This time she shrugs. "They didn't spend their time talking."

She's hugging herself, rubbing her arms like the temperature on this August morning has dipped somewhere south of zero. I think about that copper pitcher, the one that made her catatonic. I don't know what they did to her, but I've got a pretty twisted imagination.

They're going to pay. Pay until it hurts. Way past that point. I'm going to kill the cocksuckers. I could do it with my bare hands. That's what krav maga's taught me, Beast or no fucking Beast.

But first, I have to push Alix for more, even if it makes me sound like a heartless bastard. "Anything you can remember, any detail, no matter how insignificant it seems."

Her face goes slack. I meant what I said—any detail might help my private investigator track down the motherfuckers. But I can imagine what she's recalling when she closes her eyes. I see her belly tighten, like she's absorbing body blows. I watch her face hollow in remembered pain.

"Okay," I say, letting her off the hook. I hate myself when I can't make my voice be as gentle as she deserves. "Let me know if you think of anything that might help."

She opens her eyes and nods, but the ghosts stay closer than I'd like. I reach across her to the computer keyboard and forward the email from her account to mine. I'm tempted to delete it from her screen forever, so she never has to think about the video again. But she's a strong and independent woman. She has the right to keep her own emails. And deleting it from her account won't make it go away.

"Here's what I don't get," she says, and I'm glad she's thinking again, instead of reliving the past. "How'd they get the footage? Didn't Sawyer Best say the cameras he found in the dining room were from the CIA?"

It's a good question and one I should have thought of. *Would* have thought of if I hadn't been focused on annihilating the fuckers who hurt her. "Best said he'd only seen equipment *like* that from the CIA. Which made perfect sense, with Thad Jackson a client."

Thaddeus Josiah Jackson oversaw the CIA before South Carolina voters elected him to the Senate. His conviction for tax fraud got him booted from the freeport—but he was still around when I added surveillance cameras here at the house.

I had the equipment installed after Alix went AWOL, after the first night she spent here. But there's no reason to dwell on that now.

She shakes her head, clearly fighting to connect the dots. "You thought a United States Senator installed cameras in your *home*?"

"Jackson's a paranoid son-of-a-bitch. Belt, suspenders, and an over-the-shoulder holster kind of paranoid. If he caught wind of my adding security, he'd piggyback on it, just in case he could use it to his own advantage down the line."

"And now you think he's in business with Jonas and Ansel."

I shake my head. "He's more of a fund-revolutionary-armies-in-Africa kind of guy than an illegal-drug-empire fuck-wad. Plus, there wasn't any evidence of the CIA being anywhere near the freeport the night Herzog died. We checked the tapes, remember? No panel van, no receiver set up anywhere close by."

"But Jackson could have had a receiver in his gallery,

couldn't he? Equipment to pick up surveillance from the bugs in here. Maybe broadcast it somewhere else."

I shake my head, but a sick certainty starts churning in my gut. "He couldn't. He cleared out his gallery when I booted his ass."

I see the instant Alix arrives at the same thought I just had. "But Herzog could. The equipment could be in Herzog's gallery."

Not bothering with a reply, I pull up a record on the computer screen. It's the security login for Herzog's gallery, the record of when his freeport space has been accessed. There's a list of entries and exits at the front gate, corresponding access to the warehouse building, to his individual gallery. The visits are frequent for the two and a half years Herzog was a client.

They stop abruptly on the night of June 21.

A red badge in the lower right corner of the screen shows that the gallery is currently locked. As expected, no one is inside the warehouse unit.

Alix has been following along. "How do we get in there?" she asks.

"Every gallery has biometric controls. We'll need a retina scan and a fingerprint."

Her lips twist into a wry frown. "And when we can't get those?"

I turn back to the phone and call Mac again. "Meet me at the warehouse," I say. "And bring an acetylene torch."

3

ALIX

The torch's brilliant white light cuts through the freeport's impenetrable lock. The spatter of molten metal sounds like bacon popping in a hot frying pan. The vaporized door smells like a nosebleed, salty iron dripping down the back of my throat.

When the torch cuts out, the corridor is strangely silent. I look up in time to catch Mac's authoritative glare as he draws his gun. He gestures for Trap and me to stand behind him. Turning sideways, presumably to present a smaller target, he flings himself around the door.

His caution triggers a tripwire in my belly. Up until now, I've believed the freeport was a safe haven. No matter how threatening their emails, Jonas and Ansel can't reach me here.

But I have to remember that Herzog got past Trap's security. He conned his way into the inner sanctum. He was invited to join the Diamond Ring. No one here saw the danger. No one recognized the threat.

It seems to take Mac an hour to work through the gallery, but a saner part of my brain knows it can only be a minute or two. Nevertheless, I'm relieved when he appears in the doorway again, his weapon holstered.

"All clear, boss," he says to Trap.

Trap acknowledges his head of security with a nod then turns to me. "You can wait out here if you want."

I shake my head. "I'm fine."

I see the set of his jaw. He wants to protect me. But Herzog's dead and buried—or cremated or sent through a wood-chipper or whatever Sawyer Best's mercenaries did to him when they finished their gristly clean-up. I need to see what my tormentor left behind.

Raising my chin, I follow Trap into the gallery.

This is the first time I've entered a client's private space within the freeport. I understand from Trap's literature that the six-floor warehouse is broken down into dozens of galleries. Each is temperature-controlled, protected from fire, water, and smoke. They're sound-proof too, with electronics to boost connectivity for phones and computers. The air-handling system refreshes one hundred percent of the air every thirty minutes.

It's called a gallery—I expect to see something like an art showroom. Plain white walls. Pinspot lighting. Maybe an austere Lucite desk.

But Herzog's gallery looks completely different.

I recognize it immediately. The walls are painted the dark burgundy of his luxurious home office. A kilim rug sprawls across the floor, anchored by a heavy oak desk, complete with a fancy executive chair. A leather armchair waits for a guest.

My knees threaten to buckle, and my arms twitch. It takes a conscious effort not to place my hands on my head, not to sink to the floor in the Presentation Posture I mastered over three long years.

Trap's watching me with the sort of attention usually

reserved for hospital patients in the ICU. I meet his gaze directly. "I'm fine," I say.

He acts like he believes me.

"Let's see what he's got in here," he says, leading the way to the back of the gallery.

I follow, telling myself I'm safe. Nothing can happen with Trap by my side, with Mac standing guard at the gallery door. Nothing can happen with Herzog dead.

The rear half of the gallery is filled with storage shelves. I've learned about arrangements like this in the past six weeks, as I've studied auction houses and museum annexes.

Sturdy walls slide on metal tracks. Grooves in the floor and anchors on the ceiling keep the walls stable. Each surface can hold one or more paintings; they can be pulled all the way out for easy viewing.

At a quick glance, I count a dozen walls, with space at the back for more to be installed. The last one is fully extended, displaying a single painting.

"Holy fuck," Trap says.

We move toward the work at the same time. It's small, no more than two feet square. The composition looks familiar—a room with gray walls and a checkerboard floor, a pair of dark paintings on the wall, one woman sitting at a harpsichord and another standing, listening to her play. The light over all of them is silvery and delicate. It almost seems like I'm looking at an aged color photograph.

"Is that…?" I start to ask. I've seen this painting in books. I've read about it in articles.

"Vermeer," Trap says, his lips tight. "*The Concert*. Stolen from the Isabella Stewart Gardner Museum in Boston in 1990."

We're close enough to touch it now, but both of us know better than to damage a world-class work of art with the natural oil on our fingertips. I glance at Trap, and I realize he isn't surprised to find this masterpiece hanging in the freeport gallery. "You knew it was here," I say.

"I suspected." He steps to the side, viewing the treasure from a slightly different angle. "The night I met Herzog, he hinted he had it. He didn't want to ship it overseas. That's why he became a freeport client. What do you think it's worth?"

He's asking me because I've spent the past six weeks in a crash course on auctioning art. I've spent hours and hours in New York auction houses, watching the valuation of paintings and sculpture. I've studied catalogs from recent sales.

"If I remember right, the museum said it was worth two hundred and fifty million, but that was years ago. A Leonardo da Vinci sold a while back for four fifty. So this Vermeer? Missing for so many years? Who knows what it would bring today?"

Trap looks over his shoulder at the other storage walls in the gallery. "What else was stolen in the Gardner heist?"

I try to remember the details. "A couple of Rembrandts. A Manet. Some drawings... The museum's still offering a huge reward—ten million dollars, I think."

Trap slides out one of the walls.

I'm pretty sure we both expect to find the missing treasures. But the paintings on display have nothing to do with the Boston museum. Instead, we're staring at a huge canvas that looks like someone spilled cans of house paint. "That's a Pollock," I say.

The next wall has a classic Rothko, big blocks of red and black blurred into each other. There are a couple of Warhols and some Picasso drawings, a pair of brightly colored Matisse interiors and a Cezanne landscape. We find three Van Goghs and Monet paintings of Waterloo Bridge and a train station.

They hang on the sliding walls, front and back. Some are large enough that they stand alone. Others are grouped, two, three, four to a wall.

We're staring at well over a billion dollars of art, completely separate from the Vermeer.

"Were they all stolen?" Traps asks.

"I don't know. I haven't read about any of them."

I take out my phone and start to snap pictures. This time, I go through the display walls methodically, sliding out the first, cataloging the treasures on the front, then the back. With Trap's help, I work my way through all twelve walls, until we're back to the Vermeer.

"Wait," I say. "We didn't see what's behind this one." Together, Trap and I walk around the wall to see if anything's hanging on the back.

And I'm hit with a surprise that nearly sends me to my knees.

The back of the gallery—the space that could be built out with more display walls if necessary—has been set up as a little room. There's a chair. And a lamp. And wooden shelves built into the back wall, cluttered with items I don't take the time to see.

The chair draws me like a magnet. It's been the backdrop of my nightmares for more than two years. Its wooden feet are shaped like claws, evil talons fastened around carved mahogany balls. It's filthy, smeared with greasy russet and brown stains that are ground into the upholstery.

My stomach lurches. Acid scorches my throat. I whirl, pushing past Trap, staggering to the front of the gallery. Starting to retch, I don't have time to find a trashcan. I stumble into the corridor and heave up peaches and coffee.

When I close my eyes, I'm back in Herzog's prison. He's bending me over that hideous chair, he and his brothers. That's where they broke me. That's where they used the copper cruet.

My eyes stream. My nose runs. I try to stand, but my stomach rebels again. I brace my hands on my thighs and lean over, choking out weak streams of bile.

I feel Trap's hand on my back, fingers spread between my shoulder blades. He's warm, when my entire body has turned to ice. He's solid, when I'm dissolving into space. He's quiet, when my brain is screaming in protest, howling about every torture I survived at Herzog's hands.

But Trap is the anchor I need.

I'm safe, for now. Herzog can never hurt me again. Jonas and Ansel aren't here. They're never getting access to the freeport.

I spit twice and cautiously pull myself upright.

The concern on Trap's face is louder than any question. He deserves to know what drove me out the gallery.

But what good will that do? What possible advantage is there for him to hear the details of how they drugged me? Of how they used me until my torn and ruined body collapsed? I don't even remember it all. I've blanked the worst parts from my conscious memory.

I take a deep breath. I'd forfeit the Vermeer in there for a handkerchief and a breath mint. Before I can say anything, though, Trap reaches past me.

"Thanks," he says, and I realize he's talking to Mac. My face flames because of the mess I've made in the hallway, but Trap just hands me a couple of paper towels. He drops several more over the remnants of my breakfast.

I mop my face, doing my best to blow my nose discreetly. I shove the used paper towel in my pocket.

"Okay?" Trap asks, the single word flooded with an ocean of concern.

I nod.

"I have to go back in there," he says. "I have to see what's on those shelves."

I nod again.

And then, because I can't let Herzog control me from his grave, I can't afford to let him win, I follow Trap back into the gallery.

I refuse to look directly at the chair. But the shelves tell their own horror story.

There are metal cuffs. Chains. Gags and muzzles and clamps with spikes. A cattle prod nearly sends me back to the hallway, my flesh remembering Herzog's heavy hand.

He could have brought me here. He could have *kept* me here, bound in this soundproof room. He could have forced me to submit to him forever.

Maybe that's what he planned the night of the Diamond Ring dinner party. Or maybe he was outfitting this dungeon for future fun and games.

I'm shivering too hard to recognize the device in Trap's hand. It's a black plastic case, with a couple of dials and a hard rubber extension. "Wh— what's that?"

"A receiver," he says.

I blink and the thing makes sense. It was only my terror that transformed it into another tool for torture.

Trap picks up another rectangular box—more dials, more gauges, another antenna, and an electric plug that runs into the wall. "And here's the transmitter." He hefts the receiver in his hand. "He picked up the signal from the bugs with this. And he boosted the signal with that."

"But why? If he knew I was going to kill him, he would have stopped me before I ever had a chance."

"He didn't plan on getting video of his own death. He was monitoring to get leverage against me. Blackmail, maybe. Trade secrets from the Diamond Ring. Whatever he thought he could sell."

It makes sense, in a terrible, twisted way.

"So what do we do now?" I ask.

"*You* are going to research those paintings. See if any others were stolen."

"And you?"

"I'm going to build a fucking bonfire and get rid of this shit." His gesture takes in the chair, the lamp, and all the garbage on the shelves. "And then I'm tracking down Herzog's asshole brothers."

4

TRAP

One good way to measure your Chief of Security: See if he has any questions when you ask him to torch a chair that looks like it was on the set for one of those *Saw* movies. Extra points if he doesn't blink when you toss in a pile of used BDSM gear. And if he starts the fire with a cattle prod before destroying that evidence too, give him a fucking raise.

Mac carried out the destruction in the back parking lot. I didn't bother pointing out that metal wouldn't burn, but I did tell him I didn't want Alix seeing any residue left behind. I'm sure he put one and one together, but he's kept his mouth shut about a lot more since Diamond Freeport opened.

Herzog's paintings couldn't stay in his gallery, not with the door torched. I could have ordered warehouse staff to move them to an unused room, but I figured the fewer people who knew about the Vermeer, the better. I moved them myself, into an unused gallery.

I haven't decided what to do with the painting yet. A Boy

Scout would hand it over to the museum as soon as possible. An everyday guy would figure out how to spend his ten mill reward.

But I'm a billionaire who can afford to look the other way, even for an eight-figure payout. And I'm running a tax haven where more than a few of my clients are engaged in shady dealings.

Handing over the Vermeer will just invite a visit from some of my old friends—the IRS, the FBI, and fuck-all other government agencies. I owe it to my clients to keep the authorities from breathing down all our necks.

Speaking of debts to my clients...

Alix is the star of the video that arrived this morning. But there are more than enough supporting roles to put plenty of people in the line of fire. The camera caught me full-face, but if I go through frame by frame, I bet I'll find mugshots for the rest of the Diamond Ring.

Every guy who was there that night got a million-dollar bump in his freeport account for his silence. But the existence of the video changes the equation. Money is hard to balance against hard time in federal prison. And if the Herzog assholes are willing to blackmail me, I doubt they'll refrain from going after my clients too.

So I need to track down Jonas and Ansel Herzog. Find out where they're living. Pay them a little visit. I'll try negotiating, getting their absurd demands down to something I can afford. And if that doesn't work, I'll take care of them the same way Alix handled their brother.

Maybe with a little less blood spatter.

Or not.

It's the least I can do to protect Alix. The freeport. My fucking clients. My entire goddamn life.

Once I'm safely behind my closed office door in the freeport tower, I take out my cell. Harry Asher answers on the first ring.

"I've got a rush project," I say.

"Sure thing, boss."

"I need a full work-up on two individuals—addresses, family members, business contacts, names of their fucking pets, whatever you can find. And I need it in twenty-four hours."

We both know I pay well enough to jump to the head of the line. I hear Asher draw on one of his cheap cigars, sucking hard before he says, "Tell me what you've got, boss."

"Names," I say. "Klaus Herzog, Jonas Herzog, and Ansel Herzog." No one knows Klaus is dead. I'm not going to spill the beans to Asher. "They've been present in Delaware in the past three years, but I don't know if they're living here. There's a chance they're German nationals. They may be involved with drug distribution in the mid-Atlantic."

"Got any photos?"

"Not yet."

"Last known location?"

In my fucking computer. I could send Asher the email, but he's more of a shoe-leather kind of guy. "Nada," I say.

"Twenty-four hours?" he confirms.

"Faster, if you can make it."

"Got it, boss," he says. He hangs up without more small talk —that's another reason I keep him on my payroll.

I'm tempted to pull up the video again, to check the fucking countdown. But there's a clock on my computer screen, and I can see I'm three and a half hours closer to life as I know it falling apart.

I debate bringing the Diamond Ring into the loop now. But what would I actually say?

Hello—just wanted to give you a heads-up that you might be getting a call from the Dover PD, or maybe the FBI.

Hey there—thought you should know that the million-dollar deposit I made to your freeport account back in June is prime evidence that you're an accessory after the fact to murder one.

Yo, rich guy. Pay your share or the video goes public.

Fuck. I'm not contacting my best clients until I can offer every one of them a real solution.

I close my eyes, and I'm back in the warehouse, standing outside Herzog's gallery with my hand on Alix's back while she pukes up her breakfast. I felt so goddamn helpless, like someone had my balls in a vise.

No. Not like that at all. Because if someone had ahold of my balls, *I'd* be the one in pain. That chair and all the fucking crap on the shelves hurt *Alix*.

I've never felt this way before. Like I'd gladly plant my palm on the steaming wreckage of a torched metal door, just to keep her from being hurt. Like I'd hand over a painting worth a quarter of a billion dollars to guarantee I'd never have to see the look of terror on her face when she discovered that fucking chair.

I'm a mean-hearted bastard who's spent the last twenty years figuring out fucked-up ways to manage the world around me. But watching Alix battle the pain of the past three years leaves me feeling like a helpless little kid.

A kid...

I glance at my computer. There are a couple hundred items demanding my immediate attention. Emails have flooded in since last night's auction—congratulations from freeport clients, queries about setting up sales on other assets, inquiries from outsiders who know nothing more than rumors.

There's a backlog of work from the past two weeks, which I spent sitting around, missing Alix like a starry-eyed teenager with a wicked crush.

I have a stack of long-term projects—a presentation I'm supposed to make in Geneva next January, a pitch to the Dover airfield for a hangar dedicated exclusively to freeport clients, progress reports on the nearly-finished freeport racetrack and its underground garage, complete with storage bays for clients' investments in luxury vehicles...

I don't want to do any of them.

I want to cross the parking lot to my house, find Alix, and

bury my face so deep in her sweet pussy that I can forget I ever opened Diamond Freeport.

But as much as my cock likes that idea, I know I won't do it. Not this morning. Not when Alix was forced to face video proof of the asshole she saved herself from. Not when she had to see that goddamn chair, had to relive memories brutal enough to leave her puking in the hall.

Any other day, I'd gladly forfeit the freeport's share of the Monet Alix auctioned last night to keep her tied to my bed for a week or ten. I'd make her happy to stay there, too.

But she's spent enough time chained for any man's desire.

She needs something else. Something entirely different. Something away from the freeport, away from any reminder of what happened here.

I shut down my computer. I say goodbye to the security guard in the office tower lobby. I cross the parking lot and enter my home by the front door.

I find Alix in the kitchen, staring into a coffee mug like she's forgotten what a cup is for. She's changed her top. Brushed her teeth, too, from the fresh, minty smell.

She looks up when I enter, her face clouded with worry. She opens her mouth to say something, but I cut her off.

"Let's go," I say.

"Go where?" She sounds wary.

"The county fair. And I'm not taking 'no' for an answer."

5

ALIX

It's dark by the time we return home from the fairgrounds, even the long summer afterglow faded from the sky. I'm exhausted as I climb out of the Range Rover, but I'm strangely restless, too. Part of me wants to collapse into bed and sleep for a year. Another part of me wants to build a campfire in the backyard and feed it endless cords of wood, fending off the darkness.

The stuffed panda Trap won for me looks even larger on the kitchen counter. Its plastic eyes glint when Trap turns on the under-cabinet lights, like the bear knows my deepest, darkest secrets.

"Thirsty?" Trap asks, already moving to the cupboard to collect a pair of glasses.

"Mmm," I say. I *am* thirsty. And hungry, too, which I wouldn't have thought possible after everything we ate at the fair. Or maybe that's another need, making my belly feel like

I'm swooping down from the top of the Ferris wheel. Thinking about what we did up there, where anyone could have looked up, where anyone could have seen...

Trap grins at me as he cracks open a bottle of Berg and pours over clear ice cubes. The twist of his lips makes him look ten years younger. "You got some sun today."

I wrinkle my nose and feel the crackle of rosy skin. "You did too." His cheeks are flushed, and his forehead looks like it might be warm to the touch.

"Maybe if we hadn't been trapped on the Ferris wheel for so long..." he says, taking a seat on the bar stool next to me.

I gulp my water, fast enough that the ice cubes shift. Water splashes the front of my T-shirt. My sunburned cheeks heat with embarrassment, and I cross my arms to hide the spill.

My motion, of course, does little to disguise the wet fabric stretched across my chest. My sports bra isn't concealing much either. It does, though, draw Trap's sharp attention to my breasts. "Quit it," I say.

He leans closer. "Quit what?"

I draw in a shaky breath. "Quit staring at me."

He reaches over and catches one of my suddenly peaked nipples between his thumb and forefinger. His pinch rockets through my body, stealing my breath and making me sway on my stool. "Is this better?" he breathes.

Before I can answer, he fishes an ice cube out of his glass. He presses it against my other nipple, holding it fast through my wet T-shirt and bra.

I gasp against the sudden burn of the cold. His grin turns wicked as he pulls me between his legs, close enough for me to feel the massive erection trapped inside his jeans.

He raises the ice cube to my lips, teasing until they purse. I suck in the crystal cube, feeling it puddle almost immediately in the hot little cave of my mouth.

He doesn't wait for me to swallow. Instead, he squeezes his

thighs to keep me from escaping. At the same time, he strips off my T-shirt with quick and efficient fingers. "Trap!" I laugh, automatically glancing over my shoulder at the wall of windows behind us.

He's told me before that no one can get into the back yard. But still, I feel like a naughty schoolgirl when he pulls my bra over my head. I start to cover my breasts, but the fierce look in his eyes stops me. He holds my gaze as he reaches for his glass, easing an ice cube past his ready lips.

And then he leans forward, sucking my nipple into his mouth.

The heat of his lips merges with the cold of the ice. He rocks the cube across my nipple, holding the ice in place with his tongue as he sucks hard enough to send darts to the needy place between my thighs.

The ice hurts, but he soothes me before I can whimper a complaint. His fingers clutch my hips, squeezing in the same rhythm of his mouth. Needing more, fearing more, I thrust my shoulders back, giving him better access to my chest. His teeth close over my nipple, and a shudder ripples through me, so intense that I have to steady myself by placing my hands on his shoulders.

My motion leaves me staring directly into the dining room.

I don't deserve this pleasure. It's wrong for me to feel this good.

I killed a man, not thirty feet from where I'm standing. My very existence endangers everything Trap has built here. He's at risk. His clients are too.

I shouldn't be melting beneath Trap's attention.

I should be punished.

I push off his shoulders, stepping back until my breast slips free with an ugly slurping sound.

"What the—" Trap starts to complain. He thinks he taught me how to appreciate these breasts, their ridiculous size, the absurd way they bounce. That was a lesson I supposedly mastered just last night.

But right now, right here, I know I shouldn't be allowed that sort of salvation. I don't deserve pleasure.

"What?" Trap asks. "Tell me what you want. Tell me how to make you feel good."

Years ago, he gave me the words. He touched my body, and he taught me how to ask for what I craved.

But I was another woman then. A good woman. Innocent. Naive.

I close my eyes, and I can see the chair we found in Herzog's gallery this morning. I see the stains, each one etched in my memory. The blood and shit on the chair merge with the blood and shit I left in Trap's dining room the night I killed Herzog.

I find the words for what I need.

"Punish me," I say. The words feel right. They match my broken body. They fit my shattered soul. So I say them again, louder, more firmly: "Punish me."

He closes the distance between us, and I have to crane my neck to look into his eyes. His face is dark, cast into dramatic shadows by the blue-white light that glows beneath the cabinets.

His fingers grip my arms, tight enough to bruise. When I realize he's going to mark me, that I'll have those purple reminders for days to come, something ripples deep inside me. If his fingers were testing my pussy instead of clutching my arms, they'd come away soaked.

His kiss is savage. It's lips and tongue and teeth, and it strips away something deep inside me. His right hand moves from my arm to my hair, and he scrabbles to pull it, but it's still too short for a truly painful yank. "Say red to stop," he growls against my stinging lips. "Yellow to slow down."

"Green," I say. "Green, green, green."

Snarling, he drags me up the stairs.

I've never been in his bed without the ritual of a shower to start. But that was when his Beast rode him, when he fought against his own traumatic memories. Tonight, he's free. He's safe. So he orders me out of my jeans and the comfortable cotton panties I wore for an innocent day at the county fair.

I stand in front of him, completely naked. I wait for him to give me what I need.

He points to the dresser. "Get the rope. Both skeins."

I cross to the deep drawer and kneel. I reach inside, past leather, past metal, past hardened silicone plugs that feel like they could split me in two. Coils of cotton rope wait at the back. They're black and thick and soft enough that I worry they can't quench the shame burning deep inside my brain. But I gather them and bring them to Trap.

I want him to talk to me, to tell me what he's planning, but I know I don't deserve that form of grace. I'd settle for him reciting all the reasons he's binding me, all the terrible things I've done, all the ways he needs to be in charge.

But he's silent as he ties me up. He takes his time wrapping my wrists, first the right, then the left. He pulls the rope tight enough to leave creases on my skin. He positions a knot over the pulse point at the base of each thumb.

When he's done, he marches me to the side of the bed. The mattress is high; the top hits the middle of my thighs. He cups the base of my skull in the V between his thumb and forefinger, forcing me to bend over.

"Spread your legs," he orders, and I do. I don't move fast enough, though, because he kicks my feet further apart. He's still wearing shoes, and the pressure on my ankles hurts.

He dips his hand between my legs, shoving into my pussy with all the sensitivity of a mechanic checking oil in an engine. I gasp at his rough touch, at the shock of his knuckles brushing my lower lips. I already know I'm drenched before he wipes my juice across my bare ass.

This is sick. Twisted. I spent three years enslaved to a man who punished me for breathing. Why the hell does my body crave this type of violence now, when I could beg for anything else?

Trap catches the free ends of the ropes before he walks to the far side of the bed. He yanks my arms tight, making short work of lashing my bonds to the iron headboard and footboard. My breasts smash into the mattress. My belly lies flat. I can barely raise my head, can barely track his motions as he pins my arms wide.

Tension rolls down my sides, rippling through the muscles that bind my ribs, but Trap is still not satisfied. He grunts as he wraps another turn of rope around each bedpost, forcing my arms to stretch more. I balance on tiptoe beside the bed, trying to compensate.

I shouldn't be excited. I shouldn't be panting for breath. I shouldn't be desperate for this, begging for this, already spinning tight to a consciousness that's trapped between my quivering thighs.

Trap crosses behind me, and I try to turn my neck, to see what he's planning. I don't have enough range to see the dresser drawer. I can't follow what he takes out before he stalks behind me.

"If you could see yourself now," he says…

"What?" I ask. I wish he had a mirror. I need to know what I look like. I need to know that I'm getting what I deserve.

"Your ass so high in the air… Good girls don't stand like that. Good girls don't leave their legs spread, their pussies bare."

"I'm not good," I say. "I'm very, very bad."

I got an A plus in Psych 103, Abnormal Psych—*Nuts and Sluts*, we students called it. I have a dozen clinical terms for all the things I'm not supposed to like, paraphilias that could warrant years of talking to a therapist.

But if this is sick, I don't want to be healed.

I deserve this.

I earned this.

"And what do bad girls get?" Trap asks, his voice low and dangerous.

"Punishment," I say when I can manage enough of a breath.

"Count," he commands. And a stripe of fire falls across my ass.

It's a riding crop. I can just turn my head enough to make out the flat tab of leather, the whip-thin rod trembling in the air. "One!" I count. My skin tingles, sharper than the sunburn that crinkles my face.

He strikes me again, igniting a furrow just below the first one.

"Two!" I cry. This time the blow burns a little deeper. The heat spreads further beneath my flesh.

Again.

"Three!" I can feel the imprint of the leather tab, separate from the crop's thin shaft. He's layering his blows, restraining the full force he could deliver in favor of careful targeting.

"You're so red," he says, caressing my ass. The tip of his finger tests my pussy. "And so very, very wet."

I'm disgusting. A self-respecting woman would never let herself be tied up and beaten, not after everything I've survived. I shouldn't have asked for this. I shouldn't submit.

Which means I need more punishment.

So I rock back on my toes just a little. I stretch my arms in their aching sockets so I can raise my ass higher. I squeeze my butt-cheeks tight and beg, "More."

He gives it to me—seven more blows. Each is harder than the one before. Each raises the flame eating me from the inside out. Each makes me tremble, makes me ache, makes me long for the ultimate release that he alone can give me.

And when I've gasped out "Ten," I beg him. "Please," I urge. "Finish me off," I plead. "Please, please, please, let me come."

But he steps back from the bed and crosses his arms, the crop still gripped in his right hand.

"Please, Trap," I beg. "I need you. I need…"

"No," he says, his voice colder than I've ever heard it. "I'm in charge now. *I* say what you need. And *I* decide what you get. That's the penalty for being a bad girl."

I love him and I hate him and I can never, ever, ever get enough of what he's giving me.

6

TRAP

Alix cries a protest, exactly the way I knew she would. She's ready for me. Drenched. Balanced on her toes to tempt me with that incredible ass.

The lines left by the crop stand out, scarlet against her smooth white flesh. I purposely didn't choose the cane. I didn't want to break her skin, but I wanted to give her what she asked for. I want her to know she can always come to me. Come *for* me. I'll always give her what she needs, even when she doesn't know it herself.

Now, I trace the length of her spine with the crop's leather tab. She arches like a cat, even though the curve must stretch her arms to the point of pain. When she's strung as tight as a bow, I balance the crop across her lower back, placing it precisely on the matched dimples on either side of her spine.

"Hold it there, Princess. If it falls, I stop."

I don't give her a chance to question my command. Instead, I drop to my knees behind her. I bury my face in the sweet cleft of her ass, pointing my tongue straight at the tight pucker of muscle.

"Red!" she calls, before I've taken my first taste. Her thighs turn to stone around my shoulders. She's frozen, not daring to take a breath.

My poor princess. The first night I had her in this bed, the Beast commanded me to close her up with a butt plug. She panicked then, safeworded before I could ease her past the pain.

The same fear has her shut down now. Her fingers curl into claws. Her toes are locked in place. She's holding her breath, every muscle tensed as she waits to see if I'll honor her safeword.

I want to break the rules. I want to rim her now. To shock her. To show her pleasure her body's never known before. I can already imagine her rippling orgasm, rolling from her well-fingered clit to her pussy to the dark channel pulsing hard around my tongue.

That's something the fucking Beast has never let me do before, with any woman. Something special. Something I'll only share with Alix.

But rules are rules. The safeword is an absolute.

I rock back on my heels.

She hasn't flexed her back. She hasn't dropped the riding crop.

And that deserves some sort of reward.

I dive into her pussy like a starving man. I suck her folds into my lips, drawing hard enough to make her gasp. I release her slowly, stiffening my tongue, exploring deep inside. I feel her moan with my entire face.

She's honey and salt, a fruit I've only eaten in my dreams. One taste primes my throat, and I swallow like I can never drink enough. I need to slow down, need to take my time, need to tease her because that's what a good man does, but it's all I can manage not to rip my clothes off and bury my throbbing hard-on in her tantalizing heat.

I tap her clit with my tongue, then lick her front to back. She groans my name, pleading, begging. I stroke her again, slower this time. Her thighs tremble. Her calves stretch.

One. More. Time.

She teeters. Reaches. Cries out on a single endless note—a question, an answer, a desperate, mindless prayer.

I purse my lips and breathe across her sweet, drenched snatch before I give her the command: "Come."

And she breaks.

Diving in for the finish, my face is washed in her heat. She's seizing above me, around me. I work my tongue past her fluttering pussy lips, and I'm rewarded with a wash of fresh, sweet nectar. She's coming and she's coming and she's coming and I can't drink enough, can't breathe enough, can't dive deep enough to ride her forever.

Finally, she slows. She shudders. She sighs.

I shift back to kiss the inside of her thigh. I sit back on my heels. I look up at the magnificent arch of her ass, at the flushed orchid between her thighs that ripples in a sudden shiver of aftermath.

And I see the stretch of her back. The tight violin curves above her hips. The riding crop, turned askew, but never dropped. Never fallen.

"Good girl," I breathe.

And I think she won't respond, because it takes her a few deep breaths to protest. "No," she says. "I'm a very bad girl."

Even now, she wants more. Needs more. Needs me to give it to her.

I rescue the crop and finger the tab. I trace the leather flap along her flanks, watching them tremble in anticipation. I follow the knobs of her spine, marveling at how she can still arch when her legs shake with exhaustion.

I twist my hand around the crop's grip, changing the angle before she has a chance to know what I intend, and I land a single leather slap to her clit. At the same time, I repeat the magic word, short, sharp, an unmistakable command: "Come."

She cries out and collapses, letting her knees bend, pressing her thighs against the edge of the bed. She's coming again, deeper, harder, so intense she's lost the capacity to sigh, to breathe, to chant my name or call on God.

I toss away the crop and rip my belt loose. The sight of her, the smell of her, the taste of her still on my tongue... I don't have time to shuck off my jeans.

I shove my pants down with my boxers, just enough to free my raging cock. My fingers close around her hips, posing her, warning her. My dick moves like a heat-seeking missile, and I plow into her, balls-deep.

She finds the air to gasp then. Her fingers clutch beneath their ropes, greedy, longing. I pull back, almost leaving her tight, trembling pussy, but when she whimpers, I give her what we both need. I ride her hard.

I can't last long, not with the memory of her breaking beneath me at the fair, not with the scent of her filling my room, not with the heat of her clutching me, pulling me in on the ebbing tide of her own release.

Five long strokes, each deeper than the one before.

One endless moment when my cock *is* her pussy, when we're so completely joined, so utterly locked that I don't know where I end and she begins.

A single second when something cracks inside me.

And then I'm coming harder than I've ever come in my life. I'm deep inside her, and my shout or my grip or my flood of white-hot heat brings her back to the very edge. One last time, I order her to come. She screams my name and bucks beneath me and her slick needy cunt milks me dry.

A century later I can breathe again. A thousand years, and I can open my eyes. Another millennium, and I can plant my hands on either side of her sweat-streaked back, pushing myself off of her, finally slip free of our mingled, puddled heat.

I climb onto the bed and fumble at her ropes, freeing her left hand first, then her right. I brace her as she lowers her arms, absorbing the stretched ache of her body with mine. I pull her spine against my chest as she starts to shiver, throwing a leg over hers to spoon her back to warmth.

She sighs and wriggles closer. Her ass presses against my cock, which for once is too spent to do anything about the very welcome attention. Folding her close with my left arm beneath us, I work the fingers of my right hand through her short hair, finding a place at the nape of her neck that makes her purr.

I'll give her a few minutes. Then, I'll get her a glass of water. Feed her a square of dark chocolate. Bring her some salve for the marks I left on her ass and take care of the—

"Oh sweet fuck." I say the words out loud, because I'm too shocked to lock them inside.

I've never fucked without a rubber. The Beast's seen to that. The Beast, and my fifth-grade health teacher who drilled into my impressionable little skull the twin certainties of disease and fatherhood.

Sex has always meant convenient foil squares. I keep one in my wallet. I've got a box in my nightstand. I never travel without a strip tucked away in my Dopp kit.

I don't drive without keys. I don't fuck without condoms.

And it never crossed my goddamn mind to stop and get one tonight. I never had a moment's hesitation. I never had a single, solitary instant where I thought I should pull back, hold off, suit up.

Alix murmurs something. I miss all the words but her final lilting, "Okay?"

I nuzzle a soft kiss to her temple. "I'm fine." But I have to go on. It's only fair for me to say, "But I fucked up. I didn't wear a rubber."

I'm not sure what I expect, how she'll freak out. She might be furious. She might be terrified. After everything Herzog put her through, she might cry.

But she rolls toward me like she's waking up after a full night's sleep. She shifts her legs to capture my thigh between hers. She folds her hands between us, planting her palms on my chest.

I try not to stare at the stripes my ropes left on her wrists as she asks, "What will make you feel safe?"

"Make *me* feel safe?"

She reaches for my hand, lacing her fingers between mine. "Is it enough just to tap? Or do you need to punch something to clear the compulsion?"

I just pumped my jizz into her unprotected body, and she's worried about how I'll calm the fucking Beast? "No," I say. "It's not that. I'm fine with that. But I don't want to hurt you. The last thing you need to worry about is getting pregnant."

Her laugh sounds like the snort of a tiny dragon. "Not a problem," she says. She guides my fingers to the soft flesh inside her upper arm. "The one gift Herzog actually gave me."

I feel a hard ridge, like a couple of matchsticks nestled beneath her skin.

"Five years," she says. "No babies. No visits from Aunt Flo."

Aunt Fucking Flo. Sometimes, my princess isn't that far removed from the woman who sat in my kitchen three years ago, so shy and reserved I guessed she was a virgin.

But we've traveled a million miles since then. She takes my hand and raises my knuckles to her lips. "I'm clean," she says. "Dr. Hanson saw to that. Do you need to see my records? I'll give her permission to release everything to you."

She's so certain. So trusting. So calm and still and sure. My throat tightens. I feel pressure behind my eyes as I flip our hands around and brush my lips across *her* knuckles. "No," I say. "I don't need anything. Anything but you."

Her laugh vibrates through me as I pull her close. I didn't expect my cock to come back on duty any time tonight, but we both feel it stir.

"No more condoms," Alix says, utterly content. And her fingers close around my dick to seal the deal.

7

ALIX

I wake in Trap's bed, alone. Sometime during the night, he pulled a sheet over us. A blanket, too. Now they're tangled round my waist and tucked between my knees. I reach for his pillow, but I'm not surprised to find it's cool. I have no idea how long he's been gone.

Stretching as I climb out of bed, I'm greeted by the protest of overused muscles. My arms ache. My sides ache. My thighs feel like I've spent hours swimming through honey.

Looking down, I find my wrists are laced with bruises, the pattern of Trap's ropes printed like rows of interlocking bracelets. I need the bathroom mirror to confirm that my ass is marked as well. I can make out purple-red blotches where the riding crop's leather tab struck me squarely, along with a forest of thin imprints left by the shaft.

I can't resist poking at the bruises with the pads of my fingers. The soft ache fills me with a secret shame. I still don't understand how I flew apart so wildly beneath Trap's punishment, how he knew exactly what I needed, how a part of me is so broken that it thrives on the type of abuse I was forced to endure in Herzog's house.

I may not understand, but I can't deny the thrill that turns lazy somersaults in my belly as I remember everything Trap did to me last night. I'm broken. Disgusting. Perverted. But still, he gave me exactly what I needed.

And now, I desperately need a shower. I don't hesitate to use the one in the Trap's bathroom. I use his soap, too. His shampoo. His razor. It feels right to stand beneath the rainfall shower head, to turn on the jets that shoot from the wall.

This is where Trap first claimed me. This is where I belong.

I wrap a towel around my body and cross the hall to the guest room. My clothes still hang in the closet where I left them when I fled two weeks ago. Then, I took only a handful of necessities—jeans, T-shirts, a shapeless pair of pajamas.

Now I stare at the closet, at the dresser, at the nightstand stacked high with catalogs from the art auctions I've attended on the freeport's behalf. Do I move my things into Trap's room? Do I wait for a formal invitation? Do I plan on staying as a guest until Trap takes me to bed again?

Because that's one thing I know for sure. I may not be certain where to leave my things, but I know Trap and I have only begun to explore the pleasure our bodies can share. The punishment he can give me. The submission I'll endure.

I pull on clean underwear and a sports bra, soft khakis, and a top that buttons up the front. I feel confident. Safe. At ease.

And ready to drop to my knees in a heartbeat, if that's what Trap commands.

I'm nearly bowled over by a surge of lust. For just an instant, I'm back in Trap's bedroom, calves aching, every muscle in my body dedicated to keeping the riding crop balanced on my back. The memory is so real my nipples peak. I'm soaked again, between my legs. If Trap were here, if he gave me his command, I'd come right now, without him touching me at all.

I shake my head because I have no idea where to find the sane part of me, the student part of me, the sister/daughter/friend part of me that I lost years ago.

I head downstairs.

I hear Trap before I see him. His voice thunders from his office, annoyance sharpening the words. "What the fuck am I supposed to do with this?"

"Sorry, boss." The man who answers doesn't actually sound sorry at all. He sounds like he smokes ten packs a day and gargles with shattered glass.

I step into the doorway. Trap is behind his desk, thumbing his way through a ream of paper. A man sits across from him, hunched in the visitor chair. He looks like a washed-up boxer, or maybe the trainer who crouches over a stool in a corner of the ring, holding a sweat-soaked sponge and a bucket of filthy water. Trap waves me forward, and I'm struck with the stench of decades-old cigars.

"This is Alix Key," Trap says by way of introduction. "Alix, Harry Asher's been looking into the Herzog brothers for me."

Trap makes the investigation sound like nothing special, like he ordered up a report on recipes for tuna salad, or changes in the corporate tax code, or federal standards for vehicle fuel consumption. I try to keep my face blank as I slip into the empty seat on the visitor's side of the desk.

The investigator huffs a greeting and glances at me with apparent disinterest. I realize, though, that he notices my hair, shorter than most women choose to wear it. He takes in my bare feet, too. And his gaze lingers on my wrists for just a heartbeat longer than necessary. My bruises feel like they've been dipped in fluorescent paint.

"Ms. Key," he says, his tone perfectly neutral.

"Mr. Asher." I'm not as good at this as he is.

"Go ahead," Trap says to the PI. "Alix is read in on this. Why don't you give us the executive summary?" He pushes the massive stack of paper away, as if it's the source of the eye-watering cigar stench. Which, come to think of it, it might be, if the paper has spent more than fifteen minutes anywhere near Harry Asher.

The detective shrugs. "Klaus, Jonas, and Ansel Herzog are German nationals. They were born in Hamburg, to a postal clerk and a high school English teacher. Klaus is forty-three years old. Jonas is thirty-eight. Ansel, thirty-six. All three were educated in the German equivalent of public schools and attended the University of Hamburg."

The facts are so mundane, so absolutely commonplace, that for a moment, I think they don't matter. Herzog and his brothers terrorized me, but they're nothing special. Nothing out of the ordinary. I was just unlucky. In the wrong place at the wrong time.

Betrayed by my twin brother.

But Mr. Asher goes on. "Separately, they're each worth northward of fifty billion dollars. Combined, they rank up there with Bezos and Gates. Musk. Zuckerberg. That type of wealth."

Trap grunts. He's a billionaire himself, but he doesn't have *that* kind of money.

Yet.

Mr. Asher continues, as if Trap actually asked him a question. "Between the three of them, they have six homes. Berlin, London, New York. Zermatt. St. Tropez. Napa. Those are the ones listed in their personal names. They probably have more— a lot more—held by their corporations."

Trap peels away the top inch of paper, making a show of studying something that looks like a family tree. Mr. Asher leans across the desk, pointing a yellow-stained index finger at the top square. "They run a construction firm in Germany, Herzog GmbH. They're into big scale stuff—World Cup soccer stadiums, Olympics venues, airports in the Middle East. The main company has dozens of subsidiaries—architecture, finance, building supplies, the usual."

Trap scowls as he takes in the scale of brothers' operations. He holds up half a dozen pages with columns of fine print. "This is private banking data?"

Mr. Asher shrugs. "I know a guy who knows a guy. Best estimate, you're looking at half their accounts. Probably less. We can't get at anything in the Caymans or Switzerland. Belize or Singapore, either."

Trap swears and pushes the listings away. "That's it?"

"That's not even the tip of the iceberg." Mr. Asher seems to enjoy Trap's exasperated sigh. "Near as I can tell, they've got the main distribution system for crystal meth in Western Europe. They've got their hands in other pies too. Heroin. Coke. Some new shit called Crash, supposed to be like acid, but it's formulated special, to mess with kids' heads. They've got something called Stag, too, like Viagra for college kids, or high school, whatever. They say it lasts longer than the blue pill and supercharges the pleasure center in the brain. Starting about ten years ago, they made a major play for the East Coast of the US. They're muscling in on established gangs from Boston to Atlanta."

"Charming," Trap says.

I don't say anything. I'm too busy trying to remember to breathe. My one experience with Crash scarred me for life, and my neural pathways are a hell of a lot more developed than the children the Herzogs are targeting.

Trap leans back in his chair. "So, bottom line. How am I getting at these assholes?"

"Bottom line," Mr. Asher says. "You aren't."

"That's not an acceptable answer."

"What do you want, boss? These guys are the real deal. International agencies at their command. Whole governments in their pockets."

"Bullshit," Trap says.

Mr. Asher takes offense. "You gave me twenty-four hours, and I came up with all this shit. Dig any deeper, and I'll probably find their private army."

"Do it," Trap says.

"Find an army?" Mr. Asher sounds tired.

"Find a wedge. A lever. I need to get to these guys, and I need to do it yesterday."

"It's gonna cost, boss."

"Do I look like I give a fuck?"

Mr. Asher stands.

Trap gives him a pointed look. "Forty-eight hours, max," he says. "Double your rate, if you get it to me in twenty-four."

I didn't expect the bandy-legged Mr. Asher could leave the room with that much speed.

Trap waits until the front door closes before he runs a hand over his face. His eyes are closed, and fatigue is etched across his features. His shoulders slump, and for just a moment I can see the twelve-year-old boy who learned the depths of the world's cruelty in a diamond mine camp in the middle of Congo.

I'm the one who's putting him through this. I'm the reason he's pushing Mr. Asher so hard. If I hadn't killed Herzog, Trap wouldn't be facing insane demands for his money. He wouldn't be at risk of losing the freeport.

Fifteen minutes ago, I was trying to decide if I should move my belongings into Trap's bedroom. Now, I'm waiting for him to go to the freeport's office building so I can pack up my things and get the hell out of his life.

"Don't," Trap says.

"Don't what?" I try to keep my tone light. I fail.

"Don't leave."

"I'm not going to—"

"Don't lie."

I swallow my immediate denial. How can he read my mind? But that's the bond between us, something powerful, something magical. It's been there from the moment I saw him outside

Debasement. It's the reason I threw away my rulebook, why I dared to go home with him, why I found my freedom in his bed.

It's why I love him.

That's why it kills me to hurt him. But I have to say, "Let's be logical. We're both better off if I'm not here."

"How the fuck am I better off?"

I gape, because the answer is so freaking obvious. "If not for me, you wouldn't have two murderous drug lords blackmailing you and trying to turn your business into a drug distribution center for the entire east coast of the United States."

He makes a sound like a broken buzzer. "Bad answer."

"It's the truth!"

"The Herzogs smell blood in the water. Even if you disappear tomorrow, they aren't going anywhere."

"But the video shows me—"

"The video shows *me*," he interrupts. "Sitting at the head of the table. Watching. Doing absolutely nothing to stop you. And they sent us what? Five minutes of tape? They've got hours, Princess. They have a complete record of everything that happened after Kelly hauled your ass upstairs. They know I consulted with Best and Wolf. They know I opened the door to Best's dark army. They know I allowed every hint of blood to be scrubbed from my home, without reaching out to the police, the FBI, anyone. They've got a complete record, up to the minute Best found the goddamn cameras."

He's right.

I know he's right. But I still want to protect him. I want to go back in time, to the first night I spent here. I want to make the world safe for both of us, forever.

"Make me a promise," Trap says.

I'm smart enough not to agree without knowing the stakes. "What?" I ask.

"Promise you won't run away. No matter how much you want to. No matter how much it seems like a solution."

It should be easy to agree. It feels impossible.

The soundtrack in my head is relentless: I'm broken. I'm damaged. I ruin everything I touch.

I'm ruining something now, just by staying silent. I can see the pain in Trap's face. I can see him fighting to find words he doesn't want to say. "Jesus, Alix. You spent two weeks in a fleabag hotel, and I thought I'd go crazy. I spent hours online, checking my credit card to make sure you hadn't left town. I drove by that rat-trap every night, just to make sure my car was still in the parking lot. Don't put me through that again. Don't put *us* through that again."

Us.

I've never been part of an *us* before. Not like this.

The closest was the bond I shared with my brother. I took Leo's side in countless arguments with my family, with my friends. And Leo disappointed me every single time. Even his dying was a disappointment. I never got to hear his twisted justification for why he sold me to Herzog.

But Trap is nothing like Leo.

He's never lied to me.

Never cut me off from the outside world.

Never hurt me, at least not in any way I didn't long for.

I stare at the bruises on my wrists. I remember the fever-fall of desire as I balanced on my toes, reaching, stretching, waiting for release in the form of a single sharp command.

Trap accepts me as I am. He *sees* me.

I nod.

"I need more than that," he says.

I find the strength to meet his gaze, to bind myself to his wild green-brown eyes. "I promise," I say. "I won't run away."

His smile is something magical. It washes away tension. It drives away fear. It's a promise and an answer and a reason to believe there's actually good in the world.

He reaches for something on the corner of his desk—a plastic card strung on a lanyard.

"What's that?" I ask.

"Your Diamond Freeport ID."

"Why do I need that?"

"You're the freeport's latest hire. You're on the books as a fine arts specialist." He picks up a pen and scribbles something on a sticky note. "I set your salary based on public figures from the major auction houses. Your compensation package includes a one percent bonus on each work you sell, retroactive to the Monet sale, plus you're eligible for annual bonuses."

I look at the number he's scrawled. It's easily double what I could hope to earn as a senior professor of psychology at one of the finest universities in the country. Plus the commission on the Monet… That's over three quarters of a million dollars.

"I can't—" I start to say.

"You can."

"I'm not—"

"You are."

"I won't—"

"You will."

He believes I belong here. He wants me to stay. And I can't imagine anywhere I'd rather be, anyone I'd rather be with.

My fingers close around the ID.

"I should mention…" Trap says, his lips quirking in a tiny smile. "Your job description is somewhat unconventional."

I match his growing grin. "How unconventional?"

"Let's just say there are 'other duties as assigned.'"

"That's a dangerous loophole to leave open," I say. "Can I get any specifics?"

He leans back in his chair and unfastens his belt. "I've got one specific in mind right now."

I want to play. I want to make him happy. But I don't deserve the sort of joking fun he has in mind.

But Trap understands. He knows me.

He snaps his fingers and points to the floor beside his chair. "Now," he barks.

I should hate this. I should despise being degraded. I should refuse to be treated like a slave.

But I rise from my chair.

I cross to his desk.

I sink to my knees, and I reach for his zipper, and something deep inside me sings.

8

TRAP

Jesus fucking Christ.

It's one thing to have Alix here, 24/7, ready, willing, and able to accommodate my slightest need. Did I say ready? Beyond ready—she's got the stamina of an Olympic marathoner. I've created a submissive little monster.

It's another thing, though, to miss out on a full night's sleep, three night's running. We both head upstairs with good intentions. We both vow we're going to keep our hands to ourselves. We both swear we're going to catch up on shut-eye, just this once, one fucking night to prove we're responsible adults.

And then I leave my belt on the bedroom floor. Or Alix looks toward the dresser drawer. Or I take her panties and twist them around her wrists, binding her hands together so I can pin them overhead with one hand while I use the other to tease her ready clit...

I'm a goddamn zombie.

But I'm absolutely not complaining.

After three years apart, I have a catalog of fantasies it'll take a while to work through. It doesn't hurt that Alix takes to every fucking variation like she's fighting for her place in the Sex Kinks Hall of Fame.

I'm sure she has some fancy psychological words for what's going on. She's owning what Herzog did to her. Claiming her sexuality for herself. Accepting her inner desires without giving a flying fuck for what society says she should want.

Something like that.

The reality is, I give her something Herzog never did. Control. She chooses what she wants, with an iron-clad option of tapping out. She's got her safeword, and she knows I'll honor it—*have* honored it, the few times she's said it out loud.

And I've learned. She'll let me leave marks. She's game for anything oral. She'll edge for hours if that's what I command; in fact, she won't come unless I give her a specific order.

But get anywhere near the precious pucker of her ass, and she shuts down immediately. Nothing—no tools, no tongue, no finger, and absolutely, definitely, no way in fucking hell, no cock.

So if it helps her to kneel beside my desk and give me a blowjob? If she wants to feel my paddle across her naked ass? If she wants me to grab those fucking amazing tits while her hands are tied behind her back?

I can work with that.

Especially because she's locked the goddamn Beast in a cage. For twenty years, that fucking animal owned my brain. It kept a stranglehold on everything I did—shaking hands in a business meeting, high-fiving at a football game, paying for a candy bar at the goddamn grocery store.

And fucking. The Beast had a field day every time I tied a woman to my bed.

Alix changed all that. Alix tamed the Beast.

If I wanted to, Alix and I could cuddle like a couple of moon-struck virgins, holding hands till the sun comes up over the trees in the backyard. I could lie beside her, prop myself on an elbow, and trace every line of her body with my glove-free palm. I could cover her with my body, chest to chest, belly to belly, and we could fuck like goddamn missionaries.

But I don't want to.

I love tying her up. I love testing her limits. I love issuing orders. And I love being the one who has the power to release her with a single four-letter word.

All of which is a long way of saying I'm chafed and horny and I-don't-know-how-many-hours-short-on-sleep when Harry Asher shuffles into my office. We're in the freeport building. I don't want to spook Alix with anything Asher says, even if she *has* promised she won't run.

"What have you got?" I ask, before the funk of his cigar smoke reaches me.

"These guys are locked up tight, boss."

"What the fuck does that mean?"

He sags in his chair, like his spine got too heavy to bother lifting. "One of 'em, Klaus. He's disappeared off the face of the earth."

That's literally true, thanks to Best's clean-up crew. But Asher doesn't need to know that.

"Disappeared?" is all I ask.

"He's got a place in New Castle County, forty-five, fifty minutes from here. Looks like a haunted house, some place the Addams family lives in when they take a trip to the country." Asher digs in his folder and hands over half a dozen color photographs. "These are from a drone. There's a brick fence around the joint, ten feet high, with razor wire on top. The gate's got biometrics and a kill zone. Whoever built it means business."

Whoever built it is dead. But I want to know what else Asher learned, so I ask, "What makes you say Klaus disappeared? How do you know he isn't just holed up in there?"

Asher plants a thick index finger on one of the photos. "I had one of my guys surveil the place, while I looked into the rest of this shit. No one's gone in or out of the property for forty-eight hours. And see these lights? They're on some sort of timer. Came on in the same order both nights, same time. Stayed on for exactly four hours and fifty-three minutes."

Rookie error, the first I've heard Herzog make. Pity, he won't have a chance to learn from his mistake.

Asher taps the photos together. "It's not just that. He's got eight cars licensed with the state, and none of them's hit a toll point in over six weeks. He flies in and out of a private airfield, keeps a long-haul Lear there, along with a Sikorsky S-76B. Over the past ten years, there've been a few months where he hasn't used the plane. But there isn't a single week the helicopter hasn't gone up—until June. His last trip was June 18, to Long Island."

I'm impressed with the records Asher pulled, especially given my time limit. But I'm also tired of the cat and mouse game; I already know Klaus Herzog's out of the equation.

"And the other two? Jonas and Ansel?"

"They're living on Long Island." Asher pulls out another sheaf of photos. As he spreads them on my desk, I wonder if I'm looking at New York or some place in Europe.

The main building looks like a castle, with three floors and two sweeping wings and sculpted stairs that lead to a garden bigger than the entire state of Delaware. There are two swimming pools and a pair of tennis courts and nine fucking holes of golf. One massive outbuilding is clearly a garage, and another looks like stables. There are half a dozen smaller buildings—guesthouses, I guess, each of them big enough to sleep twenty. And a helipad, of course.

"So the illegal drug trade pays well," I say, grudgingly impressed.

Asher taps one of the photos. "The illegal drug trade pays a fucking private army."

I'm staring at a guard tower built into the five-foot-thick stone wall. It's hard to estimate the height, but judging by the length of the AK-47 in the uniformed soldiers' arms, it's got to be twelve feet, at least. Two guys man the station, one facing in and one facing out. There are eight towers on the perimeter and two at the front gate. Add in security at the main house, and there are at least twenty armed guards.

No way in hell I'm waltzing in there to demand the Herzog brothers drop their claims.

But I say, "They can't live behind the walls full time."

Asher shrugs. "Past six weeks, they've gone to Berlin. Abu Dhabi. Kabul."

"What the fuck are they doing in Afghanistan? Not exactly the Ritz."

"My money's on dealing arms. But they could be there for the opium trade. I might be able to find out, but not by your forty-eight-hour deadline."

Cute. He's feeling put upon. Poor Harry Asher.

"Where are they now?" I ask.

"Home, near as I can tell. A pair of Mercedes limos arrived last night around five. Left around midnight." He shuffles through the photos. "Looks like some lady friends. Can't tell if that's security with them or maybe their pimps."

I can't tell either. Asher doesn't have shots of them leaving. Given what I already know about the Herzog brothers' taste in entertainment, I hope the women walked out under their own power.

I don't have time to think about the stained chair Mac burned. I can't be distracted by Alix's reaction when she saw it. By the knowledge that those motherfuckers had her under their control for years.

Asher's waiting for me to say something. I stack the photos and add them to the report he delivered two days ago. "Here's what I don't get," I say. "Your first report didn't say anything about this Long Island fortress."

He's immediately defensive. "My first report was delivered in twenty-four hours."

"Seems like a pretty big thing to overlook. Especially if this is where the assholes are actually living."

"What are you saying, boss? You think I'm on the take?"

The thought crossed my mind.

But Asher's not done yet. "I spent forty-two years on the fucking Philadelphia PD. I know what bad guys look like. *You* aren't gonna blow my head off if you catch me double-dipping, but these guys'd feed me my own dick, soon as get my PI license pulled. They're bad shit. And I've already gotten closer to 'em than I should've. Any of this blows back their way, and I'm as good as dead."

He's wrong about one thing. I *might* blow his head off if he sold me out. Or I'd hire Best to do it.

But beneath the tough-guy bluster, I see something else: Fear. Asher's fucking terrified of Jonas and Ansel Herzog.

He wraps up his self-defense: "I told you these cocksuckers have corporations wrapped in partnerships wrapped in private holding companies. The Long Island estate is right smack in the middle of all that crap. Wouldn't surprise me if New York State doesn't even know the place exists, for tax purposes."

"Okay, okay," I soothe him. "Hold your fucking horses. Got anything else?"

He doesn't, not anything major. I tell him to invoice me, and I send him on his way.

After he's left, I go through the photos, one by one. I'm looking for a back door, a secret way in so I can fuck over the Herzog brothers, once and for all. But there's nothing in the paperwork that gives me a shred of hope.

I'm working through Asher's report a third time, when I get a call on the intercom from Susan Richards. She's my new assistant, the one I hired after Pete Miller walked out on my sorry ass. She's good, applying all the skills that helped her succeed as a single mother raising three sons to adulthood. She's able to juggle a dozen different projects at once, and she has a fine-tuned sense of when to avoid looking in the shadows.

I'm doing my best not to piss her off, so I answer promptly. "What's up, Susan?"

"Just wanted to make sure you haven't forgotten your eleven thirty."

I glance at my computer screen. There's the calendar notice, in the red Susan uses when something's important. I was supposed to be in the boardroom seven minutes ago.

"Haven't forgotten it," I lie. "What's the meeting about?"

"Freeport security staff. They want increased staffing, or they're walking off the job at noon."

"Tell 'em an emergency came up."

"I told them that last week. And the week before that."

Well last week, and the week before that, I didn't have a fucking snuff video hanging over my head. I didn't have to worry about the entire freeport being shut down when the goddamn world finds out what happened to Herzog.

I don't have time for this shit.

But I don't have a freeport if I don't have security. So, swearing, I hang up on Susan and head down to the boardroom, loaded for bear.

9

ALIX

My phone rings, dragging me out of nineteenth-century French countrysides. I thought I'd just take a moment to look at a catalog of Cezanne landscapes, but I was sucked in by the color and the compositions, by the freedom of a painter depicting the world around him almost a hundred and fifty years ago, and I've lost a couple of hours.

Blinking hard to come back to reality, I answer on the third ring. "Susan?"

"Alix." She sounds uncertain. That's a first for Trap's new executive assistant. Judging from the way she handles day-to-day disasters at the freeport, I've assumed she has antifreeze in her veins.

"Is everything okay?"

"I'm sure it is, but…"

"Is Trap all right?" My nerves make the question harsher than I intend.

"He's fine!" she reassures me quickly. "It's just that he's in a meeting with the security guards. The guards are threatening to walk out at noon, and I'm afraid Trap might lose his temper and say something he regrets."

"Where are they?"

"In the boardroom." She hesitates, and I think she's about to tell me she's over-reacting. Instead, she says, "Hurry."

I shove my phone in my pocket and run my fingers through my hair, grateful it's too short to require anything complicated, like a hair dryer. Or a brush.

I half-walk, half-jog across the parking lot to the freeport office tower. My ID wakes up the security kiosk, and I gain entry by submitting to a retina scan. Sophia, one of the curators, is staffing the front desk instead of the usual security guard. Her face is pale.

"In the boardroom," she says. "Hurry."

I wonder if she and Susan compared notes to get their identical wording. It doesn't really matter if they did. I can hear shouting from this end of the hall.

"I pay good wages, dammit! The best you'll find in the business! And I refuse to be held hostage by absolutely unreasonable demands!" Trap's bellow is drowned out by a chorus of disagreement.

Wincing, I rush down the corridor.

The scene I find is actually worse than I anticipated. Trap stands at the front of the room, hands planted on his hips as if he's some sort of drill sergeant. His hair is ruffled, like he's been combing through it with angry fingers. His cheeks are flushed.

Clyde McGregor looks like a lion-tamer who forgot to bring his chair and whip to the three-ring circus. The freeport's chief of security stands to one side. His walkie-talkie is in his fist, the antenna extended like a middle finger.

"Dinna make things worse'n they are, the lot o' ye!" He raises his voice to be heard over the chaos, his accent thicker than the August humidity outside.

"I'm talking!" Trap snaps at the interruption.

His words land like a slap across Mac's face. I'm not sure if the chief meant to include Trap with his "lot o' ye" but he's sure not looking friendly now. The security guards react predictably —their grumbling becomes louder and a lot more focused.

Trap looks cornered. I see his jaw set, and I know exactly what he's thinking. If the security guards walk out in—oh, twenty-one minutes—the freeport will be absolutely stranded. It won't be safe for clients to enter the premises. And we won't be able to guarantee the protection of any assets stored on site.

It's not like Trap can turn to Security R Us to instantly hire new staff. One of the great advantages of locating Diamond Freeport in Dover is our relatively remote location. It's easier to monitor our safety here than it would be if we were on the docks in a major city.

But that advantage turns upside down when it's time to hire staff. Trap only had a dozen applicants for Susan Richards' position—and half of those were easy to toss out. It's often impossible to find qualified candidates for jobs that aren't suitable for Sherman University undergrads looking for part-time gigs or for Dover Air Force Base spouses supplementing household income until their next military transfer.

Susan is one in a million. As she proved when she got me involved in the current dispute.

"Gentlemen!" I say from the doorway. "I apologize for being late. I'm so glad you got started without me."

Trap scowls, exactly the way I knew he would. But I catch a quick look of relief on Mac's face. He senses the same high temperature in the room that I do. And he wants to put a lid on it.

As I walk to the front of the room, the security guards fall silent. I know all of them by sight and a few of them by name. I make a point of fingering my official ID on its lanyard. I want these men to think of me as a fellow freeport employee.

A dozen catchphrases run through my head, all things I learned in psychology classes about conflict resolution: mixed-

motive interactions, ego defensiveness, naive realism, high epis-
temic motivation... I can recite studies performed by countless
social psychologists and cite articles from the most prestigious
journals.

Or I can help Trap negotiate with his employees.

I smile at the guards, knowing I'll be more successful if I
address them first. Let Trap bear the snub. He's a big boy. He
can take it. "I think I understand the issues here, but I'd love to
hear from one of you to make sure I'm not missing important
details."

There's a moment of uncertainty among the men before
Dave Washington steps forward. He's one of two supervisors,
responsible for day shifts throughout the freeport. "We want to
protect the premises," he says, without preamble. "But we're
helpless if we don't have enough staff. Men are pulling double
shifts. Vacations are routinely denied. The rules say we get two
weeks of paternity leave, but Martinez wasn't able to take two
days. We need the freeport to step up and follow its own rules.
Give us what we're promised."

Trap replies before I can rein him in. "I'm paying half again
as much as anyone else in Dover. If you aren't happy with your
paycheck, Wash, go back to babysitting college kids at
Sherman."

The guards start to shout their disagreement. I muscle my
way back into the conversation. "What I hear you saying, Dave,
is that you need more bodies."

"Damn straight," he grumbles. Mac shoots him a sharp look
but has the good sense not to interrupt.

Trap, on the other hand, is bursting with the need to contradict. Purposely brushing my fingers against my lanyard—
sending a subliminal message, if not an actual audible one—I
say, "And I understand, Trap, that you're paying top dollar and
expect top service from your employees."

"That's right," he says, biting off the words.

"But Dave, it sounds like you want to protect the freeport. You value the premises and everything we do here."

He gives a grudging shrug.

"And I think it's safe to assume, Trap, that you also want to protect the freeport. You're both in agreement about that."

The look he gives me is incredulous, like I'm wasting his time. But he acknowledges that I'm right.

Excellent. I have my lever, one tool to move both men toward agreement.

It takes more time than I expect. Dave feels obligated to consult with his fellow guards. Trap is truly concerned about the consequences of looking weak in front of his employees. At least Mac stays out of it, content to let me explore what I can build.

Noon comes and goes. No one leaves the room, which feels like a victory.

I can see a solution, crystal clear. But I want the others to come up with it, to own it so it's more likely to stick. I resist the urge to just tell them what they should do.

And it takes another hour, but they end up where I hoped they would. Dave agrees that no one will walk off the job. Trap agrees to hire two new guards, with an eye toward adding two more in six months. The new hires will be junior staff—less expensive but adding a career path to the security department. And emergency needs will be filled with substitutes from Sawyer Best's Sawgrass force, until the new hires can be brought on board.

Dave and Trap shake on the deal with Mac looking on. Then every one of the other guards steps up, shaking in turn on the agreement. I'm pretty sure I'm the only one who notices Trap's left hand in his pocket, the telltale clench as he satisfies the compulsions buried deep in his brain.

Mac waits until the guards have filed out before he turns to me. "Thank you," he says. His Scottish burr has faded to nothingness, the surest sign yet that the crisis is resolved.

"My pleasure," I say. The words sound glib, but I mean

them with all my heart. I actually accomplished something here. I contributed to the freeport.

The door closes behind Mac. I stand beside the wide table, waiting for Trap to say something.

I remember this feeling: pride in a job well done and nerves that I've made a mistake, all mixed up with longing for recognition.

I felt this way in school. In my first job, scooping ice cream at a neighborhood shop. In Herzog's library, when he ordered me to do the impossible, to alphabetize all his books in a single day.

Of course then I worried I'd be beaten if I failed.

Now, I know I'm physically safe. But the power Trap holds over me is greater than anything physical. His anger, his rejection, his dismissal—they'll destroy me.

"Trap…" I finally say, not certain how to plead my case.

"Thank you," he says.

"I—"

But he cuts me off, shaking his head with a ferocity that has me guessing all over again. "No. I'm glad you were here."

I watch the words register, like he's just discovered he can speak a foreign language.

"I didn't even know it," he says. "But I needed exactly what you brought to the table. I needed *you*."

The fierce look in his eyes freezes the apology on my lips. It's always been like this between us—just the truth, just our bare emotions, none of the trappings or expectations about how the world thinks we ought to behave.

His hand falls on a control panel embedded in the table. For just a moment, I think he's overwhelmed by the beast inside his head, that the creature still demands payment for the line of guards who shook Trap's hand.

But the glass walls of the boardroom darken, closing us off in a private cave. The overhead lights gleam brighter on the table, sparkling like diamonds inlaid in the wood.

Trap moves like a panther, lithe and confident and strong. His fingers are warm on the back of my head, firm and commanding. I melt into his heat as his mouth closes over mine. My lips open as I try to drink all the urgent passion he pours into me.

He growls deep in his throat, demanding more. His free hand grabs my breast, claiming me with a primal simplicity that makes me sigh, even as his fingers pinch my suddenly alert nipple.

His hand skims my flank. He slips past the waistband of my jeans. He shoves my panties aside and fingers me, muttering something filthy when he feels how wet he's made me.

I shift my weight to give him better access. He crooks his wrist, sinking deep inside me. "Look at me," he orders.

I didn't know my eyes were closed. I meet his fierce gaze, his brutal defiance as he curls his fingers to scrape the neediest patch inside me.

"Eyes," he says as I close mine again, concentrating on the sensations spiraling up my spine.

I force myself to focus. Force myself to obey. Force myself to watch his face as he spreads me, strokes me, breaks me into elemental pieces faster than I ever thought possible.

I'm clutching his biceps. I'm balanced on my toes. I'm stretched, taut, strung tighter than the strings on a violin, waiting, watching, almost, almost there.

"Come," he whispers, and I fold around him, shuddering. My thighs clamp around his wrist as I hold him fast, hold him tight, hold him like I'll never let him go.

I'm coming and I'm coming and I'm coming, but all the while a little voice hisses at the back of my mind: This is all I've ever wanted. And I'm going to lose it soon. All this will be history, the moment Herzog's brothers release their video to the world.

There's payment to be made, and I'm not sure I can live with the cost.

10

TRAP

I stroll over to the freeport garage, where Cole Wolf is loading in his latest purchase, one of Harley Davidson's limited-edition motorcycles. I'm pretty sure I've never seen a cooler use for a spare sixty thousand dollars, and for just a moment, I wonder how Alix would look riding behind me, hands around my waist, pressing close as we lean into curves on a winding mountain road.

"You keeping that thing?" I ask. "Or looking to make some money on your investment?"

He grins, looking nothing like the computer geniuses *I* went to school with. "You in the market?"

I shrug. "I might be."

"Finish the track you've been promising for the past year and a half, and you can take it out for a ride."

"Deal," I say.

Dover Motor Speedway is just ten miles away, but it doesn't do jack for the freeport clients, who can't take their prize possessions out of the tax haven. So I hired away Dover's chief engineer to create a three-quarter mile track. A million dollars later, we're a month or two away from opening.

Wolf uses a soft cotton cloth to polish the Harley nameplate. With a practiced air of nonchalance, he says, "I doubt you came over here just to admire this bike."

I roll my neck, trying to work out a couple of kinks. "I've got a question."

Something about my tone puts Wolf on alert. He steps back from his baby. Plants his feet. Looks me in the eye. "Shoot."

"Let's say someone has a video. Something they threaten to make public."

He doesn't move, not exactly. But every muscle in his body tightens, just a little. He's focused like a laser cutting solid steel. "Go on," he says.

"And let's say they make that threat by email."

He doesn't bother answering. He just nods.

"And the person who gets the email has a pretty good idea where it was sent from. A street address. Floor plans. That sort of thing."

Wolf's lips twist into a frown.

I knew this was a shitty idea before I hunted him down. But I have to run out the ball. "Is there any way to blow up the video? Go back upstream? Fuck it up before it can be sent out wide?"

"It's a recording?" he asks. "Not something going out live?"

"Yeah." I already know the answer. It weighs on my back like a beached blue whale.

"You're fucked," Wolf says.

"No room for doubt?"

His one-shoulder shrug is a master class on dismissal. "You could go on a phishing expedition. Send them an email with malware, a virus inside. If they open it, you can fry that machine. Maybe even take out their whole network. But if they have any brains at all, they'll have a copy of the video someplace safe. On an air-gap machine. In off-site storage, at least."

"But I can slow them down?"

"Not by much. And it might piss them off. End up with them distributing whatever it is a lot more widely. Which I assume is the exact result you don't want."

"Right." As long as I've got him giving me the bad news, I ask another question and try not to sound like I'm begging. "Anything else? Any other way to take out these motherfuckers?"

"Short of a nuclear-grade electro-magnetic pulse to take out every computer on the Eastern seaboard? And even that won't help if they're storing the video outside the range. Servers on the west coast. Overseas."

If I were a criminal drug-lord with six homes from Napa to Zermatt, I'm pretty sure I'd be stashing my blackmail material on multiple continents.

Fuck.

"So what would *you* do?" I ask.

"About a hypothetical video being distributed by a hypothetical enemy showing something that might hypothetically destroy me? I'd buy them off. Everyone has a price."

My jaw tightens. "Let's say the price is too high."

Wolf's eyebrows rise. "Then I'd attack the video. Say it's a deep fake. Someone made it with AI, artificial intelligence. Or they pieced together other footage, something innocent but they make it look bad."

There's nothing innocent about the Herzogs' recording.

But Wolf has a point. I can turn this into a public relations battle. I can say they're the bad actors. They're the ones spreading lies.

I picture the spray of blood from one end of my dining room table to the wall behind the credenza. That would be one hell of a fucking lie.

"Okay," I say. "Thanks."

"Let me know if you need an expert, someone who'll stand up in court."

"Yeah. I will."

Wolf waits a beat, giving me a chance to ask more questions. I could tell him what the video is all about. Give him a heads-up that he's implicated too, that the entire Diamond Fucking Ring has an interest in proving the Herzogs' film a lie.

But it's too early to drag him in. No reason to fuck up his life yet.

Down the road, he can hire the finest lawyer money can buy. Get his own neck out of the noose. Somehow.

When I don't ask any more questions, don't give him any more details, Wolf shakes out his cotton cloth and turns back to his new baby. "Quit wasting your time with shit you can't control," he says. "Get back to the racetrack. Finish it and then you can take out one of those cars you're always bragging about. Burn off a little frustration."

If it was only so simple.

But I laugh. And I ask him about the torque on the new motorcycle's engine. And I pretend the answer's interesting enough to keep me from thinking about how the Herzogs are going to take all of us down.

11

ALIX

I'm supposed to head up to New York for the Sotheby's
auction on Provençal landscapes. But the thought of sitting
in the car all those hours, of interacting with buyers and sellers
like everything in my life is normal, of taking mental and physical notes on the auctioneers' technique, on the actual lots, on
everything I still have to learn... I'm exhausted just thinking
about it.

But if I'm staying home, I really should work. I should
research the paintings in Herzog's gallery and figure out if all of
them are stolen. The Vermeer, of course, is famous. And the
bright yellow and red poppies were almost certainly painted by
Van Gogh and stolen from a Cairo museum in 2010. I have
leads on a couple of others, but I need to find decent reproduc-
tions to be sure. And several works in Herzog's gallery don't
resemble anything reported stolen online.

I'd rather curl up with my phone and watch soothing videos

of working sheepdogs. Each little movie is a masterpiece of order and control. The shepherd blows a whistle or waves a hand, and the dog does exactly what it's learned to do, from driving an entire herd across long distances to selecting a single ailing lamb and bringing it to the human who can save it. The dogs are equal, faithful partners and I could watch them forever.

Instead, I call Susan Richards. "Could you do me a favor?" I ask.

"Of course."

"Could you cancel the car I have scheduled for this morning?"

"Consider it done. Would you like to reschedule?"

"Not today." Maybe not ever. The pile of pillows on the guest room bed is calling to me. I can leave the light off overhead. I can hide like a kid in a fort made out of sofa pillows, accompanied by no one but my trusty stuffed panda from the county fair. I can pretend that nothing else is happening, that Klaus Herzog never existed, that his brothers were never born, that no one ever invented a video camera, much less miniaturized one into a weapon that's about to destroy my life and the life of the man I love.

"Let me know if there's anything else I can do to help," Susan says, without a clue how much I wish life was that simple. But then she asks, "Is Trap with you?"

It's unusual for her to mention him. With her perfect professionalism and seemingly endless capacity to take on more responsibility, Susan usually makes me feel like I'm the only person in the world who takes up her time. "No," I say. "I think he's in the garage, meeting with Cole Wolf."

She hesitates for a split second, just enough for my ears to register. "All right, then," she says. "Thank you."

"Is there something I can help with?"

Another one of those microscopic hesitations. "No," she says. "I don't want to bother you."

"It's not a bother," I say. The words are a reflex, the sort of polite thing my mother taught me to say, like *I'm pleased to meet you* and *Yes, please, I'd love a serving of boiled Brussels sprouts.*

This time, Susan charges ahead with no hesitation whatsoever. "If you could come over to the office building, I'd be so grateful. I'm going over the sixth-floor map, trying to figure out the fairest allocation of offices for the conservators. I think I've worked it out, but I'd love another opinion so Trap can sign off on it."

"I'll be there in a minute," I say.

I have to change out of my sweatpants which, come to think of it, could desperately use a wash. I don't have time to shampoo my hair, but my raking fingers take away the worst effects of bed-head. While I'm in the bathroom, I take a moment to swipe on some mascara and a quick dash of lipstick.

I feel about a thousand times better as I head across the parking lot. Susan is waiting in her office, directly across the hall from Trap's glassed-in corner.

"Thank you so much for helping with this," she says. She sounds so warm and genuine, my throat swells. I am *not* going to cry over floor plans.

"Thanks for asking me."

Susan unrolls a map of the sixth floor and fills me in on the challenges. We have to consider staff seniority, but there's also the reality that northern light is substantially better for any artist attempting to care for paintings that are worth millions of dollars. Freeport staff has tripled in size over the past two years, and there are lingering traditions that favor people who speak the loudest, along with those who simply take what they need to get their work done.

We look at half a dozen solutions, and none of them is perfect. If Trap were here, he'd just throw money at the problem. He'd agree to knock down walls, to add expensive air-filtration systems, maybe even bring in architects to add a new floor to the building.

"Wait," I say, after almost an hour of friendly back and forth with Susan. "We're bringing on a new tax lawyer next quarter, right?"

"That's my understanding. We just put out a call for resumés."

"And Trap wants to hire an actuarial accountant too."

"That's news to me."

The instant the words are out of Susan's mouth, a cold fog of panic grips my lungs. Trap mentioned the accountant over breakfast a couple of days ago. Maybe the new position is top secret. Maybe I'm not supposed to know about it. Not supposed to share.

Before I can make up some half-hearted lie, Susan says, "You realize my loyalty is to Trap, right? I'm his executive assistant. Anything he tells me is confidential, until I hear otherwise. And it only makes sense for me to extend that same courtesy to you."

She sounds so professional. So competent and level-headed.

But there's something else in her words. She's offering me a confidence. An understanding. She's treating me like we're both adults, two women working toward a common goal.

I've never had a relationship like this before.

When I was held in Herzog's house, I worked with my fellow slaves. I taught them English, and they helped me complete impossible tasks. But Herzog's depravity robbed us of our autonomy. And in the end, he sold off every one of them, to keep me from having their friendship and support.

When I was a student, I worked on group projects. But those were always fraught, with one person—usually me, because I've always been a rules-follower—carrying the load. Inevitably, one person took the lead and ordered others to fall in line.

Leo and I were a united front when we were kids. As twins, we constantly supported each other, working together to con our parents into a trip to Baskin-Robbins or a puppy, whatever we thought we'd die over if we couldn't have it, right then, right there. But once Leo started using, he wasn't on my side anymore. Long before he sold me into Herzog's slavery, he did whatever he needed to get his next fix, without regard to how it affected me.

In a way, Susan's like my mother. She asks my opinion, assuming I'll have a useful answer. She supports me. She believes in me.

If my mother were alive, she'd be just about Susan's age. She'd probably have Susan's gray hair. Might even have her fashion sense, too, with practical dresses and blazers with pockets and no-nonsense shoes to wear for hours and hours on end.

I realize Susan's waiting for me. I'm free to acknowledge the thing she just said, the trust she's placing in me. She's the first person to accept that Trap and I are a unit, that we're more than a man and a woman who happen to work together. The rush of pleasure I feel at that recognition is utterly unexpected.

"Thank you," I finally say. "I appreciate that."

And then, like she hasn't given me an incredible gift, she says, "So if we're adding to legal and accounting…"

She lets me finish. "We could move them both to the fourth floor. Shift logistics to six. And that will give us room to add a workspace for the junior conservator upstairs."

Susan nods, studying the floor plan.

Her silence helps me to trust her even more. I can offer an idea I've had, one I haven't even shared with Trap yet. "Based on what I'm seeing in New York auctions, our clients may be acquiring more works on paper in the foreseeable future. We might hire an expert just to work with those."

I don't know if Susan realizes this is the first time I've thought about freeport business as something I have the power to build and shape. She just says, "Even more of a reason to make this shift then. Will you tell Trap?" she asks. "Or would you like me to?"

"I can," I say.

Her smile feels like an alliance. It feels like sun shining through a window on a clear spring day. It feels like approval, and I'm grateful down to my toes.

12

TRAP

I drive to Philadelphia, because some conversations shouldn't be had over open phone lines. Braiden Kelly agrees to meet me at the Hare and Harp, around the corner from the Mummer's Museum on Two Street. I walk by the place twice before I see the green lettering over the nondescript door. It's three steps down to a hardwood floor so dark it looks black. Heavy paneled walls press in from every side.

Kelly waits for me behind the scarred mahogany bar. "Guinness?" he asks as I blink in the dim light.

It's two in the afternoon. "Why not?" I say.

He pulls a pint for me and another for himself. Passing my glass across the bar, he says to the ancient man next to him, "We'll be in my office, Fergus."

The old man nods and picks up a clean glass, holding it to the fly-specked window like he's looking for spots. Kelly leads the way to the back of the bar, through a door covered with brass-studded burgundy leather.

There's storage back here and a passage that must lead to the alley. I can make out stairs heading toward a basement, steep enough to break someone's neck without a lot of trying. There's another door of solid wood, fitted out with three heavy locks. Kelly pushes that one open and gestures for me to go first.

A massive desk fills half the room. It's carved so deeply it looks like it's alive, with Celtic knotwork and fistfuls of shamrocks and buckled top hats that might have belonged to leprechauns in the old country. Papers are stacked over the surface, anchored by a computer monitor that looks like it's twenty years old. A hand-size statue of a woman in a brown robe is conveniently labeled *St. Brigid Pray for Us*. Three mass cards are tucked beneath her feet.

Instead of fighting his way behind the desk, Kelly gestures to the two leather armchairs that fill the rest of the office. I sink into the one closest to the door, letting him put his back to the wall.

He takes a deep draught of his Guinness, which gives me permission to do the same. The stuff is lukewarm and heavy as a loaf of soda bread. I could drain my pint and not need another meal till breakfast tomorrow.

"You sounded urgent on the phone," Kelly said. That's one reason I like him. He doesn't fuck around.

"I don't know if you can help me."

He doesn't answer. And that's another reason I like him. He's patient, when it pays.

I fortify myself with another gulp of Guinness before I dive in. Kelly's no fool. I have to believe we can't be overheard here, that what's said in this office doesn't go any further.

"It's come to my attention," I start, "that some business acquaintances are throwing their weight around. Interfering with my territory. I'm wondering if you know anyone who can deliver a message. One that can't be ignored."

Braiden Kelly is the captain of the Irish mob in Philadelphia, which makes him an expert at reading between the lines.

"This message," he says. "Do you want your *acquaintances* spreading the word? Or do you want their mouths shut?"

He's asking if I want the Herzogs alive or dead. And for the first time, I realize the answer is *dead*. Forget about blocking their transmission of the video. Screw negotiating a more fair payment. Jonas and Ansel will be loose ends—dangerous threats —until the day they die. It's my job to make certain that day happens as soon as possible.

"No need for them to pass on the message," I say. "Making them an example is good enough."

He nods. It's time for both of us to drink more of our Guinness. To pretend we aren't talking about killing anyone.

After he swallows, he asks, "What information do you have on these…*acquaintances*? Name? Location? Anything about their general availability for…meetings?"

I take a sheaf of papers out of my jacket pocket. They're the highlights of Asher's report—name, rank, and serial number, plus the drone photos of the Long Island compound. Men with homes like the Herzogs have greased a lot of palms. That's why I'm here, talking to Kelly, instead of going straight to Connor Boyle, head of the Irish mob in New York.

Boyle's closer to the Herzogs. Maybe close enough to take protection money from them. And I wouldn't want to put one of my Diamond Ring clients in an awkward position.

Kelly glances at the papers for less than a second before the names register. He knows what happened at our Diamond Ring meeting as well as I do. He glances through the rest of the stack without giving away a single thought.

When he reaches the last page, the overhead view of the mansion grounds, he stares at it for longer than it took him to go over everything else. He purses his lips. Starts to speak. Opts to finish his Guinness instead.

He sets the glass down on the desk with a note of finality.

I already know his answer, but I listen to him anyway. "I'm not the man for the job."

"If it's a matter of money—"

"Of course not," he snaps.

Of course it's not money. He knows I'm good for whatever he'd ask. "What, then?"

His long index finger lands on the drone photo, like he's covering a hole on a wooden flute. "Manpower," he says. He taps again. "There." Another imaginary note. "And there." An entire symphony. "All of it."

I know exactly what he's pointing at. I've studied the guards in their towers for more hours than I care to admit.

"My messengers," he says. "They're good at short, direct communication. They'll talk to you in a restaurant. When their car pulls up next to yours at a light. Maybe find you in the jacks, if you're out at the symphony or the orchestra, something like that."

I nod. Asher couldn't get me any information on how the Herzogs spend their time when they aren't busy raping women. Nothing about their favorite speakeasies, favorite golf courses, favorite anything, other than drugging the children of America with their specially formulated poison.

Kelly says, "Something like this, delivering a message at a man's home when the home's a fucking fortress..." He shakes his head. "Too easy for it all to go arsewise."

I try to bottle my frustration. "It's important," I say. "Not just for me."

His face stays flat. Unreadable. "You need more manpower, boyo."

"So I should talk to Boyle?"

For some reason, that makes him laugh. "A whole other type of messenger," he says. "We deliver letters. You want to ship a crate. You need to talk to your man Best."

Sawyer Best. With the paramilitary troops of the private military contractor he owns and operates.

Kelly's telling me I'm not staging a battle. I'm planning a war. And for the first time since I set foot in the bar, I can actually read his face. I know exactly what he's thinking.

He doesn't believe I can win.

13

ALIX

I'm sitting on a rattan chaise in the back yard, adding extra-sharp cheddar to a slice of tart apple when Trap comes through the sliding glass door. He looks exhausted as he sinks into a woven chair.

"Tough day?" I ask.

He makes the effort to put on a smile. "Better, now that I'm home."

"Can I get you a drink?"

"A double."

I go back into the house and fetch a glass from the cabinet above the dishwasher. I add two cubes of ice from the freezer. As I pad into the dining room to retrieve the Whistlepig, I smile to myself.

I love knowing where Trap keeps the glasses. That he drinks rye. That he wants it on the rocks. They're little things, nothing that will change the world in any significant way, but they make me feel like I belong here.

Back outside, I hand him the glass, and he rallies enough to ask, "How was your day?"

"Busy." Sinking back into my chair, I pass him the cheese knife and my apple. He helps himself to a slice of both as I tell him about making the final decisions for the freeport's Labor Day family picnic. He pretends like he's interested in barbecue and local craft beers, in a carnival for the kids and a raffle for the entire staff.

His glass is empty.

"Another?" I ask.

He shakes his head.

I try again. "I think I've identified another one of Herzog's paintings. It's a Monet, a view of Waterloo Bridge. I'm pretty sure it was reported stolen from a museum in Rotterdam. The art world assumed it was burned years ago, along with six others from the same theft."

I wait for him to tell me I've done good work. That he's impressed with my sleuthing skills. That there's something good coming out of Herzog's time as a freeport client.

Silence.

I can tell him how Susan helped me with a personnel matter this morning, how we worked out a more efficient schedule for the receptionists at the front desk. I can tell him the painters are coming to spruce up the freeport garage next week, that we've already sent notices to all the clients so they can either trust us to move their collections or do it themselves. I can tell him there's a conference on cybersecurity and museums in Paris in December, and I secured a spot so I can see what might affect the freeport.

But from the haunted look on his face, I know he won't care.

He didn't tell me where he went today. There was nothing entered on his calendar. In my heart of hearts, I know what that means.

He's trying to figure out a way to keep Jonas and Ansel Herzog from releasing their video. A billion dollars, the freeport's reputation—it's all on the line because of me.

If I could just go back in time...

But there isn't a good end to that sentence. Because if I didn't kill Herzog, I'd still be his slave. I wouldn't know what it's like to live with Trap. To love Trap.

And while there's a part of me that says I'm selfish, that I'm bad, that I should have found another solution during my three endless years of captivity, I know Trap would never say that. He wants me here. He needs me.

So I do the only thing I can think of, the thing that always brings us closer together, the thing that heals all the broken places inside both of us.

I sink to my knees in the lush green grass in front of Trap's chair. I reach for the buckle on his belt.

"Alix..." he says, my name starting as a refusal but ending on a sigh.

I tug on the buckle, sliding the leather easily through the loops on his trousers. I start to toss it aside, more interested in the button, in the zipper, but at the last moment, I loop the belt around my neck. I feed the end through the buckle, pulling it tight, like a choker. I press the long end of the leash into Trap's hand.

At first, I think he won't take it, that he's too tired or too depressed or too out of sorts to play. But then his fingers tighten, and he uses the belt to pull me toward him, forcing my spine to straighten as I stay on my knees. My neck is stretched, my head at an angle. The leather bites into my voice box, and I catch my lip between my teeth to keep from crying out.

He plants his free thumb on my chin, applying enough pressure to force me to open my lips. When my mouth is open, he slips his thumb inside, sliding it slowly over my tongue.

I moan. I want more than his thumb. I want my mouth full. My lips stretched. I want my throat working, fighting to take all of him.

He leans forward and drops the belt. His fingers reach for my breast, and I know he's going to tease the nipple. He'll pinch it, hard enough to make me gasp. He'll palm it, rubbing the sensitive tip until it aches.

He'll work to give me pleasure. I always long for Trap's touch. But now, tonight, when he's beaten and exhausted, I want to be the one to give something to him.

I push his fingers away with the back of my hand. I reach for his fly before he can stop me, slipping the zipper and reaching inside. His cock springs to attention like a time-lapse film of some exotic flower blooming.

He's hard and he's hot and a bead of moisture already waits for my attention. I wrap my fingers around the length of him, squeezing hard. My thumb slips through his precum, making him grit his teeth as I smooth the slickness over his rounded tip.

"Princess," he says, one hand closing over mine. "Let's go inside."

I shake my head, underlining my refusal with a fingernail that traces one of his heavy veins.

"Sweet fuck," he gasps, trying to cup my elbow in his palm. "Come on. Let me make you feel good."

My only answer is to take him deep.

I feel the tension in his thighs. He wants to be in control here. I'm breaking the rules. He's supposed to be the one who chooses what we do and when and where. He's the one in charge. My only job is to submit.

But his cock is willing to consider a change in plans.

I pull back slowly, tightening my lips as I swirl my tongue down his length. He groans as he grows thicker, pressing against the roof of my mouth. I swallow him again.

He starts to swear, a filthy prayer that lights a candle deep inside me. His hands close around my head.

He's guiding me. Controlling me. He's making me take him deeper than I ever thought I could.

"That's right, Princess," he whispers. "Your mouth's so hot. So goddamn wet... Let me fuck your beautiful face."

The dirty talk loosens my throat. His balls flirt with my chin, and I want to tongue them, want to suck them hard, but his hands deny my freedom; they're too tight on the back of my head.

I long to tell him what I'll do for him, what I'll give him, how he'll come. But the sounds vibrating in my throat only seem to stoke the fire between us.

"That's right, Princess," he says, plunging deep. "Take. It. All."

I'm the one who started this, but I've lost control. He's driving now, not me. He's pumping in and out of my lips, hitting the back of my throat.

My eyes water. My hands splay on his hips. My neck stretches, angles, working hard to give him what he needs.

His palms burn my scalp. His wrists tremble. His breath is coming fast now, short, sharp huffs that fan the flames inside me. His thighs are iron beneath my jaw.

I need to pant like he does. I need to catch my breath. I need to slow down, to speed up, to take the entire velvet shaft of him and hold it deep, deep, deep, forever and ever and ever.

He explodes inside me.

His fingers tighten like exquisite clamps, pinning my head to the angle he needs. He's holding me close, pressing my face into his lap, keeping me exactly where he wants me. He's pulsing down my throat, hot, thick, salt, and I swallow hard, jaw working to take all that he can give me.

The words flooding from his lips are raunchy, depraved, all the ways he wants to come in me, on me, all the things he wants to do with every part of my body. I'll do it—any of it, all of it. He's mine, and I'm his, and I want this moment to stretch and loop, to weave between us, binding us together forever.

He's slowing now. The heat he's pulsing against my throat fades. His fingers loosen on my head. His words fade to a rumble, a whisper, to silence.

He pulls out of my mouth slowly. I miss him even before he's gone, miss the hardness of him, miss the stretch of my lips, my jaw, my throat. I sit back on my heels, smelling the bruised grass beneath my knees. I turn my face to rest my head against his thigh.

"Good girl," he rasps, his thumb tracing the corner of my mouth. "My good, good girl."

Something unspools inside me, a longing so deep I can't give it a name. I need to be good. I need to be what *he* needs me to be. I need to say yes, yes, yes, to any question, every question he could ever dream of asking.

He lowers his hand to the belt around my throat. The leather's still fastened through the buckle, but it's loose now. Without my asking, he wraps the end around his fist. He pulls it tight, until the edge of the belt cuts off my ability to swallow.

Using the belt as a lever, he raises my head from his knee. Leaning forward, he forces my face close to his. His grasp on my leash holds me steady; I can stay where he wants or I can choke.

His eyes meet mine, their jungle fire nearly banked. I stare at him—not blinking, not breathing, not breaking the bond that burns between us.

He holds us there, waiting, balanced, perfect.

He's asking if I'm his.

I'm saying that I am, always.

And then he opens his fist and the belt falls slack between us. I sway to my right, and he slides from his chair, landing on his knees beside me. His arms are around me, and one broad hand cradles my head. He leans against the rattan chaise, bracing his back against it, and he pulls me onto his lap and he holds me, shelters me, keeps me safe from any harm.

I'm his good girl.

I'm his princess.

I'm Alix.

And I'm where I want to be forever.

14

TRAP

Two more days go by. One week now till the brothers' deadline, and I'm no closer to a solution. No negotiated peace. No guarantee I won't be on the hook for fucking life.

I keep hearing Kelly's voice inside my head: *You need more manpower.*

But calling in Sawgrass is the nuclear option. Those guys don't fuck around. They'll take out the brothers and leave behind a shitload of collateral damage.

The Herzogs' security won't go down without a fight. And taking out the brothers in their Long Island fortress will call down every cop in the county. Hell, with their connections, they might own law enforcement throughout New York state. They could have the feds in their back pockets too.

The one weapon I have is too fucking big. It's the goddamn definition of "mutually assured destruction".

So, even though I'm running out of time and I feel like I'm

trying to cross a frozen lake on roller skates, I search for an alternative.

I schedule a meeting with my banker.

I already know the answer before he delivers the news. The only way I can manage a billion-dollar payout is to put up the freeport as collateral. And if I was desperate enough to try that, I'd torpedo my entire business empire. My clients aren't the type who want their business disclosed in loan documents.

I go over the freeport's vacancies. That demand I can actually meet—a container's worth of space. I could give the brothers Klaus's gallery, carve out another one on the same floor, even two.

But I refuse to cross that bridge.

My clients aren't angels. The freeport holds plenty of stolen goods—Klaus's paintings are only the tip of the fucking iceberg. I'd be astonished if half the vehicles in the pristine garage have valid registrations. I know one client is storing liquor that's never been taxed and another could never come up with sales papers on his collection of rare watches.

I'm fucking excellent at looking the other way.

But it's one thing to close my eyes to theft and fraud. It's another to aid and abet the distribution of Schedule I controlled substances that have been specifically designed to target the brains of helpless, developing kids.

Fuck. I only got into this situation because Alix's brother was addicted to the shit. If that asshole hadn't fucked up his life, who knows what might have happened with Alix and me? She could've come home with me from Debasement, spent the night blowing my fucking mind, and stuck around for the intervening three years so I could repay the favor—over and over and over again.

No. I'm not turning Diamond Freeport into a drug distribution center, no matter what the motherfucking Herzogs demand.

And even though this shit is keeping me up nights, I can't ignore my entire goddamn business plan, just because *I'm* hanging in the wind. The Diamond Ring's monthly meeting is scheduled for Saturday night.

Weeks ago, I told Susan Richards what I want, and she's made it happen. A chartered yacht with at least one sound-proof room and a Faraday cage to block electronic transmission. Private access to a dock on the bay. Guards to watch a few million dollars worth of cars while we're on board. A Michelin three-star chef to create a world-class meal.

And a quarter million dollar buy-in, no-limit night of Texas hold 'em.

I give Alix the choice of joining us, but she opts out. And I can't really blame her.

We set sail at seven. Braiden Kelly is the first man aboard. He greets me with a handshake that puts the Beast on alert. "How's our girl?" he asks, like he and I have been friends since high school. Or maybe like he thinks of Alix as his sister.

I shrug, because he already knows I need to take down the Herzog brothers. The rest of the Ring will find out tonight. I can't get through this meeting without letting them know the danger they're in if the video gets out.

I'm spared coming up with a more complete answer because Carl Braxton strides up the gangplank. He's followed by Gage Rider and Connor Boyle arriving together, then half a dozen others in short order. Cole Wolf is the last to join us. He pulls into the guarded lot, driving a familiar Mercedes, the car he bought off Herzog's corpse to ward off awkward inquiries about the slimeball's arrival at the freeport.

"How's it drive?" I ask as he comes aboard.

"Like a dream. German engineering, you know?"

"Glad you got your money's worth."

"Herzog drove a hard bargain." He says it like the fiction he created is real, like he actually purchased the car after intense, good faith negotiations. I wonder if he's lying for my benefit, or if that's just the way his mind works. Water under the bridge. No reason to look back. No reason to dwell on the past.

I could use more of that in my life.

Too bad I'm about to fuck up his game plan. Him, and the rest of the Ring.

But forewarned is forearmed. At least that's what I tell myself as I gather my clients in the Faraday cage boardroom below deck. I make sure everyone has his drink of choice before I drop my bomb.

"Gentlemen. There's no easy way to say this, so I'll just tell you all the truth. The last meeting of the Diamond Ring was filmed without my knowledge. I'm being blackmailed to avoid the release of the video. While I have no intention of complying with the blackmailers' demands, I'm doing everything else in my power to guarantee the recording won't see the light of day."

I almost wish Alix was here, just so she could see the variety of reactions. I'm sure she could write her long-overdue thesis about how a bunch of rich fucks deal with the news that they can't control every aspect of the world around them.

Arsene Dubois laughs, like I'm telling a lousy joke with a worse punchline, and I wonder if something got lost in translation from my English to his French. Wolf's not surprised, not after the phone call we had last week. Kelly, either.

Boyle's eyes narrow. He knows the borders of his own territory; I'm sure he's come up against the Herzogs before. He rolls his shoulders like he's gearing up for a fight, and I'm glad I'm not on the receiving end of his massive fists.

Braxton takes out his cell, only to discover he's blocked from calling his lawyer or his accountant or his priest, whoever the fuck he thinks is going to help him out of this shitstorm.

Marcus shouts, "This is bullshit!" He repeats himself twice for good measure, just in case that's enough to change the threat. He owns the largest fast-food chain in the world. He probably can't imagine a problem that can't be solved by offering up an order of free fries.

Sawyer Best's steely voice cuts through the chaos. "What are they asking?"

Steve Torrington, who made his billions in insurance, says, "Yeah, what're the demands? Better to pay up than face those consequences."

I don't bother mincing words. "They want to turn the freeport into their East Coast distribution hub for illegal drugs targeting kids."

A couple of assholes clearly think it's worth the risk. I'm fully aware of the flexible ethics that make each of these guys worth ten thousand times the average US citizen. Most would sell their own mother if the price was right.

Speaking of prices... I lower the second boom. "And they want a billion dollars."

The typical guy on the street doesn't have a clue how big a billion is. But if that John Doe dumbfuck earned a hundred thousand dollars a year for fifty years, he'd bring home five million bucks. Five percent of a billion. To get to a billion, he'd have to earn fifty-five grand a *day*.

So, yeah. The Herzogs' ask is enough to knock the room silent.

Cole Wolf recovers first, but he's had a few days to think. "What's on the video?"

Again, no reason to hold back. "Herzog's front and center. There are clean shots of Alix and me. Kelly's identifiable, and Best, too. Probably Marcus and Wolf. Maybe Boyle."

Relief rolls through half the crowd anyway, until Wolf says, "That's in the footage they sent you."

Bingo. He got there fast.

But Marcus bitches, "As opposed to what?"

"As opposed to all the footage they actually have on hand," Wolf says before he turns back to me. "I assume Best's crew found the cameras when they tore your place apart. How many?"

"Three," I say. Best nods narrow-eyed agreement.

Wolf says, "So there're two more videos out there. Maybe

they don't show the main event, but reaction shots are just as damning. Any kid with a laptop can splice them together."

In case anyone's stupid enough to miss the real point, Best chimes in. "We're all accessories after the fact. And once they pocket Prince's billion, what's to keep them from coming after the rest of us?"

"Who *are* these assholes?" Marcus demands.

"Herzog's brothers." I hold up my hands, like I can ward off a million questions and demands. "I've got a dossier six inches thick, including where they're holed up and the names of their fucking dogs. But none of that does me any good if they won't come to the table."

"You've got an address?" Braxton asks. "I've got more than a few ways to smoke them out." He's an international arms dealer. I'd be surprised if he didn't.

"They have a full-time army guarding them."

I don't look at Best.

"So what the *fuck* are you going to do?" Marcus, again.

I force myself to sound calm. Confident. Like I actually have a goddamn plan. "Their demands are an opening bid. I'll negotiate. Build a solution. The same way I built the fucking freeport."

"Then why tell us now?" That's Best, playing the role of Wise Man, with his silver beard and those eyes that can cut solid metal. He's pushing me toward a different solution. Toward something a hell of a lot more active.

But I'm still not biting.

I can't.

Instead, I say, "You're my clients. My friends." At least half of that is true, so I salt in a little lie. "I have absolute faith in my ability to bring this thing to a satisfactory conclusion." That leaves me with the real reason I'm letting them know now. "You each deserve a chance to protect yourself. If anyone's been thinking about an extended visit to the UAE or Brunei or Saudi, this might be a good time to firm up your travel plans."

They're billionaires who've built their fortunes on the shady side of the street. In addition to the three countries without extradition treaties that I've named, every one of them could recite at least a dozen more. Every man in the room understands the option I've just laid out.

Boyle snorts. I can't actually picture his Irish ass in the middle of a desert, but I figured I should at least lay out the option.

Everyone else is silent until Best finally asks, "When's the payout due?"

"August fifteenth."

"That's just one week!" Marcus again.

I bite down hard to keep from congratulating him on knowing the fucking calendar. Instead, I spread my hands wide, trying to convey that I've got nothing to hide. "I'll keep all of you up to date," I say. "If you have any questions tonight, I'm happy to answer to the best of my ability."

There's grumbling, but I expected that. These are men who are used to getting their way, immediately, in all things.

Some would say I'm an idiot, for bringing them into the loop. But I prefer to think I've got a strong long-term strategy.

If I somehow manage to meet the Herzogs face-to-face and defuse the ticking time-bomb, then I'm a fucking hero. And if I fail, then every one of these guys has incentive to get revenge.

At least the ones who haven't fled the country.

"For now, gentlemen, we wait. And to help you pass the time, Chef Jean-Yves has prepared a particularly tempting dinner. And after that, you're all welcome to try to take my money at the card table."

Best waits until the others have gone up to the weather deck. He closes the door quietly, guaranteeing we can't be overheard. "You're out of moves," he says.

I shake my head. "Not yet."

His eyes look like lasers under his gun-metal hair. "What do you think is going to happen? They'll all of a sudden call you up and invite you over for a couple of beers?"

"They don't want to release the tape. They want money instead. Access to the freeport."

"Bullshit." Best puts a lot more force behind the word than Marcus ever did. "My guys can take care of this."

"Your guys hit the ground amped to eleven. The whole idea is to keep this quiet."

"We can do quiet."

"Not at that place. It's fucking Fort Knox."

"Then find out where else we can hit them."

"You think I haven't been trying to do that, from the moment I saw their fucking video?"

He holds up his hands, a "don't shoot the messenger" gesture. I've never noticed that he's missing the last joint on his left pinky. "We're good at getting information, too," he says.

I've heard the rumors. Best has personally waterboarded dozens of prisoners. Stress positions, hooding, rectal rehydration... Word on the street is, he got the fucking job done in the desert, and he gets it done here, on US soil.

The problem is, we don't have anyone to interrogate. Alix is the only person I know who's ever seen Jonas and Ansel Herzog in person. And she's already...highly motivated to share whatever information she has.

Or is she?

"What?" Best pounces.

"Nothing."

His eyes narrow like he's sighting down a firing range. "The way I see it, you've got three choices. One: You let us loose on their compound, and we do what we do best."

I shake my head. The fallout would be too much.

"Two: You find out where those motherfuckers are going to be in the next week, and you let my men remove the problem."

"And three?"

"Three. You hire the best lawyer in the world. Because once that video goes public you'll need him. You and Alix both."

I don't know if he said her name on purpose. If he's trying to egg me on, to get me to do something I really don't want to do.

But now that my mind has snagged on Alix, I can't tear myself free. She knows the brothers. She understands the way the sick fucks think. In the past three years, she must have heard *something* we can use. Something that can help. Something that can load the weapon of Sawgrass Industries and point it toward a vulnerable target.

Best hands me a card.

"What's this?" I'm staring at ten digits. There's not another mark on the white rectangle.

"A phone number."

"What the fuck am I supposed to do with it?"

"Call me when you get your head out of your ass and accept what needs to be done. Use a fucking burner. And don't wait too long."

15

ALIX

It's after two in the morning when Trap finally comes upstairs. I've spent the last three hours staring at a romance novel, pretending I can follow the plot. I keep getting to the end of a chapter and realizing I can't remember anything on the preceding pages.

I should have gone with Trap on the boat. But it's bad enough knowing video exists of the night I killed Herzog. I can't imagine socializing with the men who were in the room that night.

When Trap walks into the bedroom, I put my book on the nightstand, not bothering to mark my place. "How'd it go?" I ask.

"Exactly as well as you'd expect."

He looks exhausted. I climb out of bed and cross the room, ignoring the chill on my bare legs.

I'm wearing a soft cotton sleep shirt. I didn't think Trap would be interested in my seducing him tonight.

I'm right.

I want to tell him he smells like a still, but that won't do either of us any good. I think about asking how much he lost at poker, but I don't really care. I can't think of anything I can say to make it all better.

But he lets me loosen his tie and pull his shirt from his trousers. I undo the buttons, one by one. I don't feel remotely like a lover luring my man to bed. I feel like a mother. Maybe a nurse.

His hands close around my hips, just holding me, not trying to bring me close, not trying to fan the fire that always simmers just beneath the surface with us. He lowers his head and brushes his lips against my forehead. I fight the sudden urge to cry.

"Get into bed," he says. "Let me wash up."

I do what he says, because my obeying might actually make his life a little easier. I listen to water running in the bathroom, to the hum of his electric toothbrush, to the flush of the toilet. It feels like I belong here, like we've been settled into this life together for a million years. It feels *right*, which is impossible because the video is still out there and everything is so, so wrong.

Trap comes out of the bathroom wearing only his boxers. He climbs into bed, leaving his pillow propped behind him. Sitting up against the headboard, he reaches for me, pulling me close until my head is nestled against his chest.

His broad hand spreads over my short hair. He sighs, and a little of his fatigue seeps into me.

"I have to ask you," he says.

"What?" I answer, even as his tone sets a flurry of panic stirring inside me, a dust devil coming to life.

He shifts, and his lips touch the crown of my head. "I need to know everything you remember about Jonas and Ansel. Anything at all. I need a way to get at them, outside that goddamn fort they have on the Island."

I don't realize I've turned to stone until he slips a finger under my chin. Something crumbles inside me as he forces my gaze up to meet his.

"No matter how small it seems," he says. "I need to know everything you know."

"To kill them." My voice sounds like shattered eggshells.

"To kill them," he agrees. "That's the only way we'll be safe."

Trap has seen his share of rough behavior, of dealings that would never be accepted in a court of law. But he's not dangerous enough to take down the Herzogs.

A row of bricks rises inside me. If I say anything that puts him in the same room with Jonas and Ansel, they'll destroy him. The Herzogs will kill Trap, and I'll have another death on my soul.

"There has to be another way," I say.

"I'm sorry, Princess."

He thinks *he's* protecting *me*. But I'm the one protecting him.

I can't tell him. I can't say all the things I did in Klaus Herzog's mansion. I can't let him know all the ways I let the Herzogs use me.

I should have fought harder. I gave in too soon. I let them break my spirit. This is all my fault.

But I can't find the words to say all that. I don't know how to tell Trap that I'm broken. Ruined. That he never should have taken me in, and now that I'm here, the only smart thing to do is to throw me out the door.

"Please," he says, and his voice is gentler than I've ever heard it. "I wouldn't ask if it wasn't absolutely necessary."

He's Trap Prince. He's the one man who's offered me shelter in this never-ending storm. He's the one man I can trust, the one man who searched for me, the one man who stood by me as I murdered Klaus Herzog downstairs.

I love him. I trust him.

And so I close my eyes, and I tell him what I can.

"Jonas is a bodybuilder. A weightlifter. Something like that.

He's a couple inches taller than I am but he outweighs me by fifty, maybe sixty pounds. It's muscle. All muscle."

Each hateful word adds a brick to the wall inside me. My voice shakes, like an icy wind is blowing through the bedroom. Trap nods, but he doesn't give me permission to stop.

"Ansel's taller," I say. "Maybe six feet? He's dark, like a man who works outside. His hair is brown, not blond like his brothers."

The brick wall is up to my chest. It's pressing against my lungs. It's strangling my aching heart. I pray I've said enough, but Trap only whispers, "Good girl." I have to go on.

"They have the same eyes—that light, light blue. Like milk. Like they're blind."

"Tattoos?" Trap asks.

I shake my head.

"Scars?"

I close my eyes. "I don't think so. I don't know. I wasn't paying attention. I couldn't ask questions. I was only supposed to be there, like an animal, like a piece of furniture in the room."

The bricks are up to my eyes. My panicked voice echoes off them, throwing words back to my ears. I need to burrow, need to escape. But Trap only says, "You know more than you think you do. Start with the night you met them. Tell me what happened. Where were you? What did they say? What did they do?"

I don't want him to know those nightmares. I don't want him to think of those things every time he looks at me. I don't want to ruin what we've built between us.

"Please…" he begs, quiet and desperate and unspeakably, unbearably kind.

So I tell him.

I tell him about dressing in a catsuit. I tell him about being struck by a cane. I tell him about the Crash and the chair and the olive oil cruet. I tell him about being used by three men at once.

And all he says is, "What else?"

I close my eyes and I harden my voice and I tell him about every visit after that first one. I remember details I thought I'd stored away forever, each jagged memory a separate uranium rod encased in glass.

And every single sentence adds to the wall around me. Every last word makes my throat grow tighter. Every separate syllable shrinks me, erases me, imprisons me.

I'm no longer Alix Key. I'm not a woman in a bed with a man she trusts to love her. I'm not a survivor, a person who was kidnapped, who killed her tormentor, who found a way to live again.

I'm a column of brick. A featureless wall. A blank, empty stretch of nothing.

Because nothing I've said matters. Nothing I've said will help.

I've given Trap words. But I don't know any secrets. I don't know any special hideaways, any private clubs where Trap can take them unaware.

Trap can't save me.

He can't save himself.

Jonas and Ansel Herzog will break us, the same way they broke me in their brother's haunted mansion. But Trap knows all my horrors now. And there's nothing I can say, nothing I can do, nothing that will ever make me safe again.

TRAP

I turn off the light on my nightstand and sit in the dark, waiting for Alix's breathing to slow. That's the only way I'll know she's actually asleep.

She closed her eyes half an hour ago, when she was only halfway through answering my questions. Her face went flat fifteen minutes after that, all expression washed away by the horrors I forced her to recall. Her voice wound down as she spoke, softer and softer until I could barely make out her whisper by the time she was done.

She was a wind-up toy, spinning down to perfect stillness. She was an old-fashioned flashlight, the kind I hid beneath the covers when I was a kid, draining batteries to absolute zero as monsters oozed from beneath my bed.

I'd actually pay a billion dollars, if I could transform her stories into a child's harmless imagination. But no child should ever know about the cruelty Alix survived. No woman, either.

When I asked her for the truth, I thought I was playing a chess match against the Herzogs. I needed to place my pieces. I needed to understand their opening gambit so I could structure my defense, so I could drive them toward the inevitable checkmate.

Now, I don't care about rules. I don't care about what's legal and what's not. What's fair and what isn't.

I'm going to annihilate those cocksuckers.

I want to do it slowly. Make them suffer. Take their money. Carve away their humanity, step by tortured step, the same way they broke Alix down to her component parts.

At least she's sleeping now, breaths slow and easy for the first time since I forced her back to the past. I ease away from her side, guiding her head down to a pillow. She stirs, starts to murmur, but I whisper close to her ear, "You're safe, Princess. Go back to sleep."

I pull the sheet up to her shoulders. I tuck the blanket close to her side. I stand beside the bed, watching, waiting until she drifts away again.

Only when she's truly out do I head into the bathroom. Shucking my underwear, I move under the shower head and crank the water as hot as it'll go.

I want to scald those images from my brain. I want to boil myself clean, just for listening to what she went through. For once, it isn't the Beast that tells me I'm dirty, I'm impure, I'm doomed.

It's Alix's truth.

It's what she survived.

I plant my palms on the tiled wall, pushing hard to shed some of my rage through my shaking shoulders. Soap, shampoo, the razor sitting ready on its shelf... None of it's enough to make me feel clean.

Fuck all of this. Fuck a world where men can dream up the sort of torture Alix endured. Fuck Jonas and fuck Ansel and fuck fucking Klaus, whose fucking sick obsessions started all of this.

The shower won't run cold—modern plumbing and a tank-less water heater guarantee that. But when my skin is red, when my fingers start to pucker, when the steam billowing off the tiles seems thicker than the clouds on a rocket's launch pad, I finally turn the water off.

I dry myself, tucking the towel tight around my waist. I drape another over my shoulders.

Back in the bedroom, Alix still sleeps soundly. I resist the urge to brush her cheek with my fingers, to settle my palm along her spine. Dreaming, she doesn't need my comfort now.

I head downstairs.

I feel ashamed for what I made her do. I didn't have the right to push her that hard. I shouldn't have forced her to tell me things she wanted buried forever.

Because the worst thing is, she didn't give me any magic answer. She didn't tell me any secrets I can use. She didn't give me a single fact I can turn into a weapon to destroy the fucking Herzog brothers forever.

All that shit. All those nightmares. For nothing.

I dig in my desk for a burner phone. I keep three or four on hand.

I find the card Best gave me on the yacht. He answers on the first ring. "Best."

"It's Trap," I say.

He just waits.

"Option one," I say. *You let us loose on their compound, and we do what we do best.*

"What's your deadline?"

"They've given me till August 15."

"So no later than midnight, August 14."

"That'll do."

"Okay. I'll take care of it."

There's no discussion of fees. No explanation of how he intends to take the Long Island fortress. No details, because I don't need to know.

But just like that, I've removed Jonas and Ansel Herzog from my life.

17

TRAP

I want to make it up to her.

I want to make things right.

I want to give her back the naivete she had the first time she slept in my bed. She'd never come before she met me. She'd never imagined the torture the Herzogs could do.

I wonder what she was like when she was truly innocent. Before her brother's addiction spun her life out of control. Before her mother died, leaving her in the care of a distracted father and a cruel, uncaring stepmother.

And that's when it comes to me. The thing I can do. One gift I can give her, to make her forget everything that's happened.

And it'll be the perfect alibi for both of us, if anything goes wrong with Best's operation.

I tap my phone before I realize it's only five in the morning. Sunday morning.

Susan Richards answers on the second ring. "Hello?" She clears her throat and tries again: "Good morning."

"Sorry to wake you."

She doesn't lie. Doesn't tell me she was already up. That she couldn't sleep. Was feeding her cat. Instead, she gives me a brisk, "Not a problem."

I tell her what I want to do.

"They'll charge a fortune," she says. "Especially with such short notice."

"I'll pay."

"You'll need the plane," she says, and I hear tapping in the background. She's taking a steady stream of notes.

"We'll head down at three that afternoon."

"You'll need a car once you get there."

"With a driver."

"Of course," she says. More tapping. "You want him in costume?"

I shake my head, even though she can't see me. "I want to keep it a surprise as long as possible." As I answer, I pull up a web page on my computer, filling in some gaps in my knowledge. I give Susan a few more instructions.

"I'll get right on it," she says. "But if they say they can't do it?"

"Offer more money."

"It's not always about money," she tries to remind me.

"This is. You've got a blank check."

"I'll email the details, as soon as they're set."

"Just to me. Alix can't know anything about it."

"Of course she can't," Susan says. And for the first time since I hired her, I think she might be laughing at me.

That's okay. I deserve it, just a little, for thinking I can pull this off.

I let Susan go so she can work her magic, and I head into the kitchen. There isn't enough coffee in the world to make up for my night of booze, poker, and the detailed vision I've gained of my enemies.

But I've got to pretend otherwise. I'm the CEO of Diamond fucking Freeport. And I'm finally doing *something* to protect my business from blackmailing cocksuckers. To protect my fortune. To protect Alix.

One week, and this will all be over.

18

ALIX

Trap texts me mid-morning.

Be ready to leave at 2

Dress casual

Comfortable shoes

I send back a row of question marks, but I don't get a reply, not even three floating bubbles. I call Susan, to see if she knows what's going on. She gives me the sort of cagey non-reply that says she knows *exactly* what's going on, but it's not worth her job to share that information with me.

I put on jeans, the ones with strategically fashionable holes torn across the knees. I worry they're *too* casual and swap them out for khakis. I try on seven different tops, not sure if I should go with knit or woven, with buttons or over-the-head. I start with low heels but decide I should take Trap's warning seriously if he's actually bothering to say something about footwear. Walking shoes it is, then, with thick socks.

At least my hair's still too short to worry about.

I should be focused on the freeport. We've got less than forty-eight hours until the Herzog brothers' deadline. I should be writing down succession plans, telling people how to manage the work I've taken on, making recommendations for auctioneers and caterers and the other outside staff I've been managing.

But if Trap wanted me to handle all that, he would have said so. That's one of the best things about Trap Prince. He says exactly what he means. And he means every word he says.

I never have to play guessing games with him.

He comes back from the office building at 1:45. A quick change upstairs, and he joins me in the kitchen. He's wearing black jeans and a tight black T-shirt, the exact outfit he had on the first night we met. Something deep inside me *pings*.

He looks at my purse, a strappy little backpack just big enough for my phone, my wallet, a tube of ChapStick, and my keys. "You can leave that behind."

"But…" It feels strange to leave the house without a thing. Trap just gives me *that* look, the one that says he knows I'm questioning him, and he knows I'll give in, so why don't we just skip to the good part anyway.

I leave my purse on the kitchen counter.

In the garage, Trap walks us to his electric blue Porsche. Again, that's the car he drove the night we met.

He holds the door for me, and I slide into the low passenger seat. After we leave the freeport's front gate, I half expect him to turn toward Dover, toward the bar where I first saw him. I could use an evening out on the town. Just the thing to take my mind off the looming threat of Jonas and Ansel.

But he turns right out of the gate. Away from town.

And he drives us to the airfield.

The private jet is waiting. We're greeted by a uniformed

attendant who rapidly serves up a cheese board and champagne. The pilot comes back to greet Trap and knows him well enough not to shake his hand.

Within minutes, we've taxied down the runway, and we're airborne.

"Now do I get to know where we're going?"

"Nope." Trap smiles as he says it, but he's enjoying his control.

I realize the window shades are down throughout the cabin. He's not taking a chance that I'll recognize landmarks from the air. "Give me a hint," I say.

"Not gonna happen."

"Three guesses?"

He doesn't deign to answer.

"How about a card game? Gin rummy? If I win, you tell me."

"And when I win?"

I shouldn't be this turned on by his arrogant assumption that he'll get the best of me. But I am. "I'll take off an article of clothing."

His eyebrows arch. "Shoes count as one thing?"

He's actually going along with this. And my mother taught Leo and me how to play gin rummy when we were five years old. "Sure," I say. "Shoes count as one."

"You're on," he says. "Shuffle up and deal."

I look around the cabin. "Where are the cards?"

"You didn't bring any?"

"Of course I didn't—" From the grin on his face, he knew this was how he'd trap me from the very beginning. Even if I carried playing cards in my purse on a regular basis, they'd be stranded back in our kitchen. And my jeans are tight enough that he can tell I'm not hiding a deck in my pockets.

I cross my arms and sit back in my chair, staging a pout.

Which lasts about as long as it takes for Trap to bend down and close his hands around my ankles. One sharp tug, and I'm sliding across the leather seat. He shifts his hands, and he's caged me on his lap.

"Got any other ideas about how we can pass the time?" he asks.

His fingers are already doing disturbing things beneath my top, and part of me is grateful that I went with the no-buttons option. Another part of me is painfully aware that there's a flight attendant just the other side of the bulkhead, and she might decide to refill our champagne flutes at any moment.

"Trap…" I start, but he reads my mind. Again.

His fingers lace between mine, and he leads me toward the back of the plane, to the room outfitted as his office. As the door clicks shut behind us, I protest again. "They'll know exactly what we're doing in here!"

"You think I give a fuck?"

He's standing behind me, but he already has the button undone at my waist. One arm folds across my belly, pulling me close to his chest. The back of his wrist presses against my zipper as he slips a finger past my soaked panties. I'm ready for him, little flutters already swirling deep, and the smirk on his face says he knows it.

But I try to preserve some sense of decorum. "We can't," I say. "Not here."

He finds the hard button of my clit and strokes it between the narrow V of his index and middle fingers. "What?" he asks after laughing at my gasp. "You'd rather do this in the john?"

I'm supposed to protest. I'm supposed to say we can't do this at all. But the pressure of three fingers plunging inside me makes me forget the English language.

"Ready to join the Mile High Club, Princess?"

I'm ready to parachute out the back of the plane, if that's what he commands, if that's the tradeoff for keeping his hand between my thighs. He bends his head, moving his lips dangerously close to my ear. I hear him breathing, hard and fast, before his teeth close tight on my lobe.

The love bite makes my knees buckle. I'd fall to the floor if Trap didn't have one arm folded around my belly. His laugh is wicked as he walks us toward his desk.

"Hands on the blotter," he says.

I obey instantly, planting my palms on the leather surface. He responds by pulling his fingers out of my eager pussy, and I can't keep from whining at the loss.

"You're the one who's so worried about the people outside," he says. "One more sound out of you, and I stop."

He waits for me to nod, to accept the rules of his game. Then his hands are firm on my waist. He pulls my khakis to my knees. He kicks my feet as wide as my pants will let him.

"Don't move those hands," he warns. "Or I'll stop."

I spread my fingers wide, anchoring myself on the desk. I hear him work his own zipper, and I feel the tip of his erection against my bare bottom.

"On your tiptoes," he demands. "Or I'll stop."

I rise up on my toes, knowing that will push the curve of my ass toward his cock. His palm smooths my flesh, a lingering caress, and I catch myself just before I purr my need.

He sinks into me, filling my pussy from behind. His cock is hard and heavy and he must be close to coming because he plants one urgent hand on my hip and the other on the back of my neck.

He pulls out slowly, teasing all my deep muscles. I don't want to lose him, don't want him to leave me, so I push back from the desk. My hands don't move. I stay on my toes. But I shift my ass back, following him like I'm under his spell.

The next time he drives home, his fingers leave my hip to pinch my aching clit. The sensation makes me catch my breath. My calves stretch. My shoulders stiffen. But I don't break his rules.

He sets a rhythm then, steady, pounding. My inner walls grip him, conveying all the things I'm not allowed to say out loud. I catch my lower lip between my teeth, sparking a pain that merges with his heat, that blends with his power.

Before I know I'm ready, I'm teetering on the edge of a cliff. We're miles high in the plane, but I'm soaring higher than that, riveted in place, reduced to the tight wet channel between my thighs, to the steel-hard wires that link my clit to my savaged lip, to my trembling palms, to my arched and aching toes.

He fills me again, my perfect match and I need him to release me, I need him to say the word, but he doesn't tell me I can come and I can't do it I can't break free I can't reach the one thing I need more than air more than light more than life if he'll just say it I'll be his forever—

"Please," I moan, the word slipping past my craving soul.

He pulls out and steps away.

I whirl to face him. My heels are flat on the floor. My hands reach for his slick, hard cock.

"Trap…"

"Rules, Princess."

I take a step toward him, prepared to beg. "Please," I say again. This time I'm fully conscious that I'm saying the word.

His hand closes around his cock. His fingers work the way mine long to do. One stroke. Two. Three.

His face freezes and his grip grows even tighter. His cock pulses. Thick milk coats his hand, shooting onto the floor between us.

When he's finished, he reaches past me, plucking some tissues from a leather box on his desk. He wipes his palm clean. Swipes at his fingers. Takes a pass at the shimmering cream on the utilitarian carpet. Tosses the mess into a trashcan beside the desk.

Zipped up, shirt tucked back in, he's at the door while I'm still stunned.

"I'll meet you back at our seats," he says. My cry of protest only makes him laugh. "Think of it this way, Princess. I gave you a bit of distraction. You forgot how much you want to know our destination." Still smiling, he exits the office, closing the door behind him.

I could finish myself off. It wouldn't take much, just a few steady swipes from fingers that are already trembling—with lust, maybe, or anger. Something related to adrenaline.

But I somehow suspect that if I go into the cabin with my hands smelling like my aching pussy, there'll be another penalty to pay. After all, Trap warned me about the rules.

I pull up my pants. I straighten my top. And just as I take my seat in the cabin, the pilot makes an announcement: We've begun our descent and should be on the ground in fifteen minutes.

I consider raising one of the window shades to see where Trap has taken me. But that's a rule too. And I'm still too close to the aching edge of need to risk more punishment, with the evening and the night still stretching ahead of us.

"Cheer up, Princess," Trap says with the grin of a man who got the release he needed. "We'll be there soon enough."

19

TRAP

S awyer Best's men are moving into position, executing a plan they've had only days to perfect. They will determine our future.

But these are the things I want to remember forever: Alix's laughter as she tried to tease our destination from me with a game of fucking cards. Alix's determination to be a good girl, to follow my rules. Alix's frustration as I kept my word, knowing the next time I feel her clutch around me will be a thousand times sweeter for denying her this once because she's mine. All mine.

And I want to remember the look on her face as our dark-windowed limo finally pulls up to a nondescript door in a featureless wall with a single sign printed with anonymous letters: *Please ring bell for admittance.*

"Go ahead," I say, gesturing toward the doorbell.

The look she gives me is part laughter, part question, part

fear of the unknown. But she trusts me. She presses the smooth black button.

The door opens before she can step back. The man who greets us is dressed like a fancy English gentleman who's heading out to the horse races—morning coat, waistcoat, snow-white shirt with upturned collar, and a perfectly knotted black tie. He's got a closely trimmed beard and short red hair. His hand, which he extends to shake, is encased in a white silk glove.

"Mr. Prince!" he exclaims. "We've been expecting you. I'm Cody Samuelson and it's my great pleasure to welcome you to the most magical place on earth!"

He opens the door wide, ushering us into a reception area swamped with turquoise and gold. I gesture for Alix to go first. She pauses just inside, her eyes as bright as a little girl's doll. "Disney World?" she asks me.

"Technically," Samuelson says, "Magic Kingdom Park." He leads the way over to a table that looks like something out of an undersea cartoon. "Let's see here… Just a few details…"

He produces a gold box studded with pastel-color jewels, each the size of my thumb. It opens easily, revealing a pair of shiny metallic bracelets. "Your MagicBands," he says.

Alix looks a little stunned as she extends her arm. Samuelson makes short work out of fastening the gold circlet around her wrist. After Alix's is secure, he attaches mine. The Beast growls, but Samuelson is wearing gloves, so I tell the fucker lurking in my brain to go to hell.

"Those bands are your tickets to the entire park," he says. "You'll use them at any of the restaurants or shops. Per your request, Mr. Prince, we've given you backstage access to a wide variety of our attractions. And, of course, your bands will unlock the door to your accommodations."

I've got to give Samuelson credit. He's discreet, not giving away my biggest surprise. In fact, he turns to me with a flourish guaranteed to distract Alix if she's inclined to ask questions I'm not ready to answer yet. "As you requested, Mr. Prince, the front gates are already open to your special guests for the evening. Twelve buses have arrived out of an expected fifty-one."

"Fifty-one…" Alix repeats before she turns to me. "Who are your guests?"

I clear my throat. I'm surprised to feel heat in my cheeks. There's no reason I should be embarrassed.

Once again, Samuelson swoops to the rescue. "Mr. Prince has reserved the entire Magic Kingdom for your event tonight. But he has generously invited families currently residing in homeless shelters throughout Florida to attend the park as his guests."

"Trap," Alix says, her fingers closing on my forearm. Her eyes are shiny, and her grip makes me feel like I'm king of the fucking world.

Samuelson passes me a phone that's not much bigger than a matchbook. "I'm at your disposal for your entire stay at the Magic Kingdom. If you need anything at all, you can reach me at 222 on this device. Now, if you'd like, we can provide you with an accessibility vehicle while you're here. Or a private guide?" He barely pauses, clearly reading the room. "Or an open door, and the chance to get outside and enjoy your stay?"

And just like that, we're wandering through the park.

"Where do you want to go first?" I ask Alix as we wander down a perfectly groomed path. Someone watered the tropical flowers recently. Their petals glisten in the early evening Florida heat.

"I can't believe you did this," she says.

"I figure we've both had a lot on our plates lately."

"But you bought out the park!"

A group of kids runs past us, squealing for first dibs on the front car at Space Mountain. "Not exactly," I say. "We've got some company."

She stops in the middle of the path. When I turn to ask what's wrong, her arms go around my neck. She presses herself against me and kisses me, hard.

There's an urgency on her lips, a drive. But there's a sweetness, too. A softness. Something that reminds me of the woman I met outside Debasement a lifetime ago, the woman I thought might be too good to drag into my life. For better or worse, though, she's here. In my life. And I love her, even if I haven't figured out the right time, the right way, to say that out loud.

"Thank you," she says.

"For what?" I answer gruffly. "We haven't even done anything yet."

"For bringing me here. For making this night special. For giving us both..." She loses her nerve, then tries again. "Before the video gets out..."

"The video's not getting out," I say.

"I know we don't want it to. And right now, right here, we can both pretend it won't. We don't have to think about it until we're back in Delaware."

I lay a finger across her lips. "I'm telling you," I say, like I'm teaching her the ABCs or how to count to ten. "The video won't be a problem."

She doesn't believe me. And I can't tell her the truth. I don't ever want her burdened with the knowledge of what Best's men are doing. But she laces her fingers between mine. She holds our hands over her heart. She meets my gaze, her eyes unblinking. "Thank you," she says again. "I mean it."

I brush a kiss against her knuckles. "Then you're welcome. Where are we going first?"

She chooses Pirates of the Caribbean. The Jungle Cruise after that, and TRON, and our own front-car trip on Space Mountain, even though she told me once she didn't like roller coasters.

Between rides, we eat our body weight in Dole Whip and mouse-shaped pretzels and cheeseburger spring rolls that are so good we go back for seconds.

We huddle close in the Haunted House, laughing at the screaming kids in front of us until a jump scare makes Alix bury her face against my neck. I keep her safe in the dark, nibbling her throat until she blushes.

The sun sets. The Florida air cools. The park, already close to empty, feels a little more deserted as some of the families with younger kids head back to their buses. We're walking down Main Street, debating the merits of sweatshirts or T-shirts with Disney designs when a burst of gold lights up the sky.

Music fills the air around us as fireworks explode overhead. We turn toward the castle at the end of the road, and it's illuminated with lasers and projections from movies every kid loves.

Alix leans into me, her back pressed against my chest. She looks up and her face is soft with wonder. The music, the lights, the cheers and laughter of children stopped in their tracks around us…

For this pocket of time, in this corner of the world, everything is perfect. I've kept Alix safe. The past can't touch us. Nothing can harm us here.

The show ends with a bombardment of fireworks. The sky is gray with smoke. Our ears ring and it takes a century for Alix to step away, to stand on her own two feet.

"That was incredible," she says. And then her jaw sets. She's stifling a yawn.

"Tired?" I ask.

"No," she says automatically. But she can't catch the next yawn. She barely hides it behind her palm. "Okay," she says, laughing. "Maybe a little."

"Time to get you to our hotel room, then."

She looks behind her, toward the park's front gate. "Do we catch a shuttle?"

"We can walk from here."

She wants to tell me no. She wants to say she's too tired to walk. I see it in the quick slump of her shoulders, the split-second before she straightens with a smile. "Point the way," she says.

So I do.

I point at Cinderella's castle.

"Liar," she says.

"It's impossible to lie in the Magic Kingdom." When she continues to stare at me, I tap the band on her wrist. "Let's go. As the man said, that's your key."

The castle is bigger than it seems from Main Street. I follow the directions I received this morning, locating the elevator to the hidden suite. The ornate doors open onto a hallway shaped like Cinderella's pumpkin coach.

The rooms beyond are outfitted in careful details. A blue-and-gold marble floor... Sculpted columns beside two beds... A crystal cabinet holding Cinderella's tiara... Stained glass windows featuring images from Disney movies...

It's a cross between a child's dream-house and an engineering marvel, a fairytale brought to life. On a table in the carriage foyer, there's a crystal slipper with a handwritten note: "With our compliments."

I pick it up, because Alix seems afraid to. "I think this is yours."

"What is it with you giving me shoes?" she says. She laughs as she takes it, and I know we're both thinking about the scuffed stiletto I gave her in the crappiest hotel in Dover, the one I saved the night she ran away.

Alix holds the shoe close to her chest as she walks into the bedroom. Matching pajamas are laid out on the two queen beds —pink stripes for her and blue for me. We've got toothbrushes in the bathroom, along with toothpaste, soap, and shampoo.

"You've thought of everything," she says.

"I had a little help," I admit. "Your fairy godmother took care of the details."

She laughs. And then, because we've been walking for the last five hours without taking a break, she yawns again. "I'm sorry!" she says.

"I'm not." I nod toward the pajamas. "Get ready for bed."

Alix doesn't have to be shy in front of me. Not after everything we've shared, every way I've touched her, all the things she's done to drive me crazy.

But there's something about this setting, about Cinderella's dream castle in the middle of a magic land built to make every child in the world shout with joy…

Alix changes in the bathroom. While the water's running, I check my phone. There's nothing from Best, which I tell myself is a good sign.

I change into my own pajamas. And I brush my teeth and wash my face and comb my hair, like I'm a six-year-old little boy closing my eyes and crossing my fingers and waiting for the tooth fairy to stop by overnight.

I believe in the magic.

I want it to be true.

So when I finish in the bathroom, I climb into bed beside Alix. I spoon behind her, curling my arm over her belly. I kiss the nape of her neck and then the corner of her mouth as she smiles and worms a little closer.

She's asleep before I tap the button that extinguishes the lights throughout the castle. Lying beside her, I listen to her breathe. I try to absorb her calm. Her trust.

But I'm still wide awake three hours later, when the ring of my burner phone shatters the darkness around us.

20

ALIX

"Fuck!" Trap shouts. "Goddamn motherfucking cocksuckers!"

My heart pounds and my stomach swirls with that special type of nausea when you've been startled awake from a deep, deep sleep. Or maybe it's the second Dole Whip I had. On top of the egg rolls. And corn dog nuggets. And the crispy mac and cheese bites.

I'm tangled in sheets, snared in the silk sleeves of unfamiliar nightclothes. The only light in the room comes from Trap's phone as he stares at its flickering screen.

"God*damn* it!" he shouts, and I realize he's got someone on speaker. For just a moment I think he's yelling at Mr. Samuelson, but that can't be possible, because he's demanding, "What the fuck happened?"

"We encountered substantial unexpected opposition." The voice fills the room, careful and measured.

"You said you had this under control," Trap says.

"They had more firepower than we anticipated."

"I don't know about you, but I anticipated a hell of a lot. The guard towers were the first fucking clue."

Instead of responding, the other voice swirls into muffled conversation, like he's covering his phone to address someone close by. There's a barked command. Another. And then a deep breath, followed by a slow exhale before the man says, "I've got to go. I've still got four men unaccounted for. Will this number be active after noon?"

"No," Trap says. "I'll burn it. I'll call you."

The other man hangs up as shouts rise in the background on his side of the call. Trap stabs at one phone, cutting off the speaker. His eyes are still glued to the moving video on his other device.

"Who was that?" I ask.

"Sawyer Best," Trap says.

I pull the sheets up to my chin, suddenly chilled despite my pajamas, despite the castle's perfect air handling system. "Why was he calling?"

Trap doesn't answer.

"What happened?" I push.

Trap pokes at his screen, restarting whatever video he's staring at.

"What the hell is going on, Trap?"

When he looks at me, his face is pulled into planes by the moving light on the screen below him. I want him to laugh like a cartoon villain. To tell me a silly ghost story, like the one where the escaped lunatic's hook gets caught in the teenagers' car door or where Bloody Mary appears in the mirror. I want to laugh away the horror.

He swallows. Closes his eyes. Steels himself and manages to look at me.

"I hired Sawgrass to do some clean up."

"I know," I say, because they're the ones who erased every

shred of evidence that I murdered Klaus Herzog. "The dining room—"

"Not then," Trap says. "Tonight."

"But you said—" I protest.

"It's the only way we can be safe."

"—I didn't give you enough to go after—"

"Best worked with what he had."

"Worked where?"

"Long Island. Where Jonas and Ansel live."

I heard the chaos on that call. "But Best's men failed."

Trap nods. "Seven men down. And four missing."

"Oh God, Trap. That's what you're watching? Sawgrass men being killed?"

Trap finally seems to remember the video still flickering on his screen. He taps the phone. His face bleaches in the frozen light.

"That's not Sawgrass. It's you. Us." He turns the phone toward me. "The Herzogs released their fucking video."

21

TRAP

So much for escaping to the most magical place on earth.

Within an hour, Alix and I sneak out the back door. We surprise a sleepy security guard who asks if we're unhappy in any way. He volunteers to call Samuelson, but I don't see any reason to get our personal liaison out of bed. I tell the guard that he's welcome to the breakfast I ordered for delivery to the castle.

The drive back to the airfield seems to take forever. Alix reaches for her phone at least three times, but she doesn't have it —I made her leave it at home.

Once we get to the plane, we have to wait half an hour while our pilot files his emergency flight plan. Alix ignores the excellent cup of coffee that materializes at her elbow, courtesy of the bleary-eyed flight attendant. Instead, she extends her hand toward me. "Please," she says. "I need to see it."

She doesn't. She already knows every fucking frame of the video.

But I'm not her father, and I'm not her shrink. *I think it's a bad idea for her to watch the goddamn thing, but she's a big girl. She gets to make her own decisions.*

I hand over my phone.

The video's spreading like wildfire.

"Well," Alix says after scrolling through a dozen links. "At least they spelled my name right."

They spelled my name right too. And Klaus Herzog's. His is framed by a memorial wreath, with his birthday and date of death printed in stark black letters.

Alix starts to watch the fucking video for the thousandth time. My fingers twitch. I want to take my phone and throw it out the airplane door. Shattering its screen on the tarmac, though, won't destroy what's already out there on the internet.

"Wait," Alix says, pulling the screen closer to her face. What could she possibly be looking at? What detail doesn't she know by heart?

She shoves the phone toward me. I hold up a hand in the universal sign for stop. I'd be happy never to see Klaus Herzog's blood painting my dining room again.

"Look!" Alix says, freezing the video mid-spurt.

I look.

The freeze frame shows Herzog's face, contorted in the pain that cocksucker deserved. Alix crouches over him, her expression as flat as a chopping board. I'm visible to her right, my mouth open, like she's caught me mid-word.

"Don't you see?" Alix asks. She points past the arterial blood spray, past the horror that's centered in the frame.

And when I squint, I realize what she's talking about. Just to make sure, I tap the screen to restart the video. I watch for a full thirty seconds.

"They blurred the other faces," Alix says. "The other members of the Diamond Ring."

My nod is a tight little spasm. This time when I stop the

recording, I turn the phone upside down. Neither of us needs to stare at the black and white still.

It's a good thing I do, because the pilot chooses that moment to come aboard. "Mr. Prince," he says with a professional nod to me. "Ma'am," he greets Alix.

"Sorry to get you up early," I say. I'm not sorry. I'm doing what needs to be done. But it never hurts to be polite to the guy who's responsible for keeping you safe eight miles above the surface of the earth.

"Not at all," he says, playing along. "I've got clearance from the tower. We should have you home in two and a half hours."

Alix waits for him to close the cockpit door before she leans forward in her leather chair. "That's a good thing, right? Hiding the other men's identities?"

She's an optimist, my sweet, good girl.

Me? I'm a glass-half-empty sonofabitch. But it still makes something ache deep in my chest when I have to tell her the bad news. "By blocking the rest of the Ring, the Herzogs created a highly motivated pool of people to blackmail."

"Fuck," Alix breathes, uncharacteristically. I couldn't say it better myself.

The flight attendant refreshes our coffee and tells us she has to take her seat. Alix's fingers tighten on the arms of her chair as the Lear picks up speed on the runway. The takeoff is clean.

I wait until sunrise before I move us into the office at the back of the plane and call Samantha Mott. Alix and I will both need experts in criminal law, but Sam is the freeport's general counsel. She can get the legal ball rolling. I tell her to find the best shark on the market, whoever handled last month's case of the century, or the one before that. That's who Alix deserves.

I'll go with number two. And Sam can meet us at the freeport gate, fend off the cops in the short run. Because if Dover's finest don't have a warrant by the time we land, they'll get one soon. I want someone with legal training to make sure every fucking i is dotted, and every t is crossed.

Sam offers her usual calm reassurance that everything's under control. That's a lie, but I appreciate her making the effort anyway. I've barely ended the call when my phone rings again.

Bob Marcus. I don't have anything to say to him, not now, not with the news breaking all around us. One slash of my finger sends him to voicemail.

Another call—Sean Ferguson, one of my newest clients. We're still building out his storage gallery to his specs. The guy's been a pain in my ass since he signed his contract. Voicemail for him, too.

I turn off the ringer.

But after fifteen minutes of drumming my fingers on my armrest and watching Alix stare out the window without blinking, I give in to my curiosity. I read the messages that are piling up.

Marcus is withdrawing from the Diamond Ring. Pussy.

Ferguson is leaving the freeport altogether. Good fucking riddance.

The *Delaware News Journal* wants a comment, as does the *Dover Post.* The *Philadelphia Enquirer* isn't far behind, and the *New York Times* lands in a pile of requests with the *Washington Post*, the *Wall Street Journal*, and the *Financial Times.*

I shoot a text to Susan Richards, which I should have done when I was still wearing striped pajamas in the middle of Cinderella's dream house. I tell her to identify the top media fixer on the East Coast and get them on payroll by noon.

After that, I turn off my phone again. For real this time. Not just the ringer.

Alix and I sit in silence for nearly an hour. The flight is a hell of a lot longer when I'm not bending her over my desk here in the office.

For once in my life, the thought of making her come doesn't turn me instantly hard. We're flying into a storm, and I need to figure out how I can keep her safe.

We're somewhere over North Carolina when I remember Wolf's solution.

"We'll say it's a deep fake."

"What?" She blinks hard as she turns toward me. I don't want to know where her thoughts had taken her.

"I talked to Cole Wolf a week ago. He said we can argue it's all made up. Hollywood special effects. We never invited Klaus Herzog to dinner. Never had him in the house. And you sure as shit never took a steak knife to his jugular."

"That won't work."

Her voice sounds flat. Dead. Like she's lost all hope, and she's ready to sign a confession so she can get some much-needed sleep.

The surge of anger that tightens my fingers into fists isn't directed at her. I want to beat the shit out of all three Herzog brothers. Dig up Klaus's rotten corpse and feed him through a woodchipper. Grind the bloody pulp and force-feed it to his brothers till they puke.

I have an hour, maybe an hour and a half to convince Alix to do things my way. Because once we land, the cops will get involved. And the reporters. And a million trolls on social media.

I have to get her to agree. Because I don't know if we can survive the alternative.

22

ALIX

Trap won't let this drop. He's been hounding me for half an hour, and now he says, "I'll call Cole Wolf before we land. He'll make it happen."

Mr. Wolf might be a tech genius, but he can't work miracles. I touch my fingertips to the back of Trap's hand. I want him to know I appreciate everything he's doing. It won't work, but I know he's trying to keep me safe.

"It's not that simple," I say. "Even the best faked video leaves clues. What do they call them? Artifacts."

"Technology's getting better every day," he argues. "With AI, they can probably make it look like the president killed Herzog."

"The president didn't live in Herzog's house for three years."

"The president wasn't sold—"

"Isn't it true, Miss Key, that you claim five other women were held as slaves by Mr. Herzog?" I interrupt him because I have to make him understand. I've thought about this a lot, from the moment I first came to my senses, holding a bloody steak knife in Trap's dining room. I continue in my fake-prosecutor voice: "Isn't it true that you and your fellow *victims*"—my fingers curl into air quotes—"could have banded together at any time to leave Mr. Herzog's residence?"

Because that's just one of the questions I torture myself with in the dark hours between midnight and dawn. Could I have convinced Lilyana to fight with me? Could we have led the other women in open rebellion?

When Trap doesn't respond, I feed him another one of my late-night terrors: "Isn't it true that you were allowed to walk around Mr. Herzog's house without any restraints, without a shock collar or manacles or any bonds that would keep you from leaving at any time?"

"After he beat you into fucking submission!" The cords in Trap's neck look ready to snap.

"Isn't it true," I continue like I haven't heard a word of protest. "That Mr. Herzog left keys to his vehicles on the counter in the kitchen and you could have left the premises whenever you wanted?"

"Jesus Christ," Trap swears, because he doesn't have any real argument. Because what I'm saying is exactly what the police will say, exactly what the prosecutor will say before a jury finds me guilty of murder. But then Trap tries: "How many months—*years*—passed before he trusted you with car keys? And who's to say you could have actually gotten away, even if you got behind the wheel? There's a fence around that property. A goddamn locked gate."

Fine.

We'll keep going.

"Isn't it true," I drone. "That on the night in question you could have asked Mr. Prince for assistance the instant you arrived at the freeport? That you could have spoken to any of the security guards at the freeport gate? You could have asked any member of the Diamond Ring to protect you the night of the dinner party in question—isn't that true?"

"Sweet fucking Christ. Is this how you torture yourself? Is this the bullshit you worry about in the middle of the night? This is what you're thinking about when I wake up and find you staring into space?"

"Isn't it true—" I start again, but Trap slams his fist down on the arm of his chair with so much force I'm afraid he's broken at least one bone.

"You were the fucking *victim*, Alix! It's not your fault your junkie brother sold you to a monster! You saved yourself when anyone else would have given up, would have curled up and died a hell of a lot earlier. You're a goddamn *survivor*, not a criminal."

I jut my chin toward the phone he's conveniently turned upside-down. "How many online viewers agree?"

"Online viewers don't get to vote."

"Neither do you, Trap. Neither do I."

"Princess…"

Something inside me twists at the pet name. But I tell him what I'm thinking because that's who I am. I don't have a choice.

"I'm a good person, Trap. I follow the rules. I'm the type of person who goes to the police, who explains what happened, who relies on the system to do what has to be done."

"Princess, maybe you *were* that person. Maybe you *used* to live in a black-and-white world with absolute right and absolute wrong. But you're in *my* world now. Welcome to the world of gray."

I shake my head. "That can't be true."

He reaches out, catching my chin between his finger and his thumb. I don't want to look at him. Don't want to pull away.

"Is it right," he asks, "that I tie you up and hurt you?" Before I can answer, he tightens his grip. "Is it right that you like it? Is it right that you're getting wet right now, just thinking about what I can order you to do?"

I can't say yes. I can't say no. What we do—what we *have*—is right *and* wrong. It's good and bad. It's sane and insane, and if the only way I can keep it, the only way I can preserve that beautiful, terrifying gray is to step off this plane and tell the fractured story Trap is spinning out of whole cloth...

"Okay," I say.

"Okay?"

"Okay, I'll do it. I'll say what I have to say. I'll tell them what they need to hear."

"Good girl."

They're two simple words. Words I thought I hated when I was an independent grad student, when relationships could be sawed into perfect cubes and fit into neat little boxes.

But I need those words now. I *lust* for those words. They're the perfect capsule of everything Trap is for me, everything he does for me, everything we are together.

So I'm not surprised when he says: "Right here. Right now. We're going over your answers to all the questions you'll face from the cops."

I'm tired. And I don't believe this will work. But Trap cares about it so much—cares about *me* so much—that I sit back in my chair and nod my acceptance.

I don't realize how tense he was until he rubs his face with both hands. He tugs at his hair hard, like punishing himself will make everything better.

"Okay," he says. "First things first. The only thing you say to the press is *no comment.*"

I shrug. That's basic. And it won't be enough, not in the long run. But I can agree for now.

"I need to hear you say it," he pushes. "No comment."

"No comment."

"And if the police get you alone, your only words are *I want a lawyer.*"

I give him what he needs. "I want a lawyer."

"Now, if Samantha's with you, or your own lawyer, the one she's lining up right now, you'll have to answer questions. So will I. And it's important we both remember things the same way."

I hear every word he says. And I hear all the ones he doesn't risk out loud. I understand that we aren't just talking about whether *I'll* go free. Trap's life is on the line too.

So I sit up straighter in my chair. I drain the last of my coffee, hoping it will sharpen my thoughts. I take a steadying breath. And I say, "Ask away."

"Where did you and I meet?"

"At Debasement," I say.

"When?"

"My birthday, three years ago. June 21."

"What happened after that night?"

My brother sold me to Herzog. I spent three years in hell. I lost myself, lost everything I believed in.

That can't be my answer. I can't have any motivation to murder Klaus Herzog. I'm not supposed to know the man.

But how do I explain disappearing for three long years?

I start to tiptoe through my answer. "I went home after I left the freeport, but my landlord had evicted us, Leo and me. Leo stole the rent money. So I… I sold my phone and used the cash to buy a beat-up car. That's where I lived, for a while, anyway."

"Why sell your phone? Didn't you need it?"

"I couldn't afford the monthly plan. I used the library when I needed a computer. Because of Leo, I didn't have anyone to call."

"Why not put the car on your credit card?"

"I didn't have one. I couldn't trust my brother. I only used cash for three or four years before we were evicted."

He nods, like he's impressed by how quickly I'm thinking on my feet. But a lot of what I'm saying is the truth. My landlord *did* throw me out. I'd been toying with the idea of dropping my phone contract because I couldn't make ends meet. I really had cut up my credit cards after the third time Leo left me holding the bag for a meth-fueled spending spree.

"What about school?" Trap asks. "Didn't you have classes to attend?"

"I finished all my coursework. The only thing I had left was writing my thesis. And…" I close my eyes, threading my way between truth and lies. "I had to sell my computer, to get enough cash to eat. I kept my thesis on a thumb drive, but it got lost when my coat was stolen at work. I was so upset at the thought of losing all that work that I couldn't go back to writing."

He looks impressed. But he zeroes in on another loose end. "Where were you working?"

"McDonald's," I say, figuring no one would ever remember me from there.

"Nope," Trap says. "They're a massive corporation, with standardized job applications. The IRS would have all sorts of documentation—payroll, taxes, all that shit."

So, no McDonald's. And no Wal-Mart, Target, or even Home Depot seasonal staff. I couldn't drive for Uber or Lyft, couldn't take a Sherman University job, and I couldn't work at the Air Force base.

I could say I took money under the table, but even that raises problems. Mrs. Nguyen who ran the corner store near my old apartment would certainly tell the police she hadn't paid me. Same with the coffee shop around the corner, and any of the cute little boutiques near campus.

"I did odd jobs for cash," I finally say. "I answered ads placed on telephone poles. Walked dogs. Cleaned houses. Babysat."

Trap's still not satisfied. "They can follow up. People will remember who they trusted with their pets. Their homes. Their kids."

I realize I'm gripping my coffee cup tight enough to make

my fingers ache. This shouldn't be so difficult. I shouldn't have to lie.

Trap says, "You turned tricks near the base. No. Someone might remember you. At the train station."

My stomach aches, and I wish I hadn't finished that last cup of coffee. But Trap is right, of course. As a prostitute, I could earn enough cash to survive. And none of my customers could confirm my identity if they were just stopping through on their way north to New York, or heading south to DC.

Also, the lie skates close enough to the truth that I can deliver it with the right amount of embarrassment. Resignation. Shame.

"I turned tricks," I whisper.

"So three years pass…" Trap prompts.

How did we get together after so much time? There's no record of my applying for a job at the freeport. We don't have any friends in common. I could never have earned enough to need a tax haven.

But the answer's so obvious, I actually laugh as I say it. "You came looking for a date at the train station."

He frowns. "I've never paid a woman in my life."

I look around the plane—at the wooden paneling, the leather seats, and the fine china spread out on the desk beside us. "There are lots of ways to pay," I say.

He doesn't like my point. But he has to accept it.

"Fuck," he says. "So I saw you at the train station. And I recognized you. And I brought you home, when?"

"The night of the party. The one you hosted for the Diamond Ring. You spent the night eating oysters and drinking champagne and you wanted a little company after your clients left."

Again—stay as close to the truth as possible. Get me in the house the night I actually arrived. Keep me around the freeport as long as I'd been there in fact.

"We hit it off," Trap says. "You stuck around. We have no

idea where the video came from, but it's got to be some asshole trying to blow up the freeport, especially after you proved your worth at the Monet auction."

"It's nothing personal," I say. "Just business."

Trap looks directly in my eyes. "And you got caught in the crossfire."

We're a long way from a trial. It'll be months—if not years —before we have to swear the truth, the whole truth, and nothing but the truth, so help us God. We'll rehearse this story dozens of times before then, saw off the rough bits, polish the details to a high shine.

This is wrong. It's a lie. But in a crazy way, viewed through a warped lens, somehow, some way, it's all true.

"You can do this, Princess," Trap says. "We can do it together."

And for the first time since I saw that video flash on the screen of his phone, I believe he might be right.

The pilot's voice breaks into our silence. "We're starting our descent into Dover, Mr. Prince."

We leave the office and head out to the main cabin. To the luxurious leather seats. To the curious eyes of the flight attendant, who probably thinks we've been making mad passionate love the entire flight.

After we land, a chorus of paparazzi is gathered at the chain link fence. They're shouting questions before we step through the plane's door. Their cameras flash in the early morning light.

No comment, I think, but we're far enough away that we don't have to say a word.

A car is waiting to take us to the freeport. Samantha Mott stands just outside the front door of Trap's house. Three police cars are parked on the driveway, along with a Dover Police Department van.

Trap squeezes my fingers before we step out of the car.

It's show time.

23

TRAP

Slouching in the driver's seat of the Range Rover, I keep my head low to avoid the fucking paparazzi. They're swarming the steps in front of the police station like a cloud of biting gnats. I got out through a side door, but I bet Alix won't be as lucky.

I check my watch for the tenth time in fifteen minutes. I knew the cops would talk to us separately. I knew they'd take more time going over her story than they did mine. I knew her lawyer would need to jump in more often, need to monitor the cops' phrasing, need to decide whether to let Alix respond or take the goddamn fifth.

But it's been four fucking hours. Why the hell are they still in there?

It was easy enough for me. I didn't need to make up much—just the night that Herzog died. We expected him at the party, but he never showed. He sent his car, though. Had it delivered to Cole Wolf, the guy who bought it after seeing it at an earlier meeting.

Good food, good booze, good business with clients—it all left me wanting a little female companionship. Sure, I could call one of those high-end escort services. But I'm a simple guy. Simple tastes. And I don't want a record of who I pay and when and where and everything we do.

A drive to the train station in my Range Rover with its fully reclining seats, a couple hundred bucks, and I got the shock of my life—Alix, the woman I'd been jonesing for since we met three years ago.

A goddamn love story, if I ever heard one.

They took me back over the details a few times. When I planned the party. When Herzog said he couldn't make it. Why he sent the car, who dropped it off, how Wolf paid ninety grand for a vehicle he'd only seen once before…

The video? It had to be a fake. That much blood? That sort of destruction? It looked like a slasher film, not anything from real life.

It was easy to repeat my answers. Easy to say the same things over and over and over again.

My lawyer—some white-shoe bigshot from New York City that Sam lined up—let me talk. He and I shook hands on the sidewalk, and he caught the train back to Manhattan. We'll follow up on Monday.

But Alix is still in there. She's got her own lawyer. She's got her own story. And I'm seriously considering going back into the station, heading down a hallway to use the john, and pulling the fire alarm to get her out of whatever tiny room they're using to interrogate her.

Bad idea.

My phone rings before I can change my mind and brave the fucking paps. I'm about to ignore it—the only person I want to talk to is Alix—when I see Gage Rider's name on the screen.

I can't afford to ignore anyone who was in my dining room that night. "Prince," I answer.

"Last week," he says, without fucking around. "On the boat. You mentioned you were trying to get in touch with a couple of guys you used to work with."

Rider played hockey for six years before back-to-back concussions made him get out. But before that, he went to Dartmouth. And rumor has it that—along with owning his old team, the Atlantic City Aces—he owns entire city blocks in New York City.

He's smart. And he knows better than to say the Herzog name out loud.

"Yeah, you know them?"

"Their names sounded familiar. I did a little digging. Turns out, they're members of a club I own."

"Club?" I know from past Ring outings the guy's a scratch golfer. Given his storied real estate holdings, it doesn't surprise me at all that he owns a country club.

"It's in Brooklyn. Kynk." He spells it for me.

Well, that's an entirely different type of club.

"And you say those guys I used to know are members?" I ask.

"VIPs."

Of course they are. "Sounds like that comes with all sorts of special privileges," I say.

"We've got perks. One of the key ones is a standing invitation to our annual Masquerade."

"When's that?"

"It's short notice. But next Saturday night."

I close my eyes. Six days, and I can put myself in the same room with Jonas and Ansel Herzog. I realize my fingers are clamped so tight around my phone they hurt. I force myself to take a deep breath, to exhale on a count of ten.

"So," I ask. "What does it take to become a member at your club?"

"I've already added your name to the guest list. Well, *a* name. I figured you might not want your reputation linked to a sex club."

Fuck my reputation. But avoiding a record of being there when the Herzogs are present is an excellent idea. "What's the name?" I ask.

"Jack Strong."

I waste a moment, trying to figure out why he chose that. Then I realize there isn't a reason. A random name is best, under the circumstances. Once again, I'm reminded that Gage Rider is smart.

"And where is Mr. Strong going next Saturday night?"

He gives me an address. "Near Industry City. There's a street-level entrance if you know what you're looking for. The club's underground, in an old subway tunnel for the line they never built to Staten Island."

"Dress code?" That seems like a safer question than whether I can bring a Sig Sauer.

"It's a masquerade at a club named Kynk. Wear whatever the fuck you want. But club security enforces two rules. Everyone wears a mask. And cell phones go into a vault at the door." He pauses for barely a second before he adds, "Well, three rules, I guess. Everyone walks through a metal detector before they hit the floor."

Bingo. That's the warning I need. "Thanks," I say, pushing the word hard, so he'll know I mean it.

"If possible..." he says, and then he trails off.

"Yeah?"

"The club's been a solid investment. We pay our taxes. Stay right with the State Liquor Authority. Get an A from the health department every year."

He doesn't have to say the rest. The club's business prospects will be in the shitter if I leave the joint looking like a slaughterhouse.

"Hell of a job that must be," I say. "Health inspector for a club called Kynk. But it probably gets boring after the first year or two. Same old, same old…" That's the only promise I can give him over this open line.

But he takes it. "Like I said, the name's on the list. Anyone you want to bring with you?"

I could bring Alix.

The thought zaps something at the base of my spine. I picture her wearing one of those little black Zorro masks and nothing else. I imagine watching her in the crowd at a fucking sex club, seeing heads turn, knowing she's mine. I think about a scene I could make her play in public.

But Alix can't be anywhere near Jonas and Ansel Herzog when the cocksuckers take their fall. Not if we have a prayer of getting her off the hook for Klaus's death.

"No," I say to Rider, before he can worry the line went dead. "Just me."

"Good enough," he says.

"Thanks," I say again. That's not enough. There's no way I can say enough, on this open line or in person, now or forever. But I try to balance the books a little: "I owe you one."

He hangs up, and I'm back to watching the police station door. But now I have something to fill my time. I need to figure out how to take out the Herzogs without triggering a fucking metal detector at the door. Or leaving behind a bloodbath. Or letting anyone make any connection with me or with Rider or with Alix.

Definitely not with Alix.

The station door finally opens. She steps into the late afternoon sun, blinking like they've kept her chained in a cave. Her lawyer's at her side, briefcase in one hand, an attentive look on his face as he helps her down the steps. He does his best to clear a path through the fucking pap vultures.

I climb out of the car, ready to cross the lot and retrieve her. She sees me, though, and waves before she turns to shake her lawyer's hand. They exchange a few words—no smiles, no frowns, not a fucking hint about what they've been doing for the last five hours.

Then Alix makes a beeline to the Range Rover. I open her door and hold it while she gets settled. Biting my tongue, I wait for her to nod before I close her in.

We're out of the parking lot, heading back to the freeport, before I finally ask. "How'd it go?"

"I don't know."

"They let you go, though. Didn't say anything about arresting you?"

"They let me go."

"What did your lawyer say?"

"Nothing. Not in front of the police. Just now, he said he'd call me tomorrow. Not to worry too much. Try to get some sleep."

"Princess…" I say, because it's better than asking a dozen questions she's obviously too tired to answer.

"I hate this," she says.

"I know."

I wait for her to say more. To open up the whole right-and-wrong can of worms again. To tell me she's a bad person. That she deserves punishment. That she can't lie about killing the asshole who ruined her life.

But she doesn't.

She just looks out the window, at the dusty streets of Dover. She studies the office buildings, then the houses, then the dried-out fields of corn and the abandoned-looking chicken barns.

When we get home, she's out of the car before I turn off the engine. I follow her into the kitchen, but she doesn't stop there. I watch her head upstairs, wishing I could say something, do something, make something happen so she never needs to feel this lost again.

I hear her turn on the shower. The water's still flowing half an hour later, when I pour myself a drink and go sit outside, trying to find a way to take advantage of Gage Rider's gift.

24

ALIX

I'm sitting on the bed in Trap's bedroom—*my* bedroom now—trying to figure out which makes me feel more guilty: the fact that I lied to the police or the fact that they may have bought it.

Of course, nothing's guaranteed. They walked me through my story three separate times—from the moment I met Trap at Debasement to the night we spent in Orlando. They pushed hard for places I might have left a record—employers, friends, freaking loyalty cards at the local Food Lion. They asked a lot about my job as a sex worker.

Lucky for me, I know how to use an anonymous browser to search the internet. I found out my fees were reduced because I didn't work through a service or have a "manager" to protect me.

I could charge two hundred bucks an hour to give a guy a girlfriend experience. Four hundred if he wanted me to act like a porn star. Before I answered the first question at the police station, I'd figured out what I'd do for four hundred—deep-throating, doggy-style, let him come on my face or breasts. If I knew the guy, he could tie me up. Spank me. I told the cops I'd do anal, but that was a lie. I said there wasn't enough money in the world to make me go bareback, but that was a lie too. At least with Trap.

I believe my story. I'm pretty sure I could pass a lie-detector test. My body doesn't remember the truth anymore. I've become the lies.

But nothing changes one basic fact: I killed Herzog.

And my murdering him in Trap's dining room threatens to destroy the freeport. Threatens to bring down the man I love.

And when I think about that, I hate myself.

Trap's still outside, in the back yard. I think about packing a suitcase for myself. About taking the keys to the Porsche and fleeing. About giving the police all the leverage they need to place the blame for Herzog's death on me. I'll run for as long as I can, then take my punishment.

Because that's what I deserve—punishment. For lying to the police. For killing Herzog. For letting Herzog do all those things to me in the first place.

And there's something else too, more weight on my conscience. Sawyer Best sent men into Jonas and Ansel's compound to execute them, to save Trap and me. Eight men died and three are hospitalized in critical condition. I'm responsible for ruining eleven more lives.

But I can't leave. Two weeks ago, I promised Trap wouldn't run away, not without talking to him first. I can't abandon him again.

Nevertheless, my need for discipline remains.

Still wearing the bathrobe I pulled on after my shower, I cross to Trap's dresser and kneel beside the bottom drawer. I've never gone through it myself. I've only retrieved items that Trap commanded me to bring to him.

The drawer is divided into compartments. I find the massive

dildo he's used on me. The butt plug I'll never take. The vibrator that taught my body an entirely new way to dissolve into pleasure.

There's the riding crop.

And beneath it, so slender I almost miss it against the edge of the drawer—a cane. I slide it out of the drawer and flex it between my palms.

Trap has never used a cane on me. But Herzog did.

I know how it will sound, whipping through the air. I know how it will feel, slicing into my flesh. I know how the stripe will last for a week. Maybe two.

The cane is brutal. It's efficient. It's exactly what I deserve.

But there's something else I need to make this work. I dig deeper in the drawer, pushing aside boxes that are too small, ones that are too large. And there, in the back right corner is the one I'm looking for.

I open the flat box and stare at the deep blue velvet inside. The handcuffs sparkle, shining like they're made of polished silver instead of steel. A key is nestled deep in the lock.

I lift the cuffs out of their bed, surprised by their weight. Turning the key springs open the first hard band. I fasten the cuff around my right wrist.

My breath is coming fast now, like I ran all the way from the police station. The sun is setting in the backyard. Trap should be coming inside soon. We should be talking about ordinary things —what we'll eat for dinner, new clients at the freeport, some ridiculous email he got from the Chamber of Commerce and last-minute changes for the company picnic on Labor Day.

Dangling the cuffs by my side, I cross the hall to the guest room. I slip out of my robe and drape it over the foot of the bed I no longer sleep in. I head to the closet and find my highest heels, black ones with deep red soles, nearly five inches.

My hips sway as I head back to Trap's room. I pick up the cane from where I left it on the floor and carry it over to the bed.

It takes a moment to fit the key into the lock on the second handcuff. The mechanism springs open like a gaping metal jaw.

I can cuff my hands together.

I can bind myself to the bed, to the iron footboard or the headboard.

I can go back to the shower and chain myself to the rainfall shower head.

So many options. And none of them the full punishment I deserve.

I slip the chain around a post in the footboard, then fasten the second cuff around my left wrist. I can slide the chain up and down the post, but I can't slip it free. I can just reach the cane, on the foot of the bed. I fumble it a little because I'm also holding the key to the handcuffs.

I bend my neck, stretching to settle the cane between my teeth. Then I step close to the bed, near enough for my cuffed hands to meet at the V between my legs. I spread my feet, teetering a little in my heels. And I push the key into my pussy, sliding it deep, past my soaking wet folds.

I'm disgusting. I'm a bad girl. I deserve to be punished for so many things.

But I'm unbelievably turned on by the wrongness of hiding the key inside me.

The sun sets. The arches of my feet begin to ache. The cuffs are heavy on my wrists, and their sharp edges leave angry red lines where they press into my skin. My jaw trembles around the cane.

I can't feel the key inside me. It's warmed to match the furnace of my body. I worry it will slip out of me. I'm that wet, that turned on.

At last, I hear the sliding door open and close. I imagine Trap walking to the kitchen, leaving his glass on the counter. I hear him walk up the stairs.

And I see the surprise on his face when he comes into the

room—mouth open, lips pursed, like he's about to ask a question.

"Sweet fuck," he breathes instead. And then, "It looks like someone's been a naughty girl."

The words are enough to start a drumbeat inside me. I twist my neck, brandishing the cane so he'll know exactly what I need.

He toes off his shoes. Takes his socks with them. Walks around behind me, ogling the view.

My high heels leave my ass canted up and back. I'm on display, vulnerable to anything Trap chooses to do. He runs his palm over my ass, slipping the edge of his hand along my cleft to the front. The tip of his finger comes up coated with the honey I'm close to dripping on the floor.

"Very. Very. Naughty," he says.

I moan a little, because I'm afraid to open my mouth, afraid that if I drop the cane, he won't give me what I ache for. His laugh is like oil over river rocks. He plucks the polished bamboo from between my teeth, bending it sharply so I can see just how much it gives under his expert control.

"Please," I whisper.

"Please, what?"

"Please punish me."

His eyes flash at that, his face slipping for just a moment into a frown, into something worse. But he recovers quickly, tapping my rock-hard nipples with the tip of the cane. "Punish you how?" he asks.

I lean forward, gripping the footboard with both hands. My ass must look like a pure white target. I should be ashamed, but I'm so turned on I think I might faint.

"Eleven strokes," I say. One for each of Best's soldiers.

Trap unzips his pants. Takes out that gorgeous cock that's so hard, so dark, so huge I wonder if I can take it all when he's ready to share. "Eleven strokes?" he asks, and he grips himself tightly, tugging hard from balls to tip.

"No!" I cry, and I don't know what I'll do if I've ruined this, if he decides just to tease me, if he jerks off instead of giving me what I need. "With the cane," I say. "Because I'm bad."

He runs his thumb down my spine. I can't help it. I arch to meet him like a horny cat. "It'll hurt," he says.

"I know."

"And leave a mark."

"That's what I want."

He bends down to kiss me. This isn't a sweet kiss, a loving kiss. This is a savage claim, a vicious show that he's the one who owns me. He's the only man who can give me what I need.

"Count," he says when he steps back.

The first slash lands like a lightning bolt. It explodes across my ass and deep inside my pussy. It shatters my heart and fractures my brain into tiny sparking diamonds. It can only be a fraction of what the Sawgrass men felt when they fell in the attack on the Herzogs' compound.

"One," I gasp.

The second blow lands beside the first—short, sharp, hot, deep. It burrows through my soul. "Two."

The third strike makes my ankles sway. The fourth sinks me to my knees. The fifth makes me sob, and the sixth makes me scream.

And all that time, I feel the power growing inside me. I'm a furnace, melting bone and muscle and skin. I'm a star, shining through the velvet night. I'm the spring that winds the universe, turning tighter and tighter and tighter.

Seven makes me sob.

Eight makes me holler Trap's name like a prayer.

Nine makes me beg, saying yes, saying no, but never, ever saying the safeword that I know would make him stop.

Ten lands across the top of my thighs, aching, burning, bright.

The last blow falls crosswise over all the other marks, and I shout my victory, three jagged syllables, torn across forever: "Eleven!"

At the same time, Trap gives his own command: "Come!" and without him touching me, I burst and I shatter and I break into a million million pieces. I come until I can't see. I come until I can't breathe. I come until I wonder if I'll ever stop, if my body will ever belong to me again.

But finally I'm back in the world. I'm conscious enough to know the only thing left in the universe that I desire.

"Fuck me," I whisper, even though I don't deserve it.

He reaches for my wrists and mutters a distant curse. Crosses to the dresser. To the nightstand. To the bed. "Where's the key, Alix?"

"Key?"

I'm the key. That's my name. He knows that. He's known that since June. Why is he asking now, when we've been closer than we've ever been before?

"The handcuffs," he says. "Where's the key to the cuffs?"

I remember, and a tiny voice whispers that I'm supposed to be embarrassed, but there's nothing that can shame me when I'm with Trap. "Inside me," I say. "I put it in my pussy."

Of course he swears again. And when he slides his fingers inside me, I whimper at the pressure against my too-sensitive flesh. I shiver from the crown of my head to my toes. He presses harder, the back of his hand rough against my throbbing clit, but then he finds the prize and rescues the salt-drenched key.

"Naughty Princess," he says, brushing his hand across my flaming ass, a hint of the punishment he could choose to add.

But he doesn't reach for the cane. Instead, he opens the right cuff first, and then the left. He drops the key on the floor before he slides his hands under my armpits. He lifts me, because my legs don't remember how to bear my weight. He walks me toward the bed, supporting me until I lean forward, my fore-arms and my belly taking my weight on the mattress.

Braced there, I can take it when he knees my legs apart. I

can clutch the bedspread in my shaking fingers. I can bury my face to smother my screams as Trap does what I asked for. He fills me with his cock, pounding hard, and when he's close, he orders me again. I come around him, and he comes inside me, and we merge into something larger, something louder, something greater than the two of us apart.

Only after every nerve in my body has fired, only after I've forgotten how to speak, only after I've forgotten the Sawgrass men who fought for me, who died for me, does Trap collapse against my back. The stripes on my ass vibrate under his weight until he finds the strength to roll to one side. He pulls me with him, curling around me, draping an exhausted hand over my hip. And before either of us can speak, we tumble into sleep.

25

TRAP

I wake a few minutes after midnight. Alix is still out cold.

I can't believe the filthy things she comes up with. I nearly blew my wad getting the key out of her snatch. I've had women in this room before, women who let me tie them up, who let me use all the tools in my dresser drawer.

But I never had a woman who got the ball rolling herself. Who was so turned on by my fucked-up needs that she tied herself up. That she cuffed herself to my bed, just to give me what I need. What we both need.

When I roll over, my hand leaves Alix's hip. She frowns in her sleep. Her mouth purses, and a line grows deep between her eyebrows. She starts to stretch, but I lean close and kiss her neck at the pulse point just beneath her jaw. "Go back to sleep, Princess."

I swing my legs over the side of the bed. But when I reach for the sheet so she won't get cold, I find myself staring at the stripes I laid out on her ass.

The lines are angry. Red. They look like they'll be hot if I touch them.

To tell the truth, they're sexy as hell, and I'm proud of myself for spacing them perfectly. Proud of her for taking the punishment, for counting out loud like a good girl. But my princess deserves some salve now, or those marks will turn to nasty bruises.

She doesn't stir as I open my nightstand, as I twist the lid off a jar and scoop out some arnica balm. But when my fingers smooth her ass, she murmurs something into the crook of her arm.

"What's that, Princess?" I ask, but she's doesn't answer. I go back to working in the salve, moving my hand in long, gentle strokes. Her eyes stay closed. If possible, she relaxes even more.

Her breathing is deep and steady by the time the arnica is gone. I consider slipping my hand over her hip. I think about finding her warm, wet heat, about gathering her own sweet juice to rub her clit until she comes, then sinking my cock into her softness. But she's already milked me dry, and it would be cruel to wake her.

So I slip out of bed instead. I find my shorts and pull them on before I head downstairs to my office.

I spent hours after I got off the phone with Rider, figuring out how to use the information he gave me. I can hold my own in a bar fight. I've spent my time in a gym. Done some krav maga too.

But two against one? And from everything Alix said about those two fucks, they're suspicious cocksuckers. It'll be hard to get the drop on them. And I promised Rider to keep his club clean.

I have to even the odds.

And that means I'm back on yet another burner phone with Sawyer Best. He's got eleven good reasons to want in on the action. We both want those motherfuckers dead.

In the split second before Best answers his phone, I wonder

if he's sleeping. But he sounds alert when he snaps, "Best." And he listens to the plan I pieced together earlier tonight, when I was nursing my drink in the back yard.

"I can do that," he says. "You want to take delivery at the freeport?"

"At my penthouse in New York."

"It's safest if it comes in with a bunch of other stuff."

"Citarella's a grocery store on Broadway. No one will think twice about a few bags of food."

"Saturday afternoon?"

"We'll be there by three."

"Expect a drop-off by four, then."

He confirms I know how to use the shit, goes over everything three times so there's no chance of a mistake. We talk about clean-up on the other end.

"Pleasure doing business with you," I say once all the details are set.

His laugh is soft. "Always happy to rid the world of a couple of shitbirds."

After hanging up, I have one more thing to do. It's too late to get reservations the old-fashioned way. I shoot an email to Susan Richards, telling her what I need.

She's not Pete Miller. She can't read my mind yet. But she's already made herself so indispensable around the freeport that I'm considering doubling her salary.

Maybe I will, after next weekend. A little celebration, once Alix and I are free of the Herzog brothers forever.

26

ALIX

I'm staring out at Central Park, trying to believe I was in
Dover just one hour ago. The police executed their search
warrant seven days ago. So far, we haven't learned what they
found. Even if Sawgrass's clean-up left trace evidence behind, it
could take weeks for Trap and me to be charged. Up to a month
or more.

Guilt—and paparazzi—follow me like persistent wasps.

Klaus Herzog is dead. Jonas and Ansel Herzog are doing
their best to destroy the freeport. Eight Sawgrass men have died.
Three still lie in the hospital, somewhere between life and death.

All that loss, all that destruction, just because of me. Every
night I consider confessing to the police, but I've promised Trap
I'll play his game.

Our lawyers have advised us to be patient. To wait. That no
news is good news.

But Trap isn't good at patience. This morning, he
announced we were going to New York. When I asked what I

should take, he told me I could bring my phone, if I wanted. Everything else was waiting in the penthouse.

And he wasn't lying.

A dress hangs in the master bedroom closet. Its emerald silk is perfect for my skin tone. The tailored bodice has darts that accommodate my curves. A slit half-way up my thigh makes it easy for me to walk. The dress is dramatic and daring and sexier than anything else I own.

It's also tighter across the rear than any other dress in my wardrobe. Even the fine line of a thong would show. So I know I'm going commando which—I have to admit—makes me a little excited.

It makes Trap excited too. I can feel that as I step into his arms to thank him for his generosity. I'm about to make a joke about the hard, hot length pressing against my thigh when the doorbell rings.

"You're expecting something?" I ask as he glances at his watch.

"Just some groceries from Citarella," he says. "I figured we might not want to go out for breakfast."

The heat in his look melts something deep inside me. Forget about breakfast. I don't want to go out for dinner—even if that means never getting to wear the incredible grass-green dress in public.

He comes in for another kiss, short and sweet as the doorbell rings again. "We've got a couple of hours before our dinner reservation. Why don't you go relax in a bath?" he says. "I had Martha Gallagher send something special, along with the dress."

I can't keep myself from stealing one last peck before I let him answer the door. While he's talking to the delivery guy, I head into the bathroom.

A silver canister sits on the counter. *Costa Brazil*, the container says. *Sal de Banho*. I pry open the lid and take a deep breath. The crystals inside smell like wildflowers and sunshine.

I slip off the dress and fill the tub with hot water. Slipping beneath the surface, I let the luxury bath salts melt my muscles. My skin feels slick, like the rough outer layer has been charmed away. I don't deserve any of this, but I feel like I'm floating, like I'm sleeping on a cloud.

I must actually fall asleep, because Trap's knock startles me. "Sorry to disturb you, Princess," he says, without opening the door. "We need to leave in forty-five minutes."

"You still won't say where we're going?" I call.

"You'll find out soon enough."

Reluctantly, I pull the plug, wrapping myself in a thick bath sheet as the lukewarm water drains away. I find that Martha's magic has extended to cosmetics. A silver bag on the counter contains lipstick and blush, along with a tube of coal-black mascara and matching liner.

There's some sort of gel for my hair too. Finally, after weeks of growing it out, I have enough to style, at least a little. I roll the mousse between my palms and then transfer the moisture to my hair. The strands look tousled, like I just stepped out of the shower.

I go light with the other cosmetics; it's been so long since I've worn them. I'm a little astonished when I gaze at myself in the mirror. I look smart. Sophisticated. The type of woman who takes a Lear jet to Manhattan and then accepts gifts from her billionaire lover in his penthouse apartment.

My forty-five minutes are almost gone. I hurry into my dress. Find the shoes Martha delivered—four-inch stilettos with straps that buckle around each ankle. They're as terrifying as they are gorgeous.

Trap is standing by the window in the living room, enjoying the same view of Central Park that captured me when we arrived at this perfect hideaway. He's wearing a black suit with a snow-white shirt that reflects brilliantly in the window. His narrow black tie has a tiny silver stripe.

"Alix," he breathes when he turns toward me.

For just a moment, I forget everything hanging over our heads. I see only the hunger in his eyes, a grasping, greedy need. I see pride there as well, pure delight that I'm wearing his gifts. He holds up a single finger, spinning it in a slow circle.

Giving in to his command, I turn so he can study me from all sides. I hear his breath catch, and a completely unexpected blush heats my cheeks.

"Beautiful," he says, his throat closing over the word. I watch him shake himself back to full awareness. He offers me his arm. "Shall we?"

I tell myself my belly swoops because the elevator runs so fast, taking us to the ground floor. I'm lying.

The usual black Mercedes waits at the curb, with Charles standing by the door to help us into the back seat. "Mr. Prince," he says. "Ms. Key."

In minutes, we arrive at a restaurant. A table for two is framed in the window next to the door—intimate, extravagant, with enough china and glassware to feed an army. A balding man is too busy studying his menu to look at the silver-haired woman sitting across from him.

The door opens from inside, and a man in a tuxedo bows slightly as he ushers us toward an ebony desk. A woman greets us with a polished smile. "Good evening, and welcome to Nourriture."

This is the best restaurant in New York City, complete with three Michelin stars. Chef William Lasker's twenty-one-course fixed-price menu changes nightly.

Trap says, "Travis Prince. Party of—"

Before he can finish, the hostess's expression changes. The sculpted curve of her lips is replaced by a sour pout, as if she just bit down on a grapefruit rind. "Mr. Prince," she says, and it sounds like she's forcing his name through the eye of a needle. Her gaze hardens when she looks at me. "Ms. Key."

She shouldn't know my name. No one should.

But I've seen the expression on her face too many times in

the past week. On the paparazzi who lined the airport fence when we landed from Orlando. On the mainstream journalists who camp out in front of the freeport. On otherwise-sunny newsreaders on the nightly news.

I'm the woman who killed a man in cold blood. I'm the crazed lunatic with a knife whose video has already been viewed more than a million times. I'm the subject of dozens of memes, of online essays, of pop psychologists offering their opinion everywhere.

I'm toxic.

Trap settles a possessive hand on my waist. I don't know if he intends to give me courage, but his touch is enough to keep my knees from trembling.

The woman regains her composure almost as quickly as she lost it. She turns a page of the heavy leather book on the table in front of her, and she makes a quick mark in the margin. "If you could indulge me one moment, please."

Her tone doesn't match her oily words. She gestures, and the tuxedoed man by the door steps to her side. She whispers something in his ear. He nods and avoids looking at us, relying on the well-trained blindness of a man who lives on tips. He hurries toward the back of the restaurant.

He's gone for almost five minutes. The entire time, the hostess pretends Trap and I aren't standing there. We pretend we aren't waiting for our reservation to be honored.

When Tuxedo Man finally returns to his place by the door, he offers a tight nod to the hostess. She summons an unconvincing smile. "If you'll follow me, Mr. Prince." She clears her throat, like something's stuck sideways in there. "Ms. Key."

Whispers begin when we enter the dining room. Polite patrons keep from staring. Rude ones ogle, reaching for their phones.

The hostess pushes through the porthole door at the end of the room. She gestures for us to come with her, into the kitchen. Glaring at two stools pulled up to a stainless-steel counter, she says, "Chef Lasker would be pleased to have you join him at an exclusive chef's table this evening."

A white-aproned young woman is hurriedly placing silver-ware beside a pair of plates. One of her colleagues adds a couple of wine glasses and two tumblers for water.

"Thank you," Trap says, as if we've been offered a treasure —and plenty of Michelin fanatics would think we have been. "But we'd prefer to eat in the dining room."

"I'm sorry," the hostess says, not sounding sorry at all. "I'm afraid these are the only seats available tonight."

"We'll take the table in the front window," Trap says.

"We already have customers enjoying their meal—"

Trap turns to the woman who set our places on the kitchen counter. "Excuse me," he says, reaching into his pants pocket for his money clip. "Could you please take this to the couple sitting in the window? A small gesture thanking them for the inconvenience of trading seats?"

He peels off ten crisp hundred-dollar bills.

As the young chef hesitates, Trap says to the hostess, "Obviously, we'll pay for their dinners as well. And for your trouble." He hands a hundred to the hostess and another to his appointed messenger.

Our flurry of activity has attracted the attention of a man who can only be Chef Lasker. He's wearing traditional checked pants and a white jacket, with severe black cording and matching buttons. His tall white hat reminds me of a bishop's miter.

"I can't..." the hostess says. "We must..." she tries again. "There are reasons..." Finally she gives up and appeals to authority. "Chef?"

Nourriture's god studies Trap and me, his gaze as sharp as a filet knife. If not for Trap's hand on my hip, I would already be out the restaurant's front door, fleeing the bright lights of the kitchen for the anonymity of the street.

But Chef Lasker finally nods. "If our guests in the window

are willing to trade tables, Nourriture would be happy to serve Mr. Prince and Ms. Key in the window."

Defeated, the hostess grabs Trap's thousand dollars from the cowering young woman and scurries out to the main dining room. Another five minutes pass, filled with the clatter of a busy kitchen cooking food, plating dishes, and asking for Chef Lasker's approval.

When the hostess finally returns with a harried nod, Chef Lasker says, "Enjoy your dinner, Mr. Prince. Ms. Key."

This time, when we walk through the dining room guests have abandoned whispers; I hear my name and Trap's spoken in ordinary tones. The flash of cell-phone cameras is blinding, video too, and the quick tap of manicured nails on glass screens sounds like an insect army.

But Trap and I settle into our seats in the window. Some quick worker has secured fresh glasses, clean silverware, and a constellation of sparkling china.

A young waiter appears between the curtains to our alcove, sweating almost as much as the dark green bottle in his shaking hand. "Champagne," he says, his voice cracking as he avoids looking at our faces. "Compliments of the chef."

Trap waits until the kid has left before he raises his glass in a toast. Touching the rim of my flute, he says, "Fuck 'em if they can't take a joke."

Startled, I laugh. All of my mortification slips away as bubbles slide down my throat.

The Herzogs' video has turned Trap and me into animals in a zoo. At least a dozen people on the street outside the window do double-takes as they walk by. I see more flashes of phones, only slightly more surreptitious than those of the guests inside the restaurant.

But Trap will not yield to the morbid curiosity around us. He does nothing to attract attention, but he refuses to be ashamed of being seen in public with me.

He leans close to tell me a dirty joke. He passes me the olive from his Belvedere martini, knowing how much I'll love its salty brine. He asks me my opinion about a client matter at the freeport, about the allocation of gallery space for a new and demanding customer.

We eat oysters and caviar, lobster and quail, and the most tender lamb I've ever imagined. There are palate cleansers of blood orange sorbet and basil granita, and tiny bites of bread so airy that buttering it would be a crime. By the time we reach dessert—chocolate mousse and pecan jam and an array of delicate cookies, each no bigger than my thumbnail—I'm enchanted and sated and more than a little drunk on the perfectly matched flight of wine that accompanied every bite.

Our car is waiting at the curb when we finish, and I wonder if Trap and Charles have some sort of telepathic link. Before I know it, we're back in the magical elevator, soaring to our penthouse retreat. I sway a little as Trap gestures for me to lead the way into the living room, and my breath is stolen all over again by the sweeping view of Central Park at night, daisy chains of lights marking the few roads that cross the great green expanse.

Heat radiates off Trap's chest as he comes up behind me. My need for him is a physical ache, a hunger that can never be satisfied. I close my eyes, and I picture us tangled in his bed, his arms around me, our legs entwined.

I want him. I need him. For the first time since I've known him, I can imagine us having sane, normal sex. No bonds around my wrists. No gag. No blindfold. No cane.

I don't need to be punished. He doesn't need to tame his Beast. We can just satisfy each other. Just love each other.

He brushes a kiss against the nape of my neck and says, "Good night."

"What?" I'm so surprised, I can barely form the question.

"I have some business I need to take care of."

I felt his body respond to mine. His cock grew hard as he pressed against my back. "Now?" I ask, because I don't understand.

"I should have told you before, but I didn't want to ruin our evening."

"Ruin—"

But he's already backing away. He brushes his hand against his breast pocket, like he's checking for theater tickets. His other hand reaches into his pants; he's making sure he has his money clip.

"Trap!" I say. "What the hell?"

"I'm sorry. I'm late. I have to go."

And just like that, he's out the door—heading back to the elevator, to the lobby, to the street.

No.

Not *just like that*.

I can't accept that he's leaving me.

I can't imagine where he's going, what he's doing.

But he wants something out there more than he wants to be with me. And I barely waste a heartbeat grabbing my phone from the kitchen counter. I keep a credit card in the case. ID, too. I can go anywhere I need to go.

I get to the lobby as Charles is closing the back door of the Mercedes. I'm hailing a cab as the sleek black car gets stopped by the red light at the end of the block. I swallow hard to catch my breath, and I say something I thought was only said in terrible movies and worse TV shows: "Follow that car."

I'm not letting Trap get away.

27

TRAP

There's no good way to get from the Upper West Side to Brooklyn on a Saturday night. If I were driving myself, I'd have to concentrate on the fucking traffic. Instead, I sit in the back of the Mercedes and let Charles fight the good fight. Creeping through a sea of red lights on 11th Avenue, I have nothing to do but go over my plan, such as it is.

My advantages:

Surprise. The Herzogs aren't expecting me to show up at Kynk.

Layout. Rider sent me floor plans for the club.

Backup: Sawgrass is doing the actual wetwork. And the guys Best has waiting outside the club are motivated as hell, seeking revenge for the fuck-up on Long Island.

My disadvantages:

Knockout drugs: Real life isn't like the movies. If I jam a needle into someone's neck, they're not going to drop in seconds. Chances are, I'll hit bone or muscle, maybe the esophagus or the windpipe. Even if I manage a direct shot to the carotid it'll take almost a minute for my victim to pass out, and he'll be fighting like a motherfucker most of that time.

Flying solo: Sawgrass will be waiting on the outside, but they don't get past the front door. I'm only one guy, and I'm going after two.

Witnesses: I'm going to a fucking sex club. How many people will be with the Herzogs when I hunt them down?

Because that's what this is: A hunt. I need to find my prey, neutralize them, and get them out the side door before any civilians know what's going on.

I have a plan. I'll work my way through the club methodically, moving right to left. The public spaces will be easy. Private rooms are more of a challenge. Some doors stay open, but I'll be out on my ass if security catches me where I'm not invited.

But something tells me the Herzog brothers like an audience. I don't see them closing any doors.

So, I'll find them. And I'll wait till they're done with whoever they're fucking. When their dicks are limp and shriveled, and bystanders are out of the way, *I'll* be the one to lure them into another private room.

After all, they know who I am. They won't pass up the chance to get revenge for me watching Klaus bleed out on my dining room floor. Or for sending the Sawgrass troops last week. If Best had eleven casualties, I know the Herzogs were hit hard.

Then the real fun starts. One sharp blow to the first neck, to the carotid sinus. Turn fast, and get the other guy's throat. If the side of my hand is hard enough, fast enough, their blood pressure'll drop like fucking stones. They'll be out cold for two minutes, maybe three. I'll have time to find each carotid. To shoot them up with whatever Best gave me. And once they're both knocked out for good, I can take my time, helping my first "friend" to a little fresh air, then going back for the second.

It's a risk. But it's the best chance I'm going to get. I need to do this so the Diamond Ring can escape the blackmail that threatened Alix and me. I need to save Alix from those animals ever getting to her again. I need to punish the assholes for releasing the video.

For the thousandth time, I check the pair of syringes in my jacket pocket. The casing is plastic—no worries about Kynk's metal detector. The needles themselves are too small to register on the machine.

We're finally over water, the lights of Governor's Island to our right. Then back on shore, in Brooklyn at last. Charles weaves his way past the trendy parts of the borough. Down on the water, the old warehouses are dark. Dangerous, like sleeping wolves.

"Slow down," I say, as we approach the address Rider gave me. There's a couple standing outside. He's dressed in a tuxedo. She's wearing a handkerchief. They both look scared.

"Drive around the block," I order.

Charles takes the turn slowly, using his indicator, just like we were all taught in school. The street looks more like an alley, looming buildings on either side. Doorways are shadowed, and trash is piled in the corners. It looks like the world ended a decade ago, but no one let folks know down here.

Another turn. More deserted buildings.

A third turn. We're heading back toward the water now. A door opens and closes, flashing light onto the dark gray street. A man dressed in the dirty whites of a busboy hefts a trash bag into a dumpster.

Charles keeps his pace steady, not calling attention to our vehicle. I almost miss the black SUV in the shadows, parked facing us, three or four car-lengths from the service door. Its front license plate is splattered with mud, illegible in the dark.

"Flash your high beams," I tell Charles. "Two short, one long."

He complies without asking questions. That's why I've trusted him for over a decade.

The SUV flashes back: Long, short, long. That's the code

Best said they'd use. Those are the guys who'll do the heavy lifting.

"Okay," I say to Charles. "Back to the front door."

This time, the coast is clear. I wonder if the couple went inside, or if their car service picked them up. Who knows how far they'd have to walk to find a cab?

I pat my jacket pocket one last time. "Find some place to wait nearby," I tell Charles. "I'll call you when I'm ready. We may need to leave in a hurry."

"Of course," he says, like I just told him I'm going to the Metropolitan Museum, or I'm having dinner at Per Se, or I need him to stop at the dry cleaners.

I slip out of the back seat on the curb side. As I approach the door, I can make out a tiny brass plaque, a carefully shined oval with block letters picked out in black: **KYNK**. When I press my hand on the metal plate and push, the door whispers open. I step into a room that could double for the front desk at a boutique hotel.

If boutique hotels hired linebackers to wear tuxedos and ear wires like the pair of gorillas on either side of the door.

"Good evening," says the woman behind the desk. She's wearing a navy suit and a silk top, looking like a flight attendant. Four pins glint from her lapel—a replica of the brass oval from the front door along with three flags: Germany, Japan, and what I think is the United Arab Emirates.

Nice to know she's fluent in so many languages, but I answer in plain old English. "I believe my friend, Gage Rider, put me on the list for tonight?"

"Your name, sir?"

"Jack Strong."

She taps the screen in front of her, scrolling down to the second half of the alphabet. "Yes, Mr. Strong." Her neatly manicured nail marks me as present. "Have you played with us before?"

"No."

"Welcome to Kynk. We invite you to step into our green-room." She gestures toward a discreet mahogany door to her right. "Inside, you'll find lockers for your convenience. We ask our guests to undress to whatever level makes them feel most comfortable. Tonight, because it's our Masquerade, all club members are required to wear a mask. If you haven't brought one, you'll find a selection for your use."

She smiles like she's inviting me to test drive a car at the dealership. "We do require all of our guests to leave behind any devices that capture audio or video, including cell phones." I automatically pat my phone in its pocket. The lack of any recording works in my favor for what I have planned tonight.

"A door at the far end of the greenroom will take you to the club proper by way of a metal detector, which is installed for the safety of all our guests. Newcomers typically take some time to walk around the club. You'll find individual playrooms as well as more public areas. If there's any particular equipment you require but cannot locate, feel free to ask any Kynk staff. We're all identified with pins." She brushes the brass logo on her own lapel.

"We expect all our guests to determine their own safewords for scenes. Our security staff is present to protect you and all other guests. Please don't hesitate to ask for any assistance you may require."

I'm pretty sure Kynk security won't be on board for what I have planned tonight. But I thank her, and I make my way to the greenroom.

I don't know what I expected—maybe something like a locker room at an upscale gym. Instead, I find more dark wood and subdued lighting. A couple of guys stand to one side dressed in tuxes, deep in a conversation about convertible debentures and debt-equity swaps. Another guy sits bare-ass on a bench, his head between his hands, muttering something that sounds like a prayer my mother taught me.

The promised masks hang on the wall to my left. They look

a little creepy, like someone skinned a bunch of hunting trophies. Most are black, but a few are scarlet. A handful are finished with fake jewels.

I can be a pirate. A panther. A lion, or tiger, or bear. Some of the masks have horns; others sport metal spikes.

I grab one from the top row—a plain Lone Ranger mask, cut long at the bottom to cover my cheeks and nose. The less attention I call to myself, the better.

Beyond the masks, the lockers are full height, deep enough to sport velvet-covered hangers, with a shelf at eye height. Before I choose one, I look around for the toilets. A row of discreet doors lines the wall to my right.

I make my way to a cubicle, closing and locking the heavy wooden door. If I were at the club purely for entertainment purposes, I'd probably strip down to my silk boxers. But tonight I'm more shy than usual. Tonight, I'm wearing pants out on the floor.

I slip the syringes from my jacket to my right front pocket, taking the opportunity to double-check their red plastic caps. When I'm sure they're safe and secure, I unzip and piss. I don't expect anyone to be paying any attention to Jack Strong and his Kynk debut, but there's no reason to spark unnecessary scrutiny about what I'm doing in the crapper.

Back in the main room, I choose a locker in the middle of the row. I hang my shirt and jacket, leaving my phone on the shelf. On second thought, I add my money clip. I won't be paying for anything in the club, and the last thing I want is questions about the initials engraved on the silver surface.

I hope I can reclaim my shit at the end of tonight. There's a very real chance things will get out of hand. Maybe Rider will get my crap to the Lost and Found. I suspect more than one locker gets forgotten at Kynk.

The combination lock asks for four digits. I key in 0621. June 21. The night I met Alix.

For just a moment, something tightens in my gut. Tonight, at dinner, there were at least three times that I came close to telling her what I'm doing here. It was torture, standing next to her in the elevator when Charles dropped us at the penthouse.

The look in her eyes when I left her behind felt like a vat of lemon juice on a cut to the bone. Despite everything we've shared together, everything we've done, there's still a doubt that lingers in her eyes. She's not sure I'm staying. She still thinks she's broken, that I'll walk away from damaged goods.

Maybe after tonight, she'll believe me, once and for all. She'll understand that I'll do anything for her. For us.

Of course, the Beast will have a fucking field day out there on the floor. It's already prowling the edges of my mind, whispering oily threats like sewer gas bubbling out of cracked pipes.

I check the locker door, tugging five times—hard—on the handle. The Beast doesn't go away, but the door stays shut. I square my shoulders. I resist the urge to mutter the words the guy on the bench was saying, the prayer against evil.

And I head out to hunt.

28

ALIX

I count out the fare, plus the five extra twenties I promised the cabbie if he got me here without being detected by Charles and Trap. Before he takes my money, the guy says, "You sure you want to get out here, sweetheart? Looks like the neighborhood's a little rough."

I try to ignore the fact that I'm wearing a floor-length formal gown and heels that would make a beauty pageant contestant question her career choice. "I'll be fine."

"I can wait a few minutes," he volunteers.

"Thanks. But my friend is waiting for me inside."

I say that like I have a clue what Trap is doing here. I didn't even see the door in the shadowy alcove the first time we drove by. My trusty driver took it upon himself to turn off his lights, staying almost a block back as Trap drove around the building. We barely caught those flashing high beams from where we were, back at the intersection. Whatever the code was, it spooked my cabbie enough that he went up an extra block, cutting back to the main road just in time for us to see Trap climb out of the Mercedes.

The more I've learned about the freeport, the more I've realized Trap needs to manage underhanded business deals. He's told me about plenty of clients' less-than-legal businesses, but I know he's protecting me from the worst of what he sees. Is he meeting some crime boss here? Maybe a motorcycle club based on the dilapidated Brooklyn waterfront?

But that doesn't make sense. What business meeting would happen close to midnight on a Saturday?

"I can take you somewhere else, sweetheart," the driver says, and I realize he's been waiting patiently while I try to figure out exactly what's going on. "Don't worry if you don't have the fare. If you were *my* daughter, I'd want to know someone was taking care of you."

"Thank you," I say. "Your daughter is lucky to have a father like you. But I'll be fine."

Before I can doubt myself, I open the car door. I have to concentrate while navigating the rough city street, asphalt covering cobblestones that have heaved into hills over time. I force myself to smile when I reach the curb, and I wave at my would-be knight in shining armor.

But my face falls when I see the brass plaque on the door: Kynk.

A sex club?

I don't understand. For the first time since Trap walked out of the penthouse, my confusion is tinged with anger. What the hell is Trap doing at a *sex club*?

My driver won't leave until I find the nerve to go in. So I push on the door, half expecting it to creak like something in a haunted house. I brace myself for cobwebs and the stench of rotting sewage.

Instead, I find myself in a foyer that looks like the front room of a prestigious museum—the Frick maybe, or the Morgan Library or one of the powerhouse galleries I've come to know in my self-guided education as an art auctioneer. The woman behind the Queen Anne table has the polished look of a seasoned curator.

But that doesn't account for the two huge men standing guard on either side of the door. Their arms are crossed over their chests, muscles bulging like battleships.

And none of it explains the name on the door: Kynk. Is Trap a member of this private club? And what the hell is he getting here that I'm not giving him at home?

"Good evening," says the woman. "May I help you?"

From her measured smile to the twitch of her hand over the tablet on her desk, I'm pretty sure I'm supposed to deliver some secret password. But password to what? And how long do I have to come up with something before the guards throw me out?

At least these three aren't surprised that I'm dressed for opening night at the opera. They aren't the least bit disturbed that I've arrived at this distant outpost alone. They don't seem to see me as a threat; in fact, their relaxed stance clearly indicates I *could* be the type of woman who belongs here.

Which makes me wonder even more: Why is Trap here? How can this place satisfy the animal that lives inside his head? What the hell am I missing?

Before I can lose the good will of the welcoming committee, I settle on a story I hope sounds believable. "A friend invited me to come here tonight. Promised I wouldn't regret it. And he's never steered me wrong before." I offer my best game smile.

Behind me, one of the stone guardians presses the black loop in his ear. "Yes, Mr. Rider," he says into the mouthpiece that barely makes it halfway around his jaw. His massive rumble is probably supposed to be a whisper. "Of course, Mr. Rider. I don't know what happened. I'll come set up the platform myself."

Rider. And Trap's here. Could the mountain by the door be talking to Gage Rider, a member of the Diamond Ring? Gage played professional hockey, and he owns the Atlantic City Aces along with—rumor says—plenty of New York real estate. Does he own this place too?

The receptionist or hostess or whatever she is has an expectant look on her face, and I realize I've missed a question. "Excuse me?" I ask.

"I asked the name of your friend. So I can check it against our list."

In the last three years, I've learned a lot about lying. I can thank Klaus Herzog for that. I look directly into her eyes and say, "Gage. Gage Rider."

She's not as good at controlling the flicker of emotion on her face. She's worried she's offended her boss, which suits me just fine. "Of course, Ms...."

"Key," I say, as if I'm certain my name is on whatever list she wants to check. "Alix Key."

The giant by the door is speaking into his mouthpiece. "Well, I don't want to be the one keeping Mr. Rider waiting. Tell Harkins I need him at the door. Pronto."

The woman looks up from her tablet. "I'm sorry. Could there be another name?"

No. I have no other name. But inspired by the frustration of the guard dog who has repeated his pointed order for Harkins to relieve him, I go for broke. "Perhaps you can call Gage and tell him I'm here."

I purposely use Rider's first name. I sound casual, like I'm willing to wait all night. I make sure not to lean forward, not to glance at the tablet, not to look like I'm trying to pressure the gatekeeper in any way.

And as the volcano behind me erupts in maximum frustration, ordering whoever's looking for Harkins to get here on the fu— freaking double, the woman behind the desk makes a decision.

"No need to bother Mr. Rider. Not if he told you to be here tonight. He mentioned we might have a new kitten or two."

"Excuse me?" I ask again.

She reaches into a box beneath the table and hands me a swath of black fabric. It feels like silk. As I spread it between my fingers, I realize I'm looking at a mask. A hood, really, something that will fasten over my head, covering my hair, my forehead, and my cheeks. It has holes for my eyes.

It has cat ears.

My fingers go numb, and I drop the mask on the desk.

Herzog savaged me when I was dressed as a cat. He drugged me, and once I was helpless, he raped me, he and his sadistic brothers. It took me four weeks in a hospital bed to recover from what they did to me.

"Ms. Key," the woman says. Her voice sounds like it's coming from the far end of a tunnel, and I think she's said my name a few times. "Are you all right, Ms. Key?"

Herzog is dead. His brothers are nowhere near this place. But Trap is. My anger with Trap has evaporated. All I have left is confusion. I don't know why he's here, but if Gage Rider owns the club, this has something to do with the freeport. I'm not leaving without Trap.

I force myself to swallow and pick up the hood I dropped. "I'm sorry," I say, pushing out a weak little laugh. "I guess no one's really ready for the first time, no matter how much she thinks she is."

That must be a good answer, because the woman flashes an understanding smile. "Our guests determine safewords for all their scenes. And our security staff is always present to protect you and all our other guests. Of course, Mr. Rider will run the auction himself."

"Of course," I say, even though I have no idea what she's talking about.

"Here," she says, pointing to a number embroidered on the right ear of the mask. "You're number seven. We already have six other special visitors for tonight's Masquerade."

I murmur something that's acceptable, because the woman moves on to the next phase of a script that seems very familiar to her. "We invite you to step into our greenroom." She gestures toward a heavy wooden door to her left. "Inside, you'll find lockers for your convenience. We ask our guests to undress to whatever level makes them feel most comfortable."

There's more—I need to leave behind my cell phone, there's a metal detector, I can explore public areas and playrooms. I can ask staff for any special toys I might require; they all wear pins with the Kynk logo.

"The auction starts at midnight," she concludes. "In the Heart, the main room at the back of the club."

I thank her, and I head into the greenroom. It looks a little like the dressing room at Gallagher Samson, but the lighting here is a lot more subdued. And three of the women touching up their makeup in the long mirror to my right are wearing nothing but lacy little thongs and stilettos. A fourth has added a tiny bra to her ensemble. A fifth woman is on her way out of the greenroom wearing nothing but a pair of Manolo Blahniks with crystal heels.

And a mask. She's wearing an elaborate beaded mask with Cleopatra eyes and intricate braids.

I find an open locker.

I'm naked under my dress. I don't have a lot of options, clothing-wise.

I spent enough time in school locker rooms that it's not entirely bizarre to strip in front of the women at the counter. But my high school field hockey team never required me to put on a mask. And I never had to fight the instant wave of nausea when the mirror shows me my face framed beneath cat ears.

Trap is out there. Trap will keep me safe.

Three years in Herzog's house devastated my innate sense of modesty. When he required, I went without clothes for days. For weeks, even. What are a few hours in the carefully controlled environment of a high-end sex club? Even if I'm expected to report to some auction at midnight?

Trap is out there. Trap will keep me safe.

I close my locker. It needs a four-digit code, so I enter the first one I think of: 0621. My birthday. The night I met Trap.

I tug at my mask one last time, centering the ears on top of my head. I blink slowly, surprised by how my eyes look like they belong to a doll. I flex my toes in my shoes, feeling the thin strap rub around each ankle.

And I head into Kynk, and the Heart, and whatever else is waiting on the other side of the door.

29

TRAP

I t looks like Rider's running a quality club here—plenty of staff, top-rail booze, rubbers available in crystal bowls on every horizontal surface. But nothing can hide the smell of sweat and sex as I walk into the main room.

Even with the fucking masks, I recognize a senator standing at the bar. I'm pretty sure the guy who's paddling the blue-haired woman squealing like an overheated flywheel starred in last summer's big movie, the one about zombies settling Mars. And I don't need pinstripes to recognize the shortstop who's sliding into home doggy-style while his date's tits jiggle against the ballet barre set into the mirrored wall.

It's hard to get a view of everyone. The crowd keeps shifting. Waiters pass through with champagne flutes and bottles of water. Couples meet up, pair off, and some head toward private rooms in the back.

Fifteen minutes into my maiden voyage at Kynk, I've passed up a chance for a blowjob with a finger up my ass, I've opted out of a remote-control butt plug, and I've told a couple I'm not interested in being their third.

No one seems upset when I pass up the invitations. There are plenty of fish in the kinky sea.

Something tells me the Herzog brothers aren't in this room. This isn't their style—plenty of space, with security standing unobtrusively in the shadows.

I make my way down a corridor lined with rough-cut brick.

The first room I come to has an open door. A man with a latex troll mask kneels in front of a woman, his bare ass shaking as he suits up with a rubber. "You call that a cock?" the woman sneers, tapping a riding crop against her black-clad thigh. Her leather mask matches her corset, trimmed in silver, with dangling laces tipped with steel. When she sees me in the doorway, she digs her stiletto into the poor guy's shoulder. "Hey," she says to me. "Want to show this pathetic cuck what a real man can do?"

"No thanks," I say and make my way to the next room.

A cluster of candles is lit on a low table, red and green and blue mixed in with white. The temperature is high enough to spark sweat on my chest. A gagged woman lies on the floor, her wrists and ankles tied with purple cotton rope to convenient anchors on the walls. Clear glass cups bulge over nipples turned almost black from the vacuum. Her partner brushes hair from her face as he says, "One more minute. You can take it." She bellows as he tips a snow-white candle over her belly, adding to the scribble of wax already hardening there.

I back out of the doorway, fairly certain neither one knows I was there.

I'm halfway down the hall when a door opens and a woman staggers out, tripping in front of me. My choice is to grab her arm or let her fall. The Beast hollers as she traps my fingers between her biceps and her boob. I clench my free hand in the pocket with the syringes, squeezing out a five-count so I can breathe.

"Hey!" she says, like she's been looking for me for ages. She's barefoot, so she should be able to keep her footing. But her panties are on backwards, with the scrap that should be covering her snatch flossing her ass.

She missed a hook on the matching lace bra. Her mask used to look like a peacock, but she crushes it in her right hand as she throws her arms around my neck.

"Wanna fuck me up the ass?" she asks. "I like it dirty. I want it rough."

The Beast is carving my brain into sushi. My balls are trying to climb inside my belly. I need to get her off me, need to drop her, but her eyes roll back in her head before I can move.

"I've got this, sir," says a uniformed security guard who appears out of nowhere. He sweeps her into a fireman's carry like she weighs less than a sack of flour. Tapping a microphone on his chest, he informs Dr. Marshall that he's on his way to sickbay.

I'm punching the wall, five quick jabs to shut up the fucking Beast, when a shadow materializes at my side. It's another guard, his fingers already close to his comm unit. "Come with me, sir," he says.

"I'm fine," I respond. The last thing I need is one of these motherfuckers finding the cargo I've got on board.

He edges a step closer. His eyes go to my fist. My knuckles are red, but they haven't split. "I'm asking you to come with me, sir," he says, his voice making it clear I don't have a choice.

"I don't know what you think you saw," I say. "That woman came on to me. She was the one who wouldn't take no for an answer."

"I'm sure that's true, sir. But you were the one punching the wall. We ask our guests who are upset to take a few minutes. Come down to the security office. Drink a glass of water and catch your breath. We want to keep the club safe for everyone."

"You think I'm a fucking risk?"

"In the alternative," he says, "we can have you sleep it off in the cage."

I don't what goddamn cage he's talking about, but the guy is big enough to frog-march me through the tunnel. He can probably frisk me too—maybe not legally, but what the fuck am I going to do? Run to the cops?

So I make a show of spreading my fingers wide. I take a deep breath to prove I'm under control. I roll my shoulders, trying to shed some of my tension.

And I let the guard force me down to the security office for a fucking glass of water. I'll get back on the floor faster if I play along. But if Jonas and Ansel Herzog leave the party before I'm free, I can't be responsible for what I do this asshole.

30

ALIX

I figure Trap won't spend his time in the main room. There are too many people here. Too big a chance someone might brush against him and set off his compulsions.

I stake out the hallway on my left. There must be a dozen rooms, maybe more, cut into the tunnel's raw brick. Most of the doors are open. Some of the people inside welcome an audience. Others are so intent on their scenes they seem to think they're on a deserted island.

God knows I saw enough twisted sex at Herzog's house to last a lifetime. I have to remind myself that the people here at Kynk have chosen to play. They've paid God-knows-how-much to belong to this club and they've consented to every single act I see. If anyone goes too far by accident or misunderstanding, there are dozens of security officers standing ready to intervene.

But my palms are sweating.

My breath comes fast enough that the roof of my mouth starts to tingle.

My heart pounds so hard I feel it in my toes.

Trap is out there. Trap will keep me safe.

But I have to find him first.

I make my way down the tunnel, checking room after room. I turn away the man who asks if he can come between my breasts. I pretend that I don't see the threesome beckoning from a couch covered in cling-wrap film. I shake my head when a man asks if he can fuck my sweet tight ass.

That last request leaves me too shaken to speak.

I grab a glass of champagne from a passing waiter and drain it all in one gulp. Before he can move down the tunnel, I help myself to a second flute.

I force myself to sip it. I need to keep my wits about me. I need to stay in control.

Chimes sound, four notes going up, then down. I half expect to see waiters wandering through the crowd, playing mini xylophones, like they're summoning guests to some black-tie wedding supper.

Club members begin moving toward the end of the tunnel. Toward the Heart.

I could leave now. I could go back to the greenroom. Take off my suffocating mask and pull on my dress. Call a car with my cell phone and make my way back to the penthouse.

Trap doesn't need to know I was here. I don't need to know what he's doing, what brought him to Brooklyn, why he had to come to Kynk.

But that's a lie.

I *do* need to know.

I didn't mean to, but I've emptied my second glass of champagne. Ordinarily, I might not feel the buzz, but I had a lot of wine with dinner.

Dinner.

That perfect meal at Nourriture seems like a lifetime ago. Trap standing up for me. For us. Telling the hostess and the world that he wasn't going to hide in the kitchen.

Trap is out there. Trap will keep me safe.

I follow the crowd to the Heart.

The main event is already under way when I arrive. Gage Rider stands on a raised platform, a few feet above the crowd. This must be the dais the security guard at the front door had to put together on short notice. A thick velvet curtain stretches behind the stage, inky black in the darkness at the back of the Heart.

Gage looks like a movie star in his custom-tailored tux. He's well over six feet tall. His athlete's shoulders would strain any ordinary dinner jacket. Strands of gold gleam in his dark brown hair, and I can make out the gray of his eyes from across the room. He speaks into his hand-held microphone like he was born in a theater.

"Here we are, ladies and gentlemen. For your bidding pleasure. I present to you, kitten number two!"

The velvet curtain slides to the side and the audience applauds—men and women both. A spotlight finds the kitten, a full-grown woman. She's wearing nothing but a wicked smile, a silver G-string, and her cat-eared mask. Her waist is so narrow it looks like she can't possibly have room for all her organs. Her rib cage could be a sculpture at the Museum of Modern Art. Her small, high breasts rise and fall with her rapid breaths, and her nipples are so pink I'm certain she's painted them with lipstick.

Gage speaks over the admiring buzz of the crowd. "Bidding will open at ten thousand dollars, ladies and gentlemen. Ten grand to play a scene with one of Kynk's first-time guests."

"Ten thousand," calls a voice from the back of the crowd.

"Eleven," someone counters.

The bidding works its way up in thousand-dollar increments. Kitten number two looks astonished by each new offer, her lips pursing in a perfect, knowing O. Gage only steps in when the bidding stalls at twenty-seven.

"On Masquerade night, the club stays open till eight in the

morning," Gage cajoles. "That's more than seven hours to play with this very willing kitten. Your wish is absolutely her command."

The bidding reaches thirty-eight.

"Do I have to remind you?" Gage asks. "All profits from this year's Masquerade benefit Wounded Heroes United. Kitten number two wants to help our bravest men and women in uniform. Won't you help fulfill her dream?"

The auction closes at fifty-two thousand dollars. Gage congratulates the winner, who steps to the podium with a spiked dog collar attached to a leash. Kitten number two kneels before her new master, accepting the restraint with another one of those sly grins and a gracefully bent neck. A roar of approval goes up as she's paraded through the crowd.

I'm no professional auctioneer, not by any means, and my chosen area of expertise is art, not eager young women. But I admire Gage's casual confidence, his easy rapport with the crowd. He calls after kitten number two and her buyer: "Wait until the last kitten before you start your scene. I don't want you two stealing my bidders' attention!"

The man holding the leash pretends to consider his options. But then he points to the floor in front of him. Kitten number two kneels, and he rests an easy hand between her cat ears. "Just for you, Gage," the man calls. "We'll wait just for you."

The crowd laughs. And then the auction for kitten number three begins. She's shorter than I am and outweighs me by at least thirty pounds. The garter belt around her ample waist attaches to fish net stockings. Her breasts overflow a tight-laced leather corset. Gage starts the bidding at fifteen.

Kitten number three brings in sixty-one thousand dollars.

Kitten number four backs out at the last minute, stepping off the podium and seeking comfort in the arms of three friends.

Kitten number five adds forty-eight thousand to the total.

A young woman steps up beside me as Gage starts the

bidding on kitten number six. "Number seven?" she asks. "If you could come with me?"

It's an offer. An invitation. I can decline, the same way number four did.

But I've spent almost an hour prowling through Kynk, and I'm no closer to finding Trap. No nearer to knowing why he came here, what he thinks he needs.

But I'm certain of one thing: If I step onto that stage, Trap will win my auction. He'll make the highest bid without a second's hesitation.

And that's what I want.

I want him to know I followed him here. I want him to know I accept whatever drew him to the club. I want him to know I love him, despite his being here, maybe even *because* he's here. I can meet him on his territory and be the woman he needs me to be. There's nothing he can ask that I won't give him.

Even if that means standing naked in the spotlight.

Even if that means playing out a scene with club members looking on.

He's the man I've chosen. He's the man I love. With him, I can do anything.

So I let the staff member guide me behind the velvet curtain. I lick my lips as Gage closes the sixty-eight-thousand-dollar auction on kitten number six.

Trap won't embarrass me. He'll make sure I go for the night's highest value.

I hear Gage say, "And our last kitten of the night, kitten number—" I catch my breath as the curtain sweeps to the side. I blink hard, blinded by the spotlight.

"Alix?" Gage says, my name echoing through the Heart as he's startled out of his casual emcee chatter.

A whisper licks through the crowd like fire in a hayloft. No one noticed me when I was slinking through Kynk's shadows. But here, onstage, pinned beneath a merciless light, people recognize the woman's who's been front-page gossip since the Herzog murder tape was released.

But Gage recovers quickly. "Kitten number seven!" he says. "Bidding will start at—"

"One million dollars."

The crowd falls silent. Gage clears his throat and stammers into his mic. "O— only serious bids here. Let's start at twenty—"

"One million dollars," the voice repeats.

But that can't be right. That's not Trap's voice, filling the suddenly silent Heart.

Instead, it's a voice from my past. A voice from my nightmares. A voice that freezes me on the platform, stealing my thoughts, crushing my plans, smothering any vestige of my free will.

The crowd parts, and Jonas Herzog steps forward to claim his prize.

31

ALIX

The Heart spins around me. The room is too large, too hot, too loud. There are dozens of people here, maybe a couple hundred, and every eye is trained on Gage. He's speaking into his microphone, white teeth flashing in a wide, strained smile, saying something about wounded heroes and the Masquerade's generous donations and this calls for a fresh round of champagne.

As the crowd applauds, Gage hands off his microphone and hurries to my side. "What the hell are you doing here?" he demands.

At the same time, Jonas pushes forward. "Come to Master, *mein kätzchen*. It's time to trim your claws."

My gut turns to water. I know the rules. I know the consequences if I don't submit.

"Alix," Gage says, his voice full of concern. He closes his hand around my trembling biceps and whispers, "This is what Trap planned?"

Before I can lie, Jonas reaches my side. "Hands off, Rider. That's my kitten you're talking to."

I haven't seen Jonas Herzog in four months, maybe five. He must have spent that entire time pumping iron at the gym. His thickly muscled shoulders ripple with the deadly strength of an anaconda. His mask is some bird of prey, an eagle or a hawk. He's entirely naked, and the deadly beak of his mask echoes his thick erection. His eyes shine out from the black silk, a blue so light they look white.

"Alix?" Gage tries again.

"Trap is out there," I say. "Trap will keep me safe."

The words don't mean anything anymore. I've repeated them so long they've lost their meaning. But Gage takes an uncertain step back. He looks around the Heart, like he's searching for Trap in the crowd.

Jonas shakes his head at my declaration, lips twisted in a cruel smile. As if to contradict me, he clicks his tongue against the roof of his mouth.

My reaction is immediate, conditioned by years of submission, by the deep gulleys a double dose of Crash carved in my brain. I drop to my knees and plant my hands on my head. I throw my elbows back and display my breasts for Jonas, for Gage, for anyone watching in the shadowed Heart.

Gage looks down at me, confused. But Jonas grips my arm tight enough to bruise bone. "Let's go, kitten," he says.

I let him drag me through the crowd. He transfers his grip to the back of my neck and leans close to whisper in my ear. "We've been waiting to get our hands on you, you filthy cunt."

Only then do I realize Ansel is waiting up ahead. He's darker than I remember. Slighter. He has an even more vicious twist to his mouth. His mask is a demon, with four wicked horns matching the curve of his angry hard-on. His milk-blue eyes gleam as Jonas parades me to him.

Ansel closes his pincers on my left arm and leans close to hiss, "Let's see how brave you are in our private room." He licks my face from the corner of my mouth to the edge of my black kitten mask, all the while crushing my biceps, grinding muscle against bone. He lowers his voice even further. "What you did to Klaus is nothing compared to what we'll do to you."

Jonas picks me up like I weigh no more than a Barbie doll, throwing me over his shoulder so my head dangles halfway down his back. His sausage fingers dig into my bottom as he carries me out of the Heart. I struggle, once, but he makes that sound again, that clicking of his tongue.

I freeze.

I'm supposed to be safe in this club. I'm supposed to be protected by the number of people, by security guards, by safewords.

But the memory of Crash whispers in my skull. Master trained me to take this sort of abuse, this embarrassment and pain. I know how to close off rooms in my brain. I know how to survive this.

And I know one more thing: I deserve this.

I played a game, and I lost. I killed Master, cut open his throat, carved off his cock, and stabbed the bloody remains until they were nothing more than mangled meat. Trap and I can hire all the lawyers in the world, but the truth is, I'm a killer.

Trap.

Trap was supposed to be out there. Trap was supposed to keep me safe.

But I know the monsters that wrestle in his brain. What is his Beast doing to him even now? He must have seen Jonas and Ansel paw me. He saw me submit. Jonas is right. I am *filthy*.

Trap isn't out there. Trap won't keep me safe.

Jonas carries me to a room at the end of the tunnel I was exploring when the auction began. The sharp smell of alcohol mixes with the lingering funk of sex. Every surface gleams—the hard-edged black couch, the iron chain suspended from the ceiling, the array of tools spread on the laminate table in the corner. A crystal bowl rests on a stand beside the door, brimming with foil-wrapped condoms.

Kynk's staff has done its job. Those efficient people have cleaned the room. They've made everything ready for a new game. For me.

Jonas dumps me on the floor like I'm a sack of dirty laundry. He plants his foot on the back of my neck as if I might try to crawl away.

He's wrong, though. I won't escape. Can't escape. I'm doomed.

My body remembers what these men did to me in the past. My ribs ache with bruises planted years ago. My face burns from the smack of ancient fists. The void between my legs screams in remembered agony, stretched and torn and bleeding from abuse no woman should have to survive.

Ansel straddles my hips. He clutches my right wrist, yanking hard, like he expects me to resist as he wraps a length of rope tight around my wrist.

But he's wrong. I have no resistance left.

Trap isn't out there. Trap won't keep me safe.

I don't deserve protection. I'm a murderer and a slut and I've already let these men use every part of me for their cruel pleasure. They've come in my mouth and my pussy and my ass before. They've cuffed me. Beaten me. Broken me in more ways than I can count.

So Ansel grabs my left wrist too. He ties my hands together, yanking hard enough to force a moan as my shoulders burn in their sockets. My protest, small as it is, lights some fuse inside him. He shifts off my back and smacks my ass, three times, hard enough to ignite the barely healed stripes Trap put there just six nights ago.

This is the punishment I deserve. This is the degradation, the shame, the price of submitting to the Herzogs.

I'm frozen inside. I'm hard and shriveled, like a three-year-old crust of bread. I'm garbage.

Jonas shifts his weight off my neck. He hauls me to my knees and snaps an order to Ansel, telling him to fetch something from the table in the corner. It's an O-ring gag, and as he fastens it tight around my head, he makes the steel cut into the tender flesh at the corners of my mouth.

"Remember this, bitch?" he sneers as he pulls it even tighter. "Remember how you screamed for it?"

Tears leak from beneath my mask. I remember. I remember everything.

Ansel slides an iron hook under the bonds around my wrists. I hear a chain slide through a pulley near the ceiling, and my arms are forced up behind me. My ribs rise, and my chest pushes out, desperate to ease the pressure on my shoulders.

Jonas asks, "Showing off your tits, you horny cunt?" He stalks to the table, and I'm not surprised to see him return with a cane.

I close my eyes, bracing for the fire I know he'll deliver. In the darkness, I hear people moving behind me.

I'm not in Master's study. I'm in a private room at Kynk.

"She's just a kitten," a man says.

"She knows she can safeword, doesn't she?" a woman whispers.

"Do something," someone says, urgent and afraid.

But no one does anything. No one stops the scene. I can't safeword because we never set an escape. Because I have no limits. Because Jonas and Ansel Herzog are avenging angels, because fate's a bitch, and so am I. Because I killed Master and this is what I deserve tonight and tomorrow and all the rest of my life.

Ansel leans forward and hisses in my ear. "You're ours, Slave. Ours till the day you die."

Because Trap's not out there. Trap won't keep me safe.

The cane whistles through the air, giving me a single heart-beat's warning before it sets my breasts on fire.

Trap will never be here, because I'm filthy.

Another blow, directly on top of the first.

I'm disgusting.

A third blow, and something detonates deep inside my skull, icy crystals shredding whatever remains of my brain.

I'm lost.

I'm.

Lost.

I'm...

32

TRAP

Gage Rider storms into the security office, waving a plastic earpiece and a hard, black battery pack. His eyes are narrowed beneath his Zorro mask. "What the hell is wrong with comms—?" He draws up short when he sees me in the holding cage. "What the fuck?"

"Get me out of here," I growl.

"He punched Flynn when we searched him," tattles the asshole who locked me up. "Broke his fucking jaw."

"Give me the keys." Rider holds out his hand.

"This is what he was hiding," Numbnuts says, like he didn't just receive a direct order from his boss. He gestures toward the two syringes lying on the metal desk. Their bright red caps look like they're made of blood.

"Rider," I say. "I'm running out of time to find them."

"Find them?" he says. "Holy fuck. How long have you been down here?"

A knife slides between my ribs, the tip hovering over my heart. "What happened?"

"They bid a million bucks on Alix."

"Alix? *Bid?*" He's lost his fucking mind. Alix is back at the penthouse, hopefully sleeping off a three-star dinner from Nour-riture. Probably nursing a grudge for my walking out on her tempting proposition.

"You don't know." His face drains to match the color of his shirt.

I don't know. But I'm getting a fucking good idea. "Get me out of here!" I bellow.

"Boss," the piece-of-shit security guard says. "Want me to call the cops?"

"Where is she?" I holler as Rider springs the lock.

He doesn't waste time with words. "Come on."

The guy spent half his life as an elite athlete, but I match him step for step as he sprints up the stairs. No time for the fucking elevator.

Club members scatter in front of us. A waiter whirls out of the way, losing his balance and sending a tray of crystal cham-pagne flutes to the floor. Three security guys fall into line behind us, but they lose ground as Rider pounds down the tunnel.

A crowd has gathered outside one of the rooms. A woman's crying, mascara ruining her daisy-covered mask. The guy she's with keeps patting her back, like that ever does any good.

Other people push forward, resting their hands on shoul-ders, trying to get a better view. A pair of guards keeps the crowd at a distance, fists on hips, arms akimbo to show they mean business.

Aside from the crying woman, the group is nearly silent. That makes sense, I guess. Everyone knows you don't interrupt someone else's scene. Breaking a Dom's concentration can fuck with his carefully calculated restraint. Screwing with a sub's mental and emotional balance can be a hell of a lot worse.

Rider shoulders his way into the room like he's fighting for a puck in the crease. I follow before the crowd can close again.

"Get off her, you cocksucker!" The words are out of my mouth before my brain processes everything I see. My shout is loud; I want it that way. But it sounds like a fucking freight train, because everyone behind me is goddamn silent.

Jonas Herzog has his cock halfway down Alix's throat. His fist is twisting her mask, ripping off one of her pointed little cat ears. He's stretching her neck, fucking her face, even though she's gagging like she's about to puke.

I lower my shoulder and hit him at speed, like he's a football sled and I'm determined to shove him off the end of the world. I feel the rush of air as my momentum crushes his lungs. I hear his cock slide free, wet and sloppy. I knee him in the crotch, hoping I can drive his balls through what passes for his brain.

Before he can drop, I whirl on the other motherfucker. He was crouching over Alix's ass like a dog humping someone's leg. Now, he's cowering by the couch, his hands over his head like he's afraid I'll kick his skull in. His right palm is slimed with spit, and my overclocking brain realizes Ansel was just lubing up. He hasn't fucked her. Yet.

I shift my balance, drawing back a foot to kick his balls all the way to Staten Island. Before I can land the blow, though, a redwood tree falls across my throat. I'm dragged back three full steps, my feet scrambling for purchase on the floor. I try to jackknife, try to throw an elbow, try to turn into the neck hold and throw the motherfucker, but Rider's security guard knows his fucking business.

Instead of keeping up the fight, I try to talk to the only person in the room who matters. "Alix," I say.

She doesn't answer.

She's strung up like a fucking turkey, jute rope tight enough around her wrists to turn her fingers blue. I've never used anything that rough on her; she'll have fibers trapped in bruises for days.

Her arms are suspended above her body like she's a display in a medieval torture museum. I pray to God the fucking Herzogs knew what they were doing because if they didn't, her shoulders might be dislocated.

They've got her in an O-ring gag, the type she hates. I don't know what they gave her, but she looks stoned out of her mind. She's staring straight ahead, like I haven't just come close to killing two fucking excuses for men to get to her. I haven't seen her blink yet.

"Alix," I say again. "Princess."

She flinches at that. But she still doesn't blink. And she doesn't turn around, doesn't look at me, doesn't acknowledge I exist.

"Dammit, Rider!" I shout, when I can't break free of the goon who's holding me. "Cut her fucking loose."

He does better than that. He crosses to the tie off, the anchor where the rope is secured against the wall. He unwinds the lashing, then cautiously adds some slack to the line from the pulley to Alix's wrists. He's lowering her arms slower than I would. Giving her a chance to adapt. To adjust. To save her fucking tendons and ligaments and whatever else the stress position was designed to destroy.

When her hands rest on the small of her back, Rider starts to step forward, to unwind the goddamn hemp. Alix bucks like he's hit her with a cattle prod. Swearing something under his breath, he stops. Glancing behind me, he signals to someone out in the hall.

A guard steps forward. She's uniformed. Built like a pro wrestler. Hair pulled back tight enough that it might cut off blood to her brain. She kneels beside Alix, putting one hand on her shoulder to brace her, to steady her. With the other, she unwinds the rope, moving with maximum efficiency and minimum emotion.

"Can you stand?" the guard asks.

Alix doesn't answer. But when the uniform climbs to her

feet, Alix copies her. My princess sways hard enough on her high heels that the guard has to steady her with a hand under her elbow. At the guard's silent urging, Alix sits on the black vinyl couch. The guard fetches her a bottle of water.

It's the first time I register the stripe across her chest. The wound is weeping beads of blood and I swear to God if those fuckers scarred her incredible tits, I'm going to rip off their cocks and make them eat each other's balls.

In fact, I might be halfway there already. The cumwipe, Jonas, is still moaning on the floor, hands tight between his legs, where I kicked him. Rider snaps out a command to his staff. "Get them medical attention."

And then he raises his voice to reach the people behind me. "Everything's fine, people. The scene just got a little out of hand."

The crowd whispers back to life.

"Come on, folks," Rider says. "Back to your party. Masquerade only comes once a year." And then he calls to someone in the hallway. "Rachel? It's time to pour the Cristal."

I don't know if it's the promise of vintage champagne or the fact that all the excitement is over, but the crowd quickly disperses. Rider flashes a quick gesture to the gorilla behind me who finally releases his grip around my throat.

I crane my neck left and then right, swallowing hard before I say, "I want to press charges."

"Fuck you!" says Ansel. I feint a half-step toward him, and he cowers back in his corner. But he must trust in Rider's security because he whines from his sanctuary, "We only gave her what she asked for."

"Alix never asked to be fucked up the ass," I growl.

"She never told us to stop!"

Rider steps over to the guards by the door, asking a couple of quick questions, too quiet for me to catch. The men answer in short, sharp phrases. They hold their story, whatever it is, even when Rider challenges them.

He turns back to the rest of us, his face suddenly lined with exhaustion. "Help the Herzogs to their feet," he says to a pair of extra guards.

"What the fuck?" I demand.

"Go on." Rider ignores me. "They can wait in my office."

"What the *actual* fuck?" My fingers forge into rock-hard fists.

"Will you shut your goddamn mouth?" Rider snaps.

I seethe as Jonas and Ansel are half-dragged, half-escorted out of the room.

"I don't have a choice," Rider says, as soon as the jizzstains are gone.

"What—"

"They're club members. They were following club rules. Alix never used a safeword."

"Like they took the time to set up a safe, sane playing environment," I sneer.

"She never said anything," Rider says. "There were fifteen, twenty people watching. She never gave any indication she wanted out."

I glance over at her. She's still sitting on the edge of the couch. Still holding her water bottle like it might turn into a butterfly if she's careful enough. Still staring into space like she's halfway to the planet Zargox.

"They drugged her," I say.

"They didn't. Everyone was watching. They saw the auction. They saw everything that happened after. Alix wanted this."

"No one in her fucking right mind would want this," I snarl.

"She dropped to her knees without a second's hesitation," he says. "I watched her."

"And you didn't intervene? After what you saw—"

"I have to ask you to leave now," Rider says.

"What the—"

"The club has rules. It's dangerous to interrupt someone else's scene. You assaulted the Herzogs. Alix could have been hurt."

"Alix *is* hurt, asshole!"

"Hey!" Rider says sharply. "I'm the good guy here. I'm the only friend you've got in the room. And I'm telling you, it's time for you to leave. Go back to the greenroom. Get your shit out of your locker. Call your ride. And get the hell home."

"I'm not leaving without Alix."

Rider obliges me, turning toward my princess. "Alix." When she doesn't respond, he repeats her name with a hell of a lot more force. "Alix!" Her head wobbles as she turns toward him. It takes a lifetime for her to focus on his face. "Do you want to leave with Trap?"

She doesn't speak. But she does climb to her feet.

Rider gentles his voice, like he's talking to someone high on a ledge. "You don't have to go with him, Alix. We'll make sure you get somewhere safe."

In slow motion, she shakes her head. And then, like she's learning a new language, she says, "No. I'll go with Trap."

Rider frowns, but he says to the female guard, "Take her back to the greenroom. Get some salve on that wound. And get her dressed and back in the lobby."

Alix follows the guard like a well-trained dog.

"Trap—" Rider starts to say.

"Fuck you."

He sighs and starts to make some excuse. But I'm tired of excuses. I'm tired of assholes, all the way down. I shoulder past the guards and make my way to my own fucking greenroom.

I've got Charles and the Mercedes waiting by the curb for almost half an hour before Alix comes out. She's wearing her dress. Carrying her shoes by their ankle straps. She's ditched her mask and washed her face and she looks like maybe she just spent a wild night drinking and dancing.

I can just catch the edge of the mark left by Herzog's cane, peeking out above her bodice. It's red and it looks painful, but whatever ointment the guard applied seems to have made a difference.

Alix climbs into the back seat without using the hand I offer to help. I punch the button that raises the smoked glass screen between us and Charles. But I wait until we're out of Brooklyn before I start.

"What the fuck were you thinking?"

She doesn't answer, which only makes me angrier.

"Why did you follow me?" I demand.

Nothing.

"What the hell did you think would happen?"

Silence.

"How the *fuck* did you end up in that room with those cocksucking cumstains?"

She flinches at *cocksucking*. But she doesn't say a word.

"*Goddammit*, Alix! You killed Klaus Herzog with a steak knife, but it was too hard to ask a fucking guard to step in tonight?"

Her eyes glisten. Her lips move. I have to lean close to hear what she says. "I thought I could trust you."

I reel back. "You *can* trust me!"

She shakes her head, just a fraction of an inch. "You weren't there. You didn't keep me safe."

"I didn't know you followed me! Jesus fuck, woman, what were you thinking?"

She blinks. "I wasn't."

"Wasn't what?"

"Wasn't thinking." And then, like she's just figured something out: "I'm broken."

"The fuck you are," I say, loud, because I want to be right.

"My brain doesn't work right."

"Your brain is just fine."

She shakes her head. And this time, when she looks at me, I finally get the feeling she sees me. "I need to go back," she says, with more focus than I've heard since dinner.

"There's no way in hell Gage Rider's letting either one of us back in that club."

"No. Not the club."

I wait.

"I need to go to Herzog's house."

"What the actual fuck do you think—"

"That's where I lost it."

"Lost *what?*"

I see her test answers in her mind. I can practically hear all the things she doesn't say: *My dignity. My value. My mind.* But out loud, she says, "Take me there, and I promise I'll never ask for another thing again."

"Goddammit, Alix—"

I see her knees twitch beneath that fucking green dress. I watch her hands lift, on their way to her head. She fights back. She stops herself. But she's shaking from the effort.

I don't want to be the man who tortures her. Not tonight, when she's already been through so much. Not ever. "Alix…"

"Please," she begs.

And God help me, I do it. I lower the screen between us and Charles. I give him the fucking address. And I lean my head back, close my eyes, and try to believe I'm doing the right thing.

33

ALIX

Trap's given in, but he's angry with me. Emotions vibrate off him like heat. His knuckles are bruised, and I wonder who he punched. I hope he hasn't burned his bridges with Gage Rider. The freeport shouldn't lose another top-ten client over me.

After fifteen minutes of silence, Trap mutters something under his breath. He leans forward and breaks into the limo's well-stocked cooler. When he passes me a bottle of water, I shake my head, but he says. "Take it."

I do.

And I have to admit, I feel better after I drink it.

I'm trying to remember everything that happened at the club. Everything's crystal clear, right up to the moment Jonas Herzog clicked his tongue. After that, it's like I'm watching myself from a drone that hovers near the ceiling. I can see what the Herzogs did. I watch how I reacted. But I don't remember anything about how I felt.

I'm tired. So tired. I think that if I fall asleep, all of this will drift away. I won't even have the drone view anymore. I'll be back in the penthouse, sad that Trap stepped out for a business meeting. I'll be ready for bed after a fabulous dinner at a world-class restaurant.

I lean my head against the window, but the vibration of the moving car keeps jolting me upright. Trap swears again and wriggles out of his jacket. He thrusts it at me, but I don't reach out. Once again, he orders: "Take it."

I fold his coat neatly and use it as a pillow. I'm asleep before we pass Newark Airport.

When I jerk awake, I can't figure out where I am. The car has stopped. I'm shivering, like I've been walking to the North Pole. My entire body aches, but there's a special pain flaring deep inside my armpits. My dress feels like it's flayed the skin off my chest, like it's rubbing against the bare bones of my sternum and ribs.

"Where are we?" I ask, peering out the window.

"Herzog's house," Trap says. He sounds like his throat is lined with shattered glass.

I open my door and step onto a paved driveway. My feet are bare. I'm pretty sure I'm never strapping stiletto heels around my ankles again.

My teeth start to chatter. Trap reaches inside the car and retrieves the jacket I used as a pillow. I drape it over my shoulders, but he makes me put it on all the way, slipping my arms through the sleeves.

It smells like his rosemary soap. I immediately stop shivering.

An iron gate blocks our way. A brick fence stretches to the right and left, at least ten feet high. It's topped with razor wire.

"So?" Trap asks. "How do we get in?"

"I don't know. I was never allowed out here."

There's a security pad to the left of the gate. When I cross to it, a floodlight snaps on, streaming down from the top of the brick fence. I shield my face with my hand, trying to blink away my sudden blindness. This type of spotlight feels familiar, and I realize I'm thinking of the kitten auction, of standing onstage next to Gage Rider.

"There's no number pad," I say. "No combination."

Trap scowls. "Those are biometric scanners. Fingerprints at the bottom. Retinas in the box above."

I should know that. I've seen the scanners at the freeport. My brain isn't working right.

There's a button by the scanner. I push it.

"Don't bother," Trap says. "According to Asher, the place is abandoned."

But before we can turn back to the car, a reedy voice trembles through the speaker: "*Wer ist da?*"

Trap swears. My stomach churns with sudden acid. I think I know that voice. I press the button again. "Ursula?"

It takes a moment, but the speaker crackles again. "Who is there?"

This time I'm certain. "Ursula? It's me. Alix."

"Alix!" she says. "*Lobe Gott!* You're back, *liebes Mädchen*. You come home!" Her accent always bristled, but now it's as thick as the wall beside me.

"Can you let me in, Ursula? Can you open the gate?"

"Is *Meistern* with you?"

Trap waves his hand in a hurry-up gesture. If I say no, I don't know if Ursula will open the gate. I lie and say, "Of course."

There's a pause, where I wonder if she understood me. But then gears start to move, and the iron gate slides to the side. Trap looks back at Charles, who's standing beside the Mercedes. Trap says to me, "Can you make it, walking up to the house?"

I don't know. I say, "Yes."

Traps issues an order to Charles. "Wait for us here."

"Of course, sir."

I wish we could drive all the way there, but I understand the danger. We don't want our getaway car trapped inside the gate if we need to escape fast.

We start to walk up the driveway. Weeds break through the asphalt. The grass on either side of the path grows up to my knees.

We round two bends before we can see the house. In the three years I lived there, I never ventured past the huge lawn that surrounds the mansion. At first, I wasn't allowed outside at all. Then, I didn't care about anything that lay beyond my prison.

The yard is growing wild now. The house looks deserted. But as we approach the great circular driveway, the front door opens. A black shape is framed in the golden light that streams down three weed-strewn steps.

I wait until Trap and I are on the bottom one before I say "Ursula?"

She steps back, just enough for me to see her face. I know those Slavic cheekbones as well as I know my own. I recognize the flat brown eyes, the mouth carved into a permanent frown, the hair pulled back in a painfully severe bun.

But the woman on the steps has lost at least twenty pounds since I saw her in June. Her intimidating biceps bulge over bat-wing flaps of loose skin. She missed a button when she pulled on her shirt. We must have woken her. It's four in the morning.

She's secured her khaki pants with a slash of fabric to keep them from falling over her hips. It's not until I step into the foyer that I realize she's using one of Master's ties as a belt.

"Alix," she says. "You walk? Where is car?" She glances at Trap, like she's just now realized he's not the man she expects. "You! Where is Master?"

Her voice rises in panic. For three long years, I hated the way she enforced Master's laws. But something about the terror on her face snags a hook deep inside my gut.

I'm trying to think of a gentle way to tell her, but Trap doesn't hesitate. "He's dead," Trap says.

Ursula's hand flies to her mouth. "*Nein!*"

Trap pushes past her like she's a moth-eaten curtain. "Your *master* won't be coming home again," he says.

His mouth twists on the title. He doesn't know Master's power. He doesn't understand why Ursula crumples to her knees.

"Please," she says, reaching for the hem of my emerald dress. "You leave with Master. He take you to party. He tell me dress you like the pretty one, the lady from the movies."

Her words are tumbling, faster and faster. Trap looks disgusted, but all I feel is pity.

"I wait for him," Ursula says. "For him and you, both. I keep house clean. I pay electric bill and gas. Water too. For Master, so house is nice when he come home."

Trap starts to say something, but I rest my hand on his arm. "Thank you, Ursula," I say. "You've done a good job. Now go back to sleep. I'll tell you everything that happened when we eat breakfast."

"I make you good breakfast," she says. "Master likes all his girls eat big meal. I make bacon and potatoes. Toast with lots of butter. We have no egg, but I make you good, good breakfast."

"Thank you," I say again. "But go to sleep now. I want to walk Trap through the house."

Ursula frets, but she shuffles off to her room behind the kitchen. Trap waits until she's gone before he says, "What the fuck is this shitshow?"

"This shitshow was my life."

He shakes his head like he's waking from some bad dream. But I know the nightmare is only beginning.

"Let me show you around," I say.

We start on the third floor. I show him Master's bedroom. Ursula has kept everything exactly the way it was the day Master drove us down to Dover. His clothes hang in the closet, shirts sorted by color, starched and ironed until they practically stand on their own.

I open the panel built into the back of the closet. I show Trap all of Master's toys—the paddles and the riding crops, the restraints made of leather and steel, the dildos meant to hurt, and the butt plugs designed for maximum penetration.

"Holy shit," Trap says. But he doesn't understand. Not really. Not yet.

I find the glass-faced device that Master used, still resting on its charger where he left it when we drove to the freeport. I palm it, and I say to Trap, "Let me show you where I lived."

We walk down to the second floor. My fingers find light switches automatically. My feet remember that the third step from the bottom squeaks. Master will beat me if I make noise while he's sleeping.

I know the house is empty, except for Ursula. I know the other women were sold off long ago. But I see Rayna in her bedroom, offering half the chocolate bar her *gadzhe* brought her just this afternoon. Simona is lying on her bed, applying bright blue nail polish even though she knows she'll have to cover it with pink before Ursula calls us for dinner. Lilyana laughs when we pass by, delighted to see me, promising to tell me all the stories I've missed while I've been gone.

"Here," I say, when we reach my room. "This is my bed." I gesture toward the mattress. "My closet." My matching blue smocks still hang there. Those are my only clothes, of course. Master doesn't believe in underwear. No bras. No panties—just like tonight, while Trap and I sat in the window at Nourriture. Like tonight at Kynk.

I reach for the black plastic band I stored on its charger before Master took me through the gates. It's heavier than I remembered. The clasp feels more secure as I fasten it around my wrist.

"Tap it," I say, passing the palm-size screen to Trap. A display springs to life, a schematic diagram of the house. "Pick a room. Any room."

Scowling, he drops a finger on Library. My wrist buzzes, and

I laugh. "That's too easy. I can get there in thirty seconds. Forty-five tops. I was never punished for being late to the library."

"This is fucked up," Trap says.

I nod, because he's right. "Let me show you the ground floor."

I whisper outside the kitchen, keeping my voice low so I don't wake Ursula. "This is where we took our meals, all us women together, until Master sold the others. I taught them English here. We had three meals a day, all big. Master likes his slaves to have a little flesh."

Trap barely glances at the table. "Come on," he says. "Let's get out of here."

"But we aren't done yet," I say.

I take him to the library. The books are on the shelves, exactly how I left them. "This is where I spent most of my time. With these books, I could travel anywhere in the world. I went to Paris. To London. To Moscow and Madrid. I lived a hundred years ago and five hundred, centuries before Master was born."

"Let's go, Alix," Trap says.

"We're almost done." It's sweet that he's so upset.

I take him into Master's study.

"This is where Master held his special meetings," I say.

"Come on, Princess."

"The chair's new, of course. You saw the old one, in Master's gallery at the freeport."

"I think I understand now."

"There's the fireplace poker," I say. "Why don't you pick it up? Feel how heavy it is. Imagine shoving that inside me. Imagine me licking it clean, after you're done."

"Alix—"

"Look! There's a letter opener. Do you think it's sharp enough to draw blood? Why don't you press harder? Come on! Really, really try."

"I'm not—"

"The frame's still here! The last time Master tied me to it, he kept me hanging for two full days. He made me drink my piss when I couldn't hold it in anymore."

"Okay," Trap says. "I get it. I understand. I heard what you told me before. I listened to the words, but I didn't realize just how sick that cocksucker was. Of course you can't forget what happened here. I had no right to ask why you didn't fight back at the club tonight. I was a fucking idiot to judge you."

The words should be a balm. They should soothe me, the way arnica soothes a cane's burning stripes. I should feel some sort of release.

But I need something else. I need something more.

I turn to Trap, pressing against him, taking him by surprise. I find his mouth with mine, and I melt the ice of his lips. My tongue tangles with his, and I breathe his breath and I know he's breathing mine. His hand splays across the back of my head, and my fingers push into the hard muscle of his back. I'm greedy and I'm grateful and I'm drinking deeper than I can ever remember drinking before.

But that's not it. That's not all I need. He has to understand me. He has to know exactly what happened, here in Master's house.

We come up for air, panting like we've run a marathon tied together at the knee. I rest my forehead against his. I trace the line of his jaw with my fingernail. And I whisper what I need to make it real, to take it back, to make Trap understand, once and for all and forever.

"Use me, Master. Tie me to the frame. Fuck me with the poker. Keep me hanging till I beg for mercy, and leave me for another full day. Take me down, and fuck my ass and call me Slave forever."

34

TRAP

"Jesus Christ!" I stagger back, banging the side of my knee on the coffee table. Pain spikes up my leg, but it doesn't matter. It's nothing, compared to the torture this room has witnessed.

I don't realize I pushed Alix until she catches herself against the fireplace mantel. "Please," she says, stumbling toward me. I reach out to help her balance, but she sinks to her knees. She grasps her head with both hands, pushing her elbows back to raise her perfect tits. This is something else Herzog did to her, something he required. "Fuck me, Master," she begs. "Fuck your helpless slave up the ass!"

I'm the one who taught her those words. She lay in my bed, blushing, whispering, and I taught her it was okay to say what she wanted. I said she could talk about her pussy, her tits, and yes, she could use the word ass.

But I never thought she'd beg for the one thing that terrifies her.

I can't tell her what she wants. I can't say what she needs. But I can say I won't be the one who breaks her. "I'm not your fucking master," I growl.

She crawls forward. She kisses my dirty shoe.

I smother the reflex to kick her away. Alix isn't the enemy. I won't fight the woman I love.

But it's a damn good thing she already shredded Klaus Herzog on my dining room floor. Because if she hadn't, I'd hunt the cocksucker down, tie him to his goddamn frame, and take him apart with a pair of red-hot pliers.

"Alix," I say, sinking onto the floor beside her. "Princess."

She's sobbing, desperate, pressing her face into the fucking rug. Her begging sounds like the world's most fucked-up prayer; she wants me to do things that can't be possible, that no human body can bear. The fact that she can even *say* those words turns my stomach, and I fight the urge to puke.

I catch her wrists, pulling them close to my chest to keep her from grinding her mouth into the carpet. "Stop it!" I shake her shoulders to reinforce the order. When she tells me how she wants me to rip apart her snatch, I bellow, "Shut your fucking mouth!"

She cowers before me, trembling with terror or the after-rush of adrenaline. I don't know which of us is breathing harder; we both sound like hurricanes. Still gripping her wrists, I shift so that my back leans against the leather chair.

"Alix," I say, searching for words. "Sweet, sweet Alix. You don't deserve this. You don't deserve any of this."

She wails. The sound starts low, but it slides high. It's the sound of utter sorrow, of perfect loss. It's broken dolls and buried pets and mean girls whispering by lockers. It's choosing a brother over the rest of a family and losing him to the devil. It's losing innocence, day after day, night after night, minute by fucking minute in this hellhole.

"What can I do?" she finally asks. "How can I be worthy?"

I don't understand. Her words make no sense.

Until they do.

I said she didn't *deserve* to suffer. I meant it wasn't right. It wasn't fair. But she's too broken to hear that. She heard she isn't worthy. She's not good enough to torture.

"Fucking Christ." I don't know where to start. I don't know how to clear the rubble, how to reach her fractured foundation. But there's no way to build anything on an utterly shattered base.

"I thought you loved me," she whispers.

I'm almost too tired to say the words out loud, but I owe them to her. "I do."

"I thought you'd do anything for me."

The truth is nearly too heavy to lift. "I thought so too."

"But you won't do this."

"No. I won't."

"I'm asking for it. I accept it. I'm giving myself to you, making you my master."

"I can't do it."

"Can't? Or won't?"

"Jesus Christ. Does it matter?"

"You were happy enough to hurt me when it helped you. When your Beast told you to do it."

"This is different."

"How?"

"I always gave you a safeword, gave you protection. I never took away your choice. You were never my slave. You are my partner."

"Are," she says, repeating the verb I just used.

I hear the meaning. She's giving me a choice.

I can rewrite our story. I can change the rules. Make *are* into *were*. She *was* my partner. Now she's my slave.

"No," I say, like she asked me a question.

"Please?" she asks, as if it's that simple.

I bend my head. I kiss her wrists, both of them, just above

where my grip has left a red mark. Her skin is raw from Jonas and Ansel's fucking jute rope. "Let's go home," I say.

She shakes her head slowly. "I'm staying."

"You can't do that." I don't bother shouting. She's talking about doing the impossible.

"I can. There's food. Water. The roof doesn't leak." Her lips actually quirk into something that resembles a smile. "Ursula's here."

"What the fuck are you going to do here?"

"Live."

I start to tell her everything she'll miss, but the list is so long, I don't know where to begin. It doesn't matter, though. None of it does.

Herzog broke her more than I ever imagined.

"I have to go," I say, praying she'll change her mind. Knowing she won't.

"I'll miss you." She takes my hand. Turns it over. Brushes her lips over my knuckles, the ones I split fighting to free her from Jonas and Ansel.

I push myself to my knees, to my feet. I cross to the door. I try one more time. "It isn't safe."

"Nothing ever is," she says, from her place on the hearth. She closes her fingers around the poker that lies on the floor before she meets my eyes with perfect deliberation. "Master."

She offers me the metal rod. It's her final bid.

I leave, because that's the only choice I have.

35

ALIX

I stay in the study long after the front door closes. I imagine Trap walking down the winding driveway. I picture him getting into the Mercedes. I hear him telling Charles to drive him home, to the freeport.

I miss Trap already.

But I've never been good at holding on to the people I love.

I loved my mother, but she got sick and died.

I loved my brother, but he sold me to Master and died.

Did I love Master? Do I still?

I feared him. I fought him—at least for the first year. I hated the way he hurt me, the physical pain he caused my body.

But Master gave me strength I never knew I had. Because of him, I outlasted every woman on the second floor, every pawn.

I became the queen.

Master formed me. Shaped me. He taught me how much my body can take.

He gave me all that power—even, in the end, the power to

kill him. He made me the woman I am today. I have to love him for that. It's a sick love. A twisted love. A desperate love. But a true love, all the same.

Dead mother. Dead twin. Dead Master.

With a track record like that, I can't let myself love Trap anymore. I can't give him what he needs. He won't give me what I need.

I couldn't explain while he was here. But in the gray light of dawn, as I shiver on the hearth, as my arms and legs ache with cold and exhaustion and the aftermath of what Master's brothers did to me in New York...

Now I know the words I should have said. The explanation of why I need what I need. The true meaning of love.

This is what I should have told Trap: The worst things in the world can happen to me, but I can survive them if I know I have your love. Hurt me in the most terrible way I can ever imagine being hurt, but be there in the morning. And then, at last, I'll finally be free.

My mother didn't stay. My brother didn't stay. Master didn't stay.

But I truly believed that Trap was the one. Trap was my true love. Trap would stay.

But he didn't.

He left.

And now I'm alone forever.

When my teeth start to rattle in my head, I pull myself off the hearth. My bones ache from staying in one position for so long. I have to hold the banister, hauling myself up the stairs.

In my bedroom, I strip off my emerald dress. It's filthy. The hem is ripped out. The seam of the bodice has split.

I pull on my blue smock. I touch the lifeline that still circles my wrist. And I walk downstairs to take my place at the long pine table, waiting for Ursula to make me breakfast.

36

TRAP

M y entire life, I've known right from wrong.
It was right to stay in that stinking hut in Congo,
even though I was scared out of my twelve-year-old mind, even
though I knew people were dying around me and I might never
see my father again.

It was right to ditch management training at an investment
bank and go with my gut, opening Diamond Freeport as a tax
haven for billionaires.

It was wrong to look the other way when some of my clients
skated on the shadier side of the law, but all we're talking about
is money and who really gives a fuck?

But hearing Alix beg me last night… Listening to the things
she needed me to do… Walking out of that house of pain and
torture, leaving Alix there, accepting her decision even though
every cell in my body told me I'd die if I walked away… I don't
have a clue if that's fucking right or wrong.

She's a grown woman. She's been through more than any

human being I know. She's allowed to exercise her own free will, to ask for what she needs, to demand it.

But I can't hurt her the way she needs to be hurt. I can't be that man. Can't live that life.

Jesus Christ, how can I live with losing her?

I only wake at noon because the sun is shining straight in my eyes. I check my phone before I hit the john, hoping, actually *praying* Alix has sent a text.

I can get back to Herzog's in thirty minutes. Fuck the speeding tickets. If she wants to go to the penthouse instead, I'll send the helicopter to pick her up. Hell, she can have the jet and any destination in the world.

She hasn't sent a text.

But I've got three unanswered calls from Rider. The last one was three hours ago and he left a two-word voicemail. "Call me."

I start pacing my bedroom. There are two ways this can play out. One: He wants to rip me a new asshole for fucking up his sex club Masquerade. Two: He wants to pull his holdings out of the freeport, screw my business the way I screwed his. Either way, fuck him.

But the phone rings while I'm still staring at it, and his name fills the screen. Apparently, he's not going to get the hint—I don't want to talk. So I stab the green icon and say, "What?"

"Is Alix all right?"

The question knocks me back on my ass. She's totally fucked up. And there isn't a thing on earth I can do to save her.

But that's not what Rider's asking. He wants to know if she'll be calling the cops. He wants to know if he needs to bring in his lawyer. Maybe his insurance adjuster. But he won't. Not for Alix. "She's fine," I say. But the lie tastes like shit, so I change it. "She will be."

I hear his exhale, long and slow, before he asks, "And you?"

What the fuck? "I'm fine." Those gorillas he hires know how to apply a chokehold without putting a guy in the hospital. Or worse.

"I want to make sure we're okay," he says. "You and me. I had to throw you out for breaking the scene—club rules."

"Fuck your club rules. They were killing her."

"*I* saw three consenting adults."

"Then *you* need to get your fucking eyes checked."

"Trap—"

"Look. Grown-ups have the right to do whatever they want with their own bodies. I don't give a shit if Rutherford T. Wellington wants to dress in diapers and let his sister Bunny shove diamond-tipped dildos up his ass while he sings the French national anthem. Keep your greenrooms and your kitten auctions and your fucking vintage champagne. But when you choose to drink with a pair of fucking rapists and make *me* walk... That's when we're *not okay*."

"You feel better now, getting that off your chest?" His tone reminds me that he's used to fighting on a solid sheet of ice, holding a five-foot club with a carbon-fiber blade on one end.

"Fuck you," I say, too tired to come up with anything better.

"For the record," he says. "I wouldn't drink with those two if you paid me a million dollars."

"You'll just take their million for the club."

"For Wounded Heroes United, yeah. The club won't keep a penny."

"Just their membership dues, then. That's all you put in your pocket. What's that, fifty grand a year?"

"A hundred," he says. "Each." Before I can sneer a response, he adds, "And you should be damn glad I take it."

"Why's that?" I'm honestly curious about what bullshit he'll feed me.

"Because members come back. Members RSVP to exclusive events. Members can be found in predictable places at predictable times."

He's telling me the door's still open. He'll let me take another shot at those fucking scumbags.

Maybe, just possibly, Rider was thinking more clearly than I was last night.

And just in case I've missed the fine print, he says, "You headed out in such a hurry last night you left a couple of things behind in security. I'm afraid they got lost in all the confusion."

The syringes. He destroyed the fucking evidence his goons took off me.

"Thanks," I say.

"Let me check the members list for our Halloween event. I'll let you know if that's a good one for you to check out."

"I appreciate that," I say. And I do.

"And let me know if you'll be around the freeport next Wednesday," he says. "I'm meeting a dealer to add a Flowing Hair Silver Dollar to my collection. Dinner's on me, if you're free."

I know a peace offering when I hear it. I take him up on his offer, and I hang up confident there's one relationship I didn't totally fuck up last night.

Next up: I need to call Best. I have to explain why I never showed at the club's service door with two packages in urgent need of transportation by the best wetwork team in North America.

At least *this* clusterfuck didn't result in eight guys dead.

When the fuck did that become my standard? No eight bodies, so everything's great.

Nothing's great.

Alix is gone.

And I can't come up with any way I'm ever going to see her again.

ALIX

In Master's house, I'm completely free.

If I want to, I can sleep all day. I can stay up all night. I can open every window in the house, letting the air conditioner labor as the late August heat fills the rooms with heavy humidity. I can seal the house shut and lower the temperature to sixty degrees.

There's no reason to charge my cell phone. I don't want to talk to anyone. No one will ever call me.

I don't have to worry about dressing for business meetings or casual day at the freeport, for workouts in the gym or fancy dinners out. I don't need to decide between sandals and sneakers, between stilettos and practical pumps. I just wear my blue smock.

Ursula cooks three meals a day—breakfast at eight, lunch at noon, dinner at six. Now that I'm living in the house, she has groceries delivered—milk and eggs, meat and bread. She's a good cook, and she makes enough for six people at every meal. I eat if I'm hungry. I scrape my plate into the garbage once I'm full. Ursula feeds the leftovers to Master's crows.

Ursula is the perfect companion. She spends most of the day in her room off the kitchen. Her English, never strong, has grown brittle in her time alone. She asks nothing of me. Accepts me, exactly as I am.

I spend most of my time in the library. I learned a lot about art in the first three years I spent in this house. I applied that knowledge when I lived at the freeport. Now, it's time to read for fun. I spend an entire day studying Hieronymus Bosch's *Last Judgment*. I spend another on Rothko's *Untitled (Red)*.

I wear my lifeline, keeping it fastened to my right wrist, even though no one will ever call me to any room in the house. No one will ever demand I offer up my body.

One night, I get a flogger from Master's closet, the one with the spiked steel tips. I try to strike my nipples, but I can't build enough momentum. My clit takes one blow sharp enough to steal my breath, but once I know the pain to expect I can't find it again. It's a waste of time to sling the leather strands over my shoulder. I feel nothing when the metal claws my back.

I try some of Master's tricks. I can make my eyes water by clamping binder clips onto my clit and nipples. But no matter how determined I am to keep them there, how hard I bite my lip, how deep I dig my nails into my bleeding palms, I free myself before Master ever would.

I use the giant dildos. Butt plugs too. I never let myself use lube, not even spit, because Master would not approve. No matter how I force my pussy or my ass, I can't generate one thousandth of the pain Master could deliver with a single twitch of his little finger.

But that's what I need: Pain. Something to remind me I'm alive. Something to tell me everything happened for a reason. Something to say this is why I killed a man, why I gave myself to his brothers without fighting, why I lost Trap and will live the rest of my life lonely and alone.

Alone except for Ursula.

After the first week, I think of one more thing to try. I find Ursula in the kitchen and ask, "After lunch? Will you help me in the shower?"

She nods gruffly and goes back to making our Cobb salads.

When we've eaten—just a few tense bites for me—she follows me upstairs. She runs the water while I take off my smock. She shakes her head at what she sees, then frowns and reaches for the familiar plastic jar: Brazilian Bikini Wax.

The warm wax is more soothing than arnica. When Ursula rips off the papers, I literally see stars. Every nerve from my knees to my navel sings a long-forgotten note. My muscles scream for mercy.

After, when she lets me rinse with cool, clear water, I feel like I've been born again.

That night, Ursula is extra-jumpy at dinner. She's made sauerbraten and spaetzle, braised red cabbage and three types of potatoes. I manage a bite of everything, but I push back from the table while she's still organizing bottles of mustard on a tray.

"You cannot go!" she says.

"I'm full."

"Not full. You wait for sweet. I make apple dumplings, just for Master."

Trap told her Master's dead. He said the words flat out. She can't have any doubt.

But she hasn't asked me about Master, not once in the past week. And now she says, "I wax you in shower. You clean for Master. He come home tonight."

I shake my head. "No. He's not coming home."

"You lie!"

"It's not a lie. Ursula, I promise you. Master will never come home again."

She shakes her head like a toddler refusing spinach. "He gone many days now. Weeks. But this is night he come home. You make new movie tonight. You make many new movie."

The only "movie" I've ever made is the one that proves Ursula dreams in vain. I need to show her the video of Master dying in Trap's dining room. Maybe then she'll believe me.

But she's babbling on, happy with the fantasy she's weaving. "So many movies. So many men."

"What are you talking about?"

"Master make movie."

Has she seen the viral video? Is she trapped in some strange fantasy about Master's death? "Master didn't make that," I say. "Master's *brothers* made it."

"Yes!" she says like I've just recited the entire Bible in German. "*Mein* Jonas. *Mein* Ansel. You make many movie with them."

"Not *with* them." I'm getting frustrated.

"With them! Yes! See! Come see!"

She grabs my hand and drags me toward her bedroom. The Ursula I live with now is greatly diminished from the woman who ran Master's domain, but she still has more strength than I can resist. She pulls me into her room and forces me to sit at the little desk beside her bed.

A laptop computer sits open in front of me. The screen has shifted to a picture of Master, his milk-blue eyes staring out like he's trying to read my mind. Ursula kisses her fingertip and touches Master's lips on the screen. Then she scrapes the track-pad, forcing the computer to wake.

A video is framed on the screen.

"Movie!" Ursula says proudly. "You watch movie!"

I'm looking at Master's study, at the leather chair that replaced the one with claw feet. A man sits deep on the cushion, his legs spread, his head thrust back.

A woman kneels between his legs. She's wearing a headband studded with a unicorn horn. Her tight white top is fastened at the neck with a plaid necktie. Her matching schoolgirl skirt has flipped up, exposing her ass. Her butt is plugged with a metal cone that ends in a stream of horsehair.

She's stroking the man's giant erection.

She's making whinnying sounds.

She's saying, "Thank you, Daddy. Thank you for my pony."

She's me.

She's me, and that's one of Master's special guests. He's the Reverend Bobby Quinton, and he's about to take Jesus's name in vain when he comes all over my pouting face while I tell him I'm Daddy's girl, his special girl, the only girl who loves him.

I sit back in Ursula's chair. "Where did this come from?"

"Master," she says. Like that's the answer to everything.

And to Ursula that *is* the answer to everything. Master is the heart of her world. The subject of her catechism. Master is the beginning and the end, the alpha and omega, the reason she wakes up in the morning, and the last thing she thinks about before she sleeps at night.

Master filmed me with his special guest. The picture is black and white. The sound is a little hollow. But the images are crisp and clear, every detail captured.

Master taught his brothers. Master showed Jonas and Ansel how to harness video to make a billion dollars.

"How many other movies did Master make?" I ask.

Ursula looks confused. "All."

I try again, digging out my few words in German. "*Ein? Zehn? Wie viele*...movies?"

"All," Ursula says again. Her fingers slip over the trackpad, and she brings up the list of files on the computer. They're all MP4 files, all "movies". The dates range over the past three years. There are at least two dozen.

I move the cursor to a file at random. "Okay?" I ask Ursula.

"You watch," she says proudly, like she's presenting me with a golden crown.

I click the file, and the screen fills with moving pictures.

38

TRAP

"Trap?" From the tone in Susan Richards' voice, she's already said my name a few times. I look up from the black-and-white display on my computer screen. My eyes feel like I've dragged them over a coral reef. I blink a few times, which doesn't help.

"What do you need?" My question is sharper than necessary, but it's too late to take it back.

"You have a Chamber of Commerce meeting in Wilmington at three," she says.

It's 2:30 now. I should have left half an hour ago.

Fuck it. "Tell them an emergency came up. I'll see them next month."

Her lips purse. She doesn't like to lie. But she knows better than to call me on it.

"Anything else?" I ask, which is a dick move, because there are about ten thousand other things I'm supposed to be doing, and I'm late on at least half of them, but none of that is Susan's fault.

Before she can answer, I'm staring at the computer screen again. I've hired an outfit that does drone surveillance. Some asshole's got a life marginally worse than mine, sitting in a dark room somewhere, managing eyes in the sky over Herzog's house in the woods.

The feed comes in 24/7. So far, no one has entered the house. No one has left. Twice, cars have been let through the gate, and I've watched that creepy German woman carry groceries up the steps.

I haven't seen Alix. Not a fucking glimpse.

"Let me know if you need anything," Susan says, before she backs out of my office.

I need someone to take point on Herzog's painting, *The Concert*. Are we giving it back to the Gardner? Taking the reward? Opening the floodgates for speculation about other stolen goods at the freeport?

Alix would know about past thefts. She'd compile a list of middlemen. She'd balance what's best for the museum, for the world of art lovers, and for the freeport's long-term health.

But Alix isn't here.

I also need someone to figure out what the fuck is wrong with the maintenance staff. Two supervisors have quit in the last three months, and there isn't a janitor who's worked here for longer than a year.

Alix would interview the current employees. She'd use her fancy psychology terms to figure out their motivations and evaluate their job satisfaction. She'd come up with charts and bullet points and presentations, and she'd stem the tide of constant turnover.

But Alix isn't here.

I need someone to talk to. Someone to shoot the shit with at the end of a long workday. Someone I can touch without the Beast going apeshit inside my skull.

But Alix isn't fucking here.

She isn't here, and she isn't coming back, and no amount of staring at a drone feed is going to change that. But I waste another hour watching black-and-white footage of Herzog's house because I can't think of another fucking thing to do.

That's not true.

I can drive up there. I can punch the button on the front gate. I can tell Alix I'll do what she wants. Give her what she needs.

Tie her to the fucking frame.

Fuck her with the goddamn poker.

Take her up the ass.

Call her Slave, and make her call me Master.

Here's the really fucked-up thing: If any other woman in the world wanted me to do that, I could. The Beast would shred my brain, and I wouldn't step out of the shower for three months after I finished, but I could do it. All of it.

But not for Alix. Not *with* Alix. Not *to* Alix.

I love her too much to play the one scene that would keep her in my life.

The intercom buzzes, but I ignore it. The workday ends. People head home to their families. They eat dinner. They watch TV. They live their fucking lives.

And I stare at the drone footage until long after the sun sets somewhere over the Delaware Bay.

39

TRAP

The freeport parking lot has turned into a carnival for the Labor Day picnic, and I'm about to lose my fucking mind.

One kid is melting down because the six-foot teddy bear he just won has a yellow bow tie instead of a red one.

Another kid is screaming because she just spilled ice cream on her favorite dress, the one that looks like Cinderella's ball gown, complete with long white sleeves.

Two girls are trying to tear apart the ring toss booth, and a boy is peeing in the dino dig sandbox.

I stalk off to the open bar and get myself another Big Oyster IPA. I'm still taking my first gulp when Mac sidles up to get his own cold one. Once he's served, he salutes me with his Solo cup and says, "Any idea where Alix is? I really want the missus to meet her."

I tell the guilty Rottweiler gnawing at my stomach to shut

the fuck up. "She couldn't make it. I'm sure she's sorry not to be here."

Mac makes a sympathetic sound, like a giant clearing his throat. "Maybe next time."

He gets a second beer and heads off to give it to his missus.

I wander around to the front of the warehouse, where the caterers have set up two dozen half-barrel grills. The smell of barbecue chicken and spareribs is enough to make my mouth water. I pick up a plate and get in line behind Amber, one of the receptionists.

She's juggling three plates, including one piled high with something that looks like broccoli salad. "Is Alix around?" she asks. "I wanted to thank her for making sure the caterer served my favorite!"

"Sorry," I say. "Something came up at the last minute. She had to head out of town."

Amber's pout is pretty. "Oh, that sucks! I'll send her an email then."

"You do that," I say, even though I know Alix isn't checking email.

She hasn't logged into her freeport account for two weeks. Her phone's dead too. She hasn't spent a penny on one of my credit cards, and there's no record of her grabbing cash from an ATM.

Electronically speaking, Alix Key has ceased to exist.

And that thought sparks the chain of waking nightmares that keeps me up at night. I'm worried about Alix. Worried about what she's doing in that shitshow of a haunted mansion. Worried that the crazy German woman guarding the door has gone psycho with a meat cleaver. Worried that Alix wants me, needs me, but doesn't know she can ask.

I slip my hand into my front pocket, where I've got the keys to the Porsche. Thirty fucking minutes.

But I can't just go to Herzog's house for a joyride. If I appear on the doorstep, Alix will think I've changed my mind.

She'll think I'm ready to hurt her like the animal she killed. She'll think that's all she has to live for—my breaking her down to be my mindless, sex-toy slave.

Susan Richards steps to my side with a stack of envelopes embossed with the Diamond Freeport logo. "Does Alix—"

"I don't know," I interrupt. "Alix isn't here. Alix isn't coming. She got called out of town. Had to leave without warning. I don't know when she's coming back, and I don't know how to reach her, and I don't know when I'll next be talking to her, so I can't help with anything at all."

Susan shifts her sunglasses to her hair, so she can look directly in my eyes. "I was going to ask if Alix wanted to run the raffle, since she's the one who came up with all the prizes. But apparently the answer is no. And I'm guessing you don't feel like playing emcee either."

I clench my fist around the Porsche key. "Sorry," I say, because none of this is Susan's fault. "I'll do it."

She stares me down like she's my mother, giving me shit for forgetting to take out the garbage. But finally, she hands over the prizes. "All you have to do is pull a ticket and read off the number. Each envelope has a certificate for the winner; they can pick up the actual prize from Security tomorrow. The name of each prize is printed on the flap."

Her manicured nail points out the words on the first envelope: Tickets for four to the Dover Motor Speedway. The handwriting belongs to Alix.

"Trap?" Susan asks, and I wonder how long I've been staring at those perfect letters.

I shake my head. "Sorry," I say again. "I've got it. Pull the ticket. Name the prize. Pick them up tomorrow."

She rests her fingers on my arm. I'm pretty sure that's the first time she's actually touched me, aside from a formal handshake when she interviewed for the job. Her hands are cool. They remind me of my mother's. Maybe that's why the Beast settles for a lazy harrumph without going berserk.

"Call her," Susan says.

My throat aches with misery. "I can't."

"Why do men always say that?"

"Sometimes it's true."

Susan presses a little harder. "I've heard the way she talks about you. I know she really cares. Whatever fight the two of you had, you'll get past it if you talk it out."

I know Susan means well. She thinks she's helping me. Helping Alix, too. There's no way I can tell her how far off base she is. I can't imagine repeating the first words of Alix's demand to this good-hearted, well-intentioned woman.

"Thanks," I say. "I'll think about it."

"Don't think. Do."

I take the envelopes and head to the stage at the front of the midway. At least I can make my employees happy, even if my own life has turned to shit.

40

ALIX

M aster recorded me giving a blowjob to a man he called
The General, who thanked me by pulling out hanks of
my hair and kicking me with his spit-polished boots.

Master recorded me with the Counselor, who tied me to the
frame in Master's office and beat me with a crop until shit and
piss ran down my legs.

Master recorded me wearing nothing but a nun's wimple,
my wrists in a yoke, kissing the amethyst ring of a man he called
Your Excellency.

Master recorded me with the Senator, arms tied behind my
back, helpless to defend myself as he bit the tits Master gave me.

There are twenty-six files in all.

Ursula is with me when I watch the last film. Her eyes are
soft, and she makes that sad gesture again, kissing her fingers
and touching Master's lips on the freeze-frame that ends the
display.

"Maybe Master home for Halloween," she says. "Make big party."

I sigh and try again. "Master's never coming home."

"But Halloween his favorite. Halloween special."

Master dressed me in a catsuit on Halloween and fucked me with his brothers. That was the night that changed everything. That was our wedding night, in the twisted, tortured world he taught me to survive.

"Master won't be home this Halloween."

"We make costume," Ursula says. "Watch movie and Master come home."

"He didn't film that party. He only filmed me with special guests."

"*Mein Ansel. Mein Jonas.* Special, special guests." As Ursula babbles, she moves the cursor on the screen. She opens a different folder, one labeled *Geschäft*. "Here," she says. "You watch. Then we make costume."

She clicks on another video file. Immediately, I'm on the screen. I'm wearing the catsuit, the corset, the impossible stiletto-heel boots. Master is there, and so are his brothers. He's recorded the whole thing—the moment I walk into the room, the blowjob I give Ansel, Jonas asking for the cruet. I watch Master force me to swallow a double dose of Crash. I hear Jonas click his tongue against the roof of his mouth.

And then I watch the things I can't remember. I see what they do to my body when I've lost all ability to respond. I see them triple-team me, shouting instructions to each other in German. I see their hands and their cocks and the tools they scavenge from the room. I see what they do with my boots.

My angel protected me that night. She wrapped me in the gauze of Crash. She blurred my mind, kept me safe, kept me alive.

I was raped. Brutally. Repeatedly. Methodically.

I was almost killed.

I can't watch what the Herzogs did and call it anything but

torture. I can't make up any more stories that offer up even a shred of comfort, that explain, that justify. I can't pretend the brothers nurtured me, helped me to find some inner strength I never knew I had.

They hurt me so badly I had to lie to stay alive. They destroyed me so thoroughly I had to forget. They broke me so completely I mistook their brutality for a twisted kind of love.

I can't lie to myself anymore.

No man who could do the things on that video could be capable of love—not even the darkest love, the most twisted love, the most desperate kind of love that squeezes a single pixel of light from a never-ending nightmare.

I see that now.

I understand.

I finally see what I asked Trap to do, and why he couldn't do it, and why I should be grateful to him for all the days of my life.

"Ursula," I say. "May I use your phone?"

She hands it to me. "You call Master now? You tell him come home?"

Ignoring her, I tap in ten digits. I pray he'll pick up a call from an unknown number. I hope it's not too late.

The call goes to voicemail.

I try again, listening to four long rings.

Voicemail again.

I call a third time, fingers turned to marble, I'm gripping the phone so tightly.

"Prince," he finally answers, the single syllable short and hot.

"It's me."

"Oh, sweet Christ. Where are you?"

"At the house. I haven't left the house."

"I'll be there in thirty minutes."

"I'll open up the gate."

Ursula claps her hands when I end the call. Her fingers fly over the computer keyboard, and she opens a window on the screen, something to do with security. She taps a red button, turning it green. "Gate open now!" she crows. "You call him! You finally call Master! Gate open for Master."

"Klaus Herzog is dead," I say. "I cut his throat with a steak knife and watched him bleed out on a dining room floor."

"*Nein, nein, nein,*" she says.

I take the computer and open up a search engine. All I have to do is type in my name and Trap's. A dozen copies of the video scroll down the page, links to websites all over the world.

I choose the first one, labeled, "Uncut! Unedited! Every drop of blood!"

I hit Play.

I know the recording by heart now. The moment I seize the knife. The instant Herzog's blood arcs into the air. The first time I stab his body, the second, the hundredth time, and the screen shows the entire bloody mess.

Ursula howls something in German. She reaches for the computer, but I snatch it away. I don't want her touching anything, erasing anything. I need to keep her "movies" to remember everything that happened in this house from hell.

Ursula tries to scratch my face, but I bat her hand away. She tries to grab my hair, but I rear back and she can't get a real purchase.

But I can grab *her* hair. I can yank out the tight bun that pulls the skin tight beside her eyes. I can twist her neck until she's staring at the ceiling, and I can shake her like she's a floppy doll.

"He's dead, you crazy bitch. And nothing you do will ever bring him back."

I open my hand and her head hits the table. I grab the computer and stalk to the front door. My lungs fill with fresh air as I step onto the porch, and for the first time in two weeks, I feel clean.

41

ALIX

T en minutes.
        Twelve minutes.
    Sixteen.

I keep opening the computer and checking the clock. Trap said it would take thirty minutes to get here. I feel like I've been standing outside for hours.

The house is eerily quiet behind me. I expected Ursula to chase after me. I'm standing with a clear view of the door so I can defend myself if she attacks. But she hasn't come outside, and when I look through the tall ground-floor windows, I don't see her moving through the house.

Twenty-one minutes waiting.

When I close my eyes, I hear Ursula's head hitting the table again. I don't think it was a deadly blow. I didn't push her. I didn't shove.

But what if she's lying there, dying?

She's a sick woman. Broken. But I have to be better than she is, don't I? I have to help her, if she's injured.

I check the computer one more time. Twenty-four minutes.

If I wait for Trap, he can check on Ursula. He can make sure she's breathing.

But I don't want Trap going back inside that house. I don't want him walking by the study door. I don't want him thinking about what I asked him to do, what I told him I needed, what I thought would make me whole.

So I put the computer on the edge of the steps and head back inside the house.

"Ursula?" I call from the doorway. My voice shakes more than I want it to.

She doesn't answer.

I force myself to take a few steps into the foyer. "Ursula? Are you all right?"

Silence.

My heart is pounding. I've seen enough horror movies to know that this is when the monster jumps out of the doorway, drops from the ceiling, explodes from the floor to destroy its female prey. I catch my breath, steeling myself to go toward the kitchen.

My throat is coated with the rotten-egg stink of gas.

I manage three steps before the sulfur makes me cough. My eyes are burning; they feel like sandpaper when I blink. My fingers tingle with adrenaline as my brain screams, "Danger, danger, danger!"

I cross the kitchen in five long strides, holding my breath as the hiss of escaping gas grows louder. I don't know how the leak started; I don't know how it got this bad so quickly, but if Ursula was groggy when I left her, she must be unconscious now.

The door to her bedroom stands open, just the way I left it. But when I look inside, there's no Ursula. She's not by the desk. She isn't on the bed. She hasn't fallen to the floor, overwhelmed by the stench of gas.

The alarm in my head is shrieking now. I have to get out. I have to save myself.

I sprint for the front door, grateful that I left it open when I began my mission of mercy. As I stoop to collect the computer, I see lights coming up the driveway. They're low to the ground, moving fast, and it only takes a moment to hear the healthy purr of the Porsche's engine.

I run toward freedom.

The car skids to a stop a few yards in front of me. Trap's feet scrabble on the overgrown driveway. Before I can say anything, his arms are around me, pulling me close, crushing me against his chest with the hard edges of the computer held tight between us.

"Alix," he says, one hand spread across the back of my head. "Thank God you called."

"Trap," I manage, like our names can be some sort of anchor.

I'm shaking. My entire body trembles like it's trying to fly apart. My feet are bare, and the cold of the driveway's stone is climbing past my knees. My flimsy blue smock offers no protection against the chilly breeze, and a tiny part of my brain wonders when summer started its fade to fall.

But none of that matters. Trap is here now, and his arms will keep me standing, and he'll take me to the freeport, and we'll be safe there together. I let my knees soften. I give my jaw permission to relax. My teeth start to chatter, and my head feels light, but none of it matters because Trap is holding me together.

"What the fuck is that?" he says. And I dig deep for the strength to open my eyes. I look into his face, and I realize he's staring over my head, at something high up in the house.

I twist my neck, because I have to know. And when I realize what I'm seeing, a sharp cry scrapes the back of my throat.

Ursula stands in the window of Herzog's bedroom. Despite the glass between us, her face is clear. Her hair is wild, snaking around her head like it's alive. Her mouth is stretched and twisting. We can't hear her, but she's shouting something.

I realize we can see her because she's framed in flickering light. She's framed in flickering *fire*. In her left hand, she holds one of the heavy brass candlesticks that stood on the mantel in Herzog's study. A flaming taper has kindled the curtains on either side of the tall window. The sheers have transformed into sheets of fire.

Her left hand holds the candle. Her right hand holds a knife.

It's a butcher knife from the kitchen. Its blade is as long as her forearm.

She shifts the knife. She raises it to her throat. She screams something we can't hear, but my heart knows she's stretching out the only word she lives for: *Meistern*.

Master.

She slashes the knife across her throat.

For one perfect second, Ursula is suspended in the window. Her arms fling wide in victory or reflex or one last supreme proof of her dedication to the man she worshipped. Blood spatters on the glass between us, black in the golden firelight. I open my mouth to scream, but the sound is sucked away by an explosion that tears the world in two.

Bricks fly. Wood splinters. Glass rains down like diamonds in the night.

Trap covers me with his body, turning his back to take the worst of the assault. We're far enough from the front door that we're spared the worst projectiles.

The heat is like a furnace. The house is engulfed.

Ursula is gone.

Trap recovers before I do. He half-leads, half-carries me to the passenger door of the Porsche. He helps me in and reaches across to fasten my seat belt. He crosses to his own door, takes his own seat, works his own belt. He keys the ignition and runs the windshield wipers to wipe debris from the windshield.

And then he turns the car around and guns the engine, racing for the gate—for the gate, for the highway, for the freeport, for home. I sit beside him, head back, eyes closed, hands clutched around the hard shell of the computer. And neither one of us says a word about the hell we've left behind.

42

TRAP

We pause on our way past the dining room. I grab a bottle at random—Belvedere, it turns out. I don't bother with glasses, don't waste time with ice. We both take a slug, grimacing at the burn before we go back for doubles.

The booze starts to work its magic immediately. Alix is steadier on the stairs. Her fingers relax around that computer, which she's gripped all the way home like it holds the launch codes for nuclear war. When we get to the bedroom, she places it on the dresser, centering it with perfect care.

Her hands finally empty, she stands in the middle of the room, looking lost. She's wearing that fucking blue hospital gown dress thing, and I want to tear it off her, shred it, cut it into tiny scraps. But I ease it over her head and carry it to the hamper. I can burn it tomorrow.

She's shivering again. We both are.

I strip off my jeans and my Diamond Freeport shirt. The Labor Day picnic seems like it happened a century ago. I drop my boxers on top of the pile and take Alix's hand to lead her into the shower.

She still has that fucking black band on her wrist. I can remember the punch to my gut when I realized how he used it, how I felt when I hit the button that called her to the library.

The library. I wonder if she's going to miss those books.

I'll buy her replacements. Ten thousand more. We'll build the largest collection of books about art the world has ever seen.

As Alix shivers on the tile floor, I turn on the water. It blasts from the rainfall shower head like a liquid blowtorch. I move us under the flow and pick up the handheld.

Cradling Alix's arm at the elbow, I blast the band with the full force of steaming water. I flood it until her wrist turns red from the heat. I give it a minute more, because I want to smash the thing into individual molecules. But I don't want to hurt her, so I finally settle for unbuckling it and slipping it from her arm. I throw it into the far corner of the shower with all my fucking strength.

Watching its glass face shatter wakes something in Alix. She looks at me like she's just startled from a nightmare. A smile starts at the corners of her lips. She spreads a hand on my chest, fingers wide, and I'm so grateful it hurts to breathe.

"Trap," she says.

"Welcome home, Princess."

"It's good to *be* home." She looks me in the eye. "I missed you. Oh God, Trap. I missed you so much."

Her lips are cold when I kiss her, but they warm beneath my touch, parting when she sighs. My tongue finds hers and my teeth find hers and I want her, I need her, I can't ever let her go.

Her hands are flat on my back, pulling me closer. My chest crushes her amazing tits and I feel her muscles go stiff. Breaking off the kiss, I look down to see an angry red line across her ripening skin. She still hasn't healed from her caning at the club.

Fuck Jonas Herzog. Fuck Ansel Herzog.

My fingers curl into fists, but I don't want to feel this anger now. I don't want revenge's cold teeth chewing on my brain. So I shove down my fury, locking it in a box I can open tomorrow.

For now, I reach for the shampoo. The rosemary gel is slick between my fingers. I work it through Alix's hair, building up the lather. She melts again, yielding up the pain from the mark on her chest. "Does that feel good, Princess?"

"It feels like heaven." Her eyes are closed. Her lips are puffed from that incredible kiss. My cock stirs, pressing against her hip.

Eyes still closed, she reaches down between us. Her fingers are steady and sure as she strokes me. I'm instantly at full mast, which makes Alix laugh. "Looks like you missed me," she says.

"More than you can imagine." I'm just telling her the truth, but it sounds like something more. Like I'm making a promise. Swearing some sort of vow.

She tilts her head back and lets the shampoo run from her hair. Some of the suds roll over her tits and down her belly, across the plane of her mound. She's waxed there, smooth as glass, and I know she must have groomed herself in memory of him.

The thought should drive me wild. But I know he's dead. She killed him. And she's with me because she wants to be here. I'm the winner in the end.

I reach for the bar of soap and roll it between my hands. The lather is thick and heavy, and I smooth it over her skin like cream. I wash her back. I wash her ass. I turn her around and slip my hands between her legs.

She pushes against me as I bathe her folds, her spine slick against the hair on my chest. My cock is more impatient now, pressing hard above the cleft of her ass, but I set my jaw and remind myself we've got all night.

She's glowing as water rinses away the suds. Her skin is pink, flushed with the heat of the shower and the sneaking tease of my fingers. Her hair is almost long enough now to curl around her face.

When I turn toward the faucet to cut off the water, her hand closes around my arm. I let her pull me around. I stand still while she fetches the smooth bar of soap, and I bite back a groan as suds foam around her fingers.

She washes my chest, teasing the chips of my nipples. She rolls down my ribs, hands steady and firm. She gathers more soap before she traces the fur from my navel to my rock-hard cock.

I want to catch her wrists. I want to push her hard against the tile wall. I want to find her mouth with mine and drink her breath as my dick plows the sweet wet crease between her thighs.

But she's the one who's driving. She's the one who handles my cock, who soaps me up and rinses me clean. She's the one who cups my balls, bathing them in the shower's liquid fire. She's the one who frees me.

I don't have to be her avenging angel, not tonight. I don't have to be her protector. I don't have to be the man who'd lie for her, kill for her, die for her.

I just have to be the man who loves her.

When the water runs clear, she's the one who turns off the faucet. We reach for towels together. I wrap her in thirsty terry, using a second towel to dry her arms, her legs, her hair. She does the same for me, wiping me dry.

Leaving the damp towels where they fall, we lace fingers and walk into the bedroom. How many times have we stood by this bed? She's only been free for ten weeks—only two and a half months since she killed Herzog—but it feels like we've been here forever.

I turn to face her. I cup the back of her neck. I match her gaze with mine and I find the words I never thought I'd say.

"I don't want to hurt you. I don't want to be that man."

It feels like I'm dying. I'm extinguishing my soul. Some truths are as basic as the sun and the moon and the stars, and this is one: I can never cause a woman the type of pain Alix craves.

But the sun will eventually die. The moon will crumble out of orbit. Every star in the sky will implode someday.

I'll become the man Alix needs. I'll do the things she begged me to do when I left her in Herzog's torture chamber. I'll hurt her because I trust myself to save her, because I've spent years measuring out a lesser type of pain. I know how to make it, to shape it, to brake.

Another man might kill her. Herzog almost did.

Losing her will definitely kill me.

So I say the rest, everything I've thought, every night of the two long weeks she's been gone. "I'll never know what you lived through, how it changed you, how it made you who you are tonight. But if you need that pain to feel anything at all…" My throat closes, but I have to go on. I have to say every last word. "I'll hate him till the day I die. And I'll hate a part of myself too. But I'll do it. For you. Because I love you." I need her to know that, I need her to understand, before I do the things that will destroy my soul. "I love you, Alix Key. And I'll be the man you need me to be for as long as you'll have me in your life."

43

ALIX

H e doesn't know. He dropped everything and drove to Herzog's, speeding through the night just because I called him.

I haven't had time to tell him about the videos. I haven't figured out the words.

I'm not the woman who stood in Herzog's study and begged him to break himself for me. I'm not the woman who was in so much pain, who was so lost, so broken that agony seemed the only path to freedom.

I cup his jaw with my palm. I touch my forehead to his, then shift back, just enough that he'll be able to read truth in my eyes. I squeeze his fingers with our linked hands.

"Thank you," I say.

And there, I see it. Just a flicker. Just a flash. I see him recognize his own damnation, accept it and embrace it, because he still thinks that is what I need.

"Thank you," I say again. "Because you trust me. You

believe me. You accept that my life is mine, that my body is mine, that I'm the only person in the world who truly knows what I need."

My voice shakes. My eyes sting. But I have to say the rest. I have to let him know the truth. I have to free him.

"I said those things because I believed them. Because everything I'd lived through showed me one dark path. But now I've seen more. I have so much to tell you, so much I need to say. But this is the one thing that's most important: I was wrong."

He freezes. He's suspended in a space outside of time. I feel it in his fingers. I feel it in the sudden pulse that leaps above his throat.

"I was wrong," I say again. "I was so hurt, so broken, so confused... Seeing Jonas and Ansel at the club... Losing control on the auction block... Looking for you... Needing you..."

I can't build a sentence, can't say what I want to say. Trap swallows hard. His eyes are gleaming. He's straining to hold back, to keep from speaking, to give me the time and space I need to find my words.

I accept his gift. I steady myself with a single breath. And then I leap into the future because *he* was brave, because he went first. "The things we do here, the scenes, the play... you opened that door for me. You taught me what my body needs to be alive."

His lips part. He starts to speak, but I settle a finger across his lips. He waits, because that's what I ask him to do. He waits because he loves me. And I tell him the rest, because it's what he deserves to know. "So when I was back in that house, when I was swamped by the memory of pain I couldn't control... I thought you could help me through it. You could be my guide. You could be my angel."

"A— And now?" Trap's voice is stretched.

"Now I know I was wrong. Herzog hurt because he could. Because he made an art of cruelty. Because he had no limits."

I'm so close to the end. So close to what I need to say. If I wanted to, I could close my eyes now. I could step off the edge and fall and fall and fall and know Trap will be there when I land.

But I don't want to close my eyes.

I don't want to step off the edge.

I want to stand here, to be here, to own the words I choose to say.

"I was wrong to push you. I was wrong to think you'd be like Herzog. You have limits. That's why I trust you. That's why I'm a stronger person with you. That's why I love you."

I can't help it. Tears spill over and start to run down my cheeks. But he gave me the words I need, the words I want to share forever.

"I love you, Travis Prince. And I'll be the woman you need me to be for as long as you'll have me in your life."

I think his kiss will steal my breath away. Instead, his lips are tender. Sweet. He tastes me like I'm the most precious nectar from the rarest flower in the world.

He eases me to the side of the bed. We sink onto the mattress together. He pets me, strokes me, worships the lines of my body. I quiver beneath his palms, humming with an inner light.

I want to feel the weight of his chest. I need to feel his legs tangled between mine, his knee pressing mine to the side. I sink back on the bed, pulling him with me, never wanting to let him go.

He leans on one forearm. He traces my hair across my forehead, around the curve of one ear. He bends forward and lowers his lips to my breasts and settles the softest kiss in the world against the cane's angry mark. He traces the line end to end, his fingertips as soft as feathers.

"It's okay," I whisper. "I won't break."

"You'll never break," he growls. "You're the strongest woman I know."

His eyelashes are frosted with unshed tears as I pull him

close for another kiss. His thighs press against mine until I shift my hips. My knees spread to carve a basket for his weight. Keeping one hand cupped to the back of his neck, I reach between us. My fingers find his ready cock and guide it to my deep wet heat.

I gasp as he enters me. He shudders as we fit together. I rock my hips to build a better angle, and he sinks all the way home.

His hands are planted on the mattress, on either side of my head. My palms flatten on his back, feeling his muscles ripple, measuring his restraint. I tighten around his heat, squeezing to set him free.

He swears because he's Trap. He whispers filthy things as he reads my eyes. He rides me, steady and hard, each thrust finding some new way to bring us closer together.

There's nothing between us—no condom, no leather, no toys to break our focus. There's only his body and mine, moving together, giving and taking, mastering perfect balance. This is more intimate than all the screaming orgasms we've ever shared. The intensity is a furnace blast, so strong, so pure, so intensely *true* that the rest of the universe spins away to nothingness.

He's pumping faster. Thrusting harder. Spinning tighter, with every muscle in his body. I'm matching him, push for push, taking everything he has to give. His face pulls tight. His neck arches back. He rises up one last time and he's framed above me, poised inside me, and I catch my breath to hold with his.

He shifts his weight to one strong wrist. He reaches down between us, to our perfect meld. He sets a fingertip against my thrumming clit, and he grits a single word: "Come."

I shatter, because he told me to. I shatter, because he's flooding deep inside me. I shatter, because this is who we are, this is what we do, this is how we share our love together.

He groans as he collapses on top of me. I sigh as I cradle his body. We lay together, utterly spent, bound for life by our twin thundering pulses, our matched lingering gasps, and the soft, lazy shudder of aftershocks in the night.

44

ALIX

Trap's gone when I wake. I start to call out for him, to see if he's in the bathroom, but I hear the shrill beep of a truck's back-up warning, coming from outside. It's Tuesday morning, after the Labor Day picnic. If he's not supervising the tear-down from the family fun and games, he must be taking care of actual business, in his office downstairs, or over in the freeport building.

I climb out of bed to use the bathroom, and I grab my robe from its hook outside the tiled shower. I'm tempted to head downstairs for a cup of Trap's perfect coffee, but there's something I want to check on first.

I frown when I realize my phone was destroyed in last night's fire. I only owned the thing for a couple of months.

But I can use the computer on top of the dresser to track down what I need. I click a button to link it to the home network and add the password with an automatic flash of my fingers. I open a browser and run a quick search.

New Castle Mansion Goes Up in Flames is the first headline.
Gas Mishap Suspected.

The articles have the bare facts—a mansion in rural New Castle County caught fire last night. The explosion was felt by neighbors who phoned authorities promptly, but by the time first responders arrived, it was too late to save the structure. The house is owned by a Delaware-registered corporation; the board of directors is being contacted to determine who, if anyone, was home at the time of the accident.

I wonder how much will survive the fire. Will they find Ursula's body? Any evidence of Herzog's crimes?

I brush my fingers over the metal case of the computer. It's a lot more precious now, if it's the only remaining documentation of what Herzog did in that house.

I wonder what sort of security Herzog had on this machine, what sort of password he used. Whatever it is, Ursula knew it. And as long as I keep the thing from rebooting, I can get into all of the files.

There are twenty-six "special guests" who would love to get their hands on this computer. It should be relatively easy to figure out who they are. I have clues from Herzog's weird forms of address. And I can run single frames through an image search to see who comes up.

I suspect Herzog planned to blackmail each of his visitors. That seems to be a cornerstone of the family business, after all.

That reminds me. I need to phone my lawyer. I hope I haven't put my legal status in serious jeopardy because of my two-week disappearance.

At least this computer holds evidence for clearing my name. Every one of these videos builds a case of self-defense—even if Herzog only appears in the one film, with his brothers.

I wonder if that's why he kept it separate. Maybe the *Geschäft* files were meant for his own personal pleasure. I don't even know what *Geschäft* means.

I type the word into an online translator.

Business.

Was Herzog planning to blackmail his own brothers? And what other *business* files does he have on this machine? It only takes a moment to work my way back to the *Geschäft* folder.

I steer clear of the video. I'd be happy never to see it again.

Most of the files are in German. They date back at least ten years, a variety of spreadsheets and documents, with the occasional media file sprinkled in. I can't make heads or tails out of most of them; we'll have to hire a translator.

But one subfolder is called *Mädchen*. I don't recognize all of the labels inside, but a few leap out: Lilyana, Marta, Pavla, Rayna, Rosa, Simona.

I click on Lilyana first. There's a photo of her—long hair, gaunt cheeks; it must have been taken when she first arrived from Bulgaria. There's a document in Cyrillic; I can only make out numbers. And another in Arabic, with different, bigger numbers.

My hand starts to shake. I'm looking at bills of sale.

I click on the other names. Lilyana's the only one who went to Afghanistan. Pavla and Rayna were shipped to New Orleans. Marta went to the Philippines. The documents for Rosa and Simona are in Spanish; it looks like they ended up in Colombia.

The dates match perfectly. I'm staring at proof that Herzog trafficked women.

I look at the other names. There are thirty-two sub-folders. Thirty-two victims. Thirty-two women who are probably dead by now, and I'm the only one who can bear witness to the fact they ever lived, ever suffered in New Castle County, Delaware.

Adriana.

Daria.

Gabriela.

Key.

My fingers freeze on the trackpad.

Herzog didn't buy me. He didn't sell me. And why aren't my records filed under A, for Alix?

I tap the folder.

There's a photo. It isn't me, but it's a face I know nearly as well as my own. It's Leo.

The picture was taken in the study. Leo is standing in front of the mantel. The metal torture frame is to his right, almost out of the shot.

My brother looks curious. He's grinning, the way he always did when he met new people. I think he looks a little scared.

I scroll down. I don't know what I expect to find. Leo wasn't a girl, a *Mädchen*. He was a man. A man who chose to work for an animal. Leo made the decision of his own free will, and that's what killed him.

So, there's no bill of sale.

But there are hundreds of other documents, nearly identical. Each one is called Key, followed by a six-digit code. A date. The first one is from a month after I arrived at Herzog's. The last one is from June 15. The Sunday before Herzog died.

I open a file. It resembles a paystub. There's Leo's name. An address in Philadelphia. Lines for each day of the week. Columns for hours worked, for pounds processed (Crash), for pounds processed (Cocaine), for pounds processed (Heroin), for market value (gross) for market value (street).

This can't be possible. Lilyana told me years ago: Leo's dead.

But Leo was processing drugs for Herzog in downtown Philadelphia, as recently as ten weeks ago.

My heart pounding, I find the computer's search icon. I type in Key and this past Sunday's date, six digits, day, month, year.

A single file shows up. I click, and I'm staring at an email from Philadelphia Distribution Center to Klaus Herzog. It arrived yesterday morning, Monday. Apparently drug kingpins don't observe federal holidays.

I click on the attachment.

My brother, my twin—the man who sold me to Klaus

Herzog to pay off a drug debt—is alive and well. And he's living in Philadelphia, less than a hundred miles away.

I hope you enjoyed reading *Conflict Diamond*. My love story with Trap Prince concludes in *Priceless Diamond*, the last book in the now-complete Kidnapped Series.

Buy *Priceless Diamond* Now!
https://alixkey.com/PB3US

BONUS SCENE

~

Remember how Trap took me to the county fair, and I ended up with a stuffed panda?

Want to see what happened at the fair (including our trip on the Ferris wheel)?

Get your bonus scene by typing:

https://alixkey.com/Bonus2

into your phone or computer browser.

MORE DIAMOND RING

∾

Looking for an Irish Mob retelling of Jane Eyre? *Irish Brute*, the true love story of Braiden Kelly and Samantha Mott, is a Kindle Unlimited read.Start the Irish Mob Series by typing

https://alixkey.com/KI4US

into your phone or computer browser.

∾

One last thing: If you want an absolutely free full-length, totally stand-alone Diamond Ring novel, featuring a gender-switch Jack and the Beanstalk retelling and starring Irish mobster Connor Boyle, I've got you covered! Just type:

https://alixkey.com/sins

into your phone or computer browser.

THANK YOU

I can't thank you enough for choosing *Conflict Diamond* from among all the dark romances out there! Without readers like you, I would never have my writing career.

You may not realize it, but *you* can be my hero. Study after study shows that the number one reason a person reads a book is because that book was recommended by a friend.

So will you tell one friend about *Conflict Diamond*?

Of course, if you're dead-set on reviewing my book on Amazon and Goodreads, I won't complain! Honest reviews are hugely helpful because many advertisers require me to have a certain number of reviews before I can buy ads.

Leave a review on Amazon
https://alixkey.com/KI2US

Leave a review on Goodreads
https://alixkey.com/GR2

Whatever you do, don't be a stranger! I look forward to hearing from you soon!

www.alixkey.com
alix@alixkey.com

ABOUT THE AUTHOR

Alix Key was born in Potomac, Maryland, where she grew up making her twin brother and all her dolls act out her favorite fairytales. When an all-grown-up Alix discovered that very real dangers lurk in the woods, she figured out how to rescue herself. She now lives outside Dover, Delaware with her own Prince Charming. When not writing dark romance, Alix serves as the Chief Operations Officer of Diamond Freeport.

You can learn more about Alix at her website, www.alixkey.com.